FORGOTTEN VOICES

Recent Titles by Jane A. Adams from Severn House

The Naomi Blake Mysteries

MOURNING THE LITTLE DEAD
TOUCHING THE DARK
HEATWAVE
KILLING A STRANGER
LEGACY OF LIES
SECRETS
GREGORY'S GAME
PAYING THE FERRYMAN

The Rina Martin Mysteries

A REASON TO KILL
FRAGILE LIVES
THE POWER OF ONE
RESOLUTIONS
THE DEAD OF WINTER
CAUSE OF DEATH
FORGOTTEN VOICES

FORGOTTEN VOICES

A Rina Martin Novel

Jane A. Adams

This first world edition published 2015
in Great Britain and the USA by
SEVERN HOUSE PUBLISHERS LTD of
19 Cedar Road, Sutton, Surrey, England, SM2 5DA.
Trade paperback edition first published
in Great Britain and the USA 2015 by
SEVERN HOUSE PUBLISHERS LTD.

British Library Cataloguing in Publication Data

Adams, Jane, 1960- author.
  Forgotten Voices. – (A Rina Martin mystery)
  1. Martin, Rina (Fictitious character)–Fiction.
  2 . Murder–Investigation–Fiction. 3. Detective and
  mystery stories.
  I. Title II. Series
  823.9'2-dc23

ISBN-13: 978-0-7278-8518-0 (cased)
ISBN-13: 978-1-84751-619-0 (trade paper)
ISBN-13: 978-1-78010-671-7 (e-book)

All Severn House titles are printed on acid-free paper.

Severn House Publishers support the Forest Stewardship Council™ [FSC™],
the leading international forest certification organisation. All our titles that
are printed on FSC certified paper carry the FSC logo.

Typeset by Palimpsest Book Production Ltd.,
Falkirk, Stirlingshire, Scotland.
Printed and bound in Great Britain by
TJ International, Padstow, Cornwall.

For A.F. and the Werewolf Pack. On account.

PROLOGUE

September

'You made it then. Sorry I didn't collect you from the airport, but you know I'm not much of a driver. Not distance anyway.'

She listened as he told her it didn't matter.

'When can I expect you? A hotel? Don't be silly. You'll stay here.' She sighed. 'All right, maybe you have a point. Call me when you're settled and we'll—'

Daphne closed her eyes and tried to control her temper. He could be such a stubborn boy. Daphne still couldn't think of her younger son as a full-fledged man. He wasn't anything like his brother. In less generous moments, Daphne found herself wishing it was Ray that the cancer had taken and not her other son, Jeb.

'Look, Ray, we need to get some things straight, right now. Right, right, OK, let me know when you're in the hotel and we'll talk.'

She put the phone down and stood in the hall staring at it accusingly. She'd had such plans too. Ray would come to stay, they'd go together to see that daughter-in-law of hers and Daphne would get the result she wanted. Once and for all, Ellen would be out of the way.

But she supposed he was right not to come to stay with her. They needed to keep their distance, Ray had said. No one knew he was back and it should be kept like that until afterwards.

Satisfied that it would all go her way in the end and that Ray was entitled to sound tired and a little dispirited after so long a journey, Daphne went back into the kitchen where she'd begun to prepare a meal for herself and her returning son. She couldn't eat all this lot herself. Daphne began to pack meat and vegetables back into the fridge. She supposed the beef would freeze. It could wait for the celebration. Later.

The woman had to go. That was all that mattered now.

ONE

September

He could not have said how many times he had sat on the ridge and looked down on the farm. It was a view he had known all his life and a house he had been into many times. From where he sat he could see a little of the track and the corner of the fence that he knew defined the vegetable garden and the orchard. Beyond that a mix of arable and rare breed stock filled the forty or so acres that remained of what had once been a considerable holding.

Manageable, she had told him. It was manageable now and he'd been forced to agree that selling off the remainder had been a sensible option.

He could see directly into the farmhouse from his vantage point. Not deeply, but a bit of the kitchen through the big window, a little of the range and the corner of the table. She had stood at the sink for a while now, her gaze mostly down and he guessed she was washing pots or perhaps peeling vegetables. Her blonde hair was tied back. He was too far away to see the grey strands that he knew were annoying her so much. She kept threatening to dye it and he had always told her that he liked it. And asking why she thought it mattered.

'Oh, there's a *man* speaking,' she would say, as she shook her head fondly.

From time to time she glanced up from her task, looking out of the window at the sunlight and flowers in the yard. She'd have the radio on; she usually did when working in the kitchen, especially when the house was empty. She liked the sense of being in company and she loved her music.

Occasionally when she glanced up he got the feeling that she was staring straight out at him, but he knew that she wasn't. Not really. That she was unlikely to have seen him. The grass was long and the leaves of the beech tree against which he sat swept down, obscuring him from view.

He loved this spot. He loved the woman he watched now.

But that was hardly the point, was it. That was not important now.

As the afternoon crept on he knew that she'd be finished with her tasks soon, would move away from the window, would get ready for the children coming home from school. He wondered if he should meet them off the bus, so that they didn't go up to the house alone.

Perhaps he would.

But he could delay things no longer. He left the ridge and followed the winding rabbit path down, climbed the low fence that separated the yard from the field and crossed towards the house.

Looking up, she saw him then. She smiled, her eyes lighting with genuine pleasure and welcome, filling him with so much happiness that he could hardly bear it.

Then, slowly, reluctantly, he raised the shotgun. He could see her clearly, even glimpse the strands of grey in her soft blonde hair.

He fired both barrels.

Glass shattered. The woman fell.

TWO

It was, Mac thought, always slightly odd to see Sergeant Baker out in the field, as it were. His usual habitat was the front office, dealing with the locals of Frantham and fielding queries and problems from the tourists that still flocked to the little seaside town at this time of the year. Sergeant Baker, exuding a teddy bear quality of comfort and care topped off with a good dollop of common sense was ideally suited to the task. He epitomized the notion of 'community policeman', being hardly able to get from one end of the promenade to the other in less than an hour because everyone had to have a word.

It took a shift of perception, therefore, to see him at a crime scene. Further, to see him taking charge of a crime scene. It was easy to forget that Sergeant Baker was an experienced and very able investigator.

Mac paused just inside the farm gate – he'd parked a little way up the narrow lane, so that he didn't block the exit for the mortuary ambulance and the two cars already on scene. The afternoon was warm and the trees on the ridge had only just begun to turn. The day still had an almost summer feel to it, enhanced by the low hum of bees as they buzzed among the tubs of flowers close by the entrance gate. A more peaceful epitome of English countryside would have been hard to imagine, Mac thought, an illusion broken as he rounded the end of the farmhouse and the shattered window came into view.

Frank Baker saw him and waved. 'I'll be right out,' he said, and disappeared.

Mac stood quietly in the yard, his back to the house, looking up at the trees on the ridge and enjoying the illusion of peace for just a moment or two longer. It was wrong that violent death should happen anywhere but it especially assaulted his sense of decency that it should happen in a spot as lovely as this.

Frank Baker joined him and Mac turned his attention back towards the house.

'The shooter probably stood about there.' Frank indicated a small area that had been cordoned off and a pathway that had been protected leading back towards the fence. 'The grass is flattened on the field edge over there. No footprints that we could see. It's been dry for days.'

'They came down off the ridge and climbed over the fence?'

'Such as it is. A toddler could get over it. But that's the thinking so far. Then shot her through the window.'

'Who found the body?'

Frank Baker, already pale and grave shook his head as though disbelieving. He looked grey, Mac thought.

'Her kids found her,' he said. 'Just home from school. The bus drops them at the end of the lane then goes on into the village.'

'Jesus,' Mac said. 'How old?'

'Eleven and thirteen. There's no mobile signal at the farmhouse, so they ran to the neighbours half a mile down the road and raised the alarm.'

'No landline here?'

'I think they just wanted to get away from the place as fast as they could. The landline is in the kitchen. They'd have had to stay where there mother was lying.'

'I see,' Mac said, nodding. 'Where are they now?'

'The Richardses, the neighbours, they kept them there. Toby Richards called me. I came up, found this.'

'He called *you*?'

'I've known Toby since we were both at school.' Frank Baker shrugged. 'It occurred to him that the kids might have got it wrong, that they might have seen something that scared seven shades out of them, but not understood what—'

'He thought they might have made it up?'

Frank shook his head emphatically. 'No, you take one look at the poor little buggers and you can see they're telling the truth. But he thought it was better to get a pair of familiar eyes on the problem, assess what was what before they called the full cavalry.'

'So you came up here and found her.'

'And then *I* called the cavalry, yes.'

'This friend of yours, he didn't come up here to check things out? I mean, I'm glad if he didn't, he'd have to be eliminated from the crime scene—'

Frank was shaking his head. 'Toby's been in a wheelchair these past three or four years. Tractor rolled with him, broke his back. He was in hospital for months. There's just him and Hilly at the cottage. He was a tenant on the Breed Estate, just across that way. Been a farmer all his life. The cottage they're in now belongs to the Breeds too, they adapted it for Toby and Hil.'

Mac raised an eyebrow. 'Guilty conscience?'

Frank snorted laughter. 'Accidents happen, Mac, and this was just one of those things. Anyway, Carrie Butler, who runs the Breed Estate now her dad's gone, she's one of the good ones. So was her dad. Her brother wasn't worth spit, but there you go.'

Mac decided he'd ask more later. He was still on a steep learning curve when it came to the local population. 'And did you know the dead woman?'

'Ellen Tailor. She was a blow-in, married a local farmer, Jebediah Tailor, about fifteen years ago. Tailor's family had farmed this place for generations. When he died it was hard for her to carry on. She sold a parcel of it off about five years ago. She couldn't farm it on her own, couldn't afford to hire help, so she kept just enough for a market garden, chickens and a few hobby sheep.'

'Hobby sheep?'

'Some rare breed things. Toby would be able to tell you about them. She and the kids show them at the local agricultural events. It keeps them involved with the local community but she doesn't have the problems of the big herds of cattle her husband used to run.'

'And you say she was a blow-in. An outsider. How did the locals like her?'

'Well, apart from whoever blasted her face off with a shotgun, I'd say she got along fine,' Frank said bitterly.

Mac nodded and took that as his cue to go and view the body.

Rina Martin closed the front door and dropped her bags on to the tiled floor.

'And, relax,' she said softly and took a deep breath of home.

The Peters sisters must have been baking; the scent of cake still hung in the air and there were fresh flowers in the vase on the hall table. Pink roses and old-fashioned sweet peas picked from Rina's bit of a garden. There'll be a second vase somewhere, Rina thought, similarly pretty and delightfully traditional; Eliza and Bethany, the two ever-youthful lady performers who resided with Rina literally never did things by halves and Rina would be expected to guess who had arranged which vase and to praise them equally.

But for now, the house was quiet and empty. Rina had timed her return precisely so. The Montmorencys – a former double act of very dissimilar 'twins' – spent Thursday afternoons at the new Marina in Frantham Old Town. They met for a so-called 'lunch club' which Rina knew from experience usually extended until tea time.

The Peters sisters, Bethany and Eliza, had recently discovered a tea dance which also took up their Thursday afternoons. Rina calculated that she had perhaps a couple of hours of quiet before the noise and chaos arrived and by that time, she thought, she would be ready for it.

Leaving her bags where they lay she went through to the large kitchen that occupied most of the space at the rear of the house. Before Rina took over, Peverill Lodge had been a genuine B&B – hence the good-sized kitchen – rather than just the home it had become since. Officially the Montmorencys and the Peters sisters were just paying guests, and to an extent they did pay their way, but Rina was under no illusions as to them ever leaving.

Not that she minded.

This was home and they were now her family.

The fifth guest, out at work on his second job, Rina guessed, was likely to be departing soon and Rina would miss him. Tim Brandon, much the youngest member of the household, would be moving in with his girlfriend, Joy. Joy's mother had helped them find and afford a little cottage nearby. A tiny little place – fortunately with an outbuilding big enough to turn into an office-cum-store for Tim's belongings – but with a very large garden. Rina had no doubt that Tim and Joy would be happy there and was incredibly grateful that they were still close by. She had grown so used to Tim's enthusiasm and support since he'd moved in a few years before and she would miss him terribly. But Rina also loved Joy, Tim's fiancée, and was just glad that he had found someone who understood him so well.

Rina filled the kettle and found the chocolate cake in the blue tin. A Victoria sponge sat cooling on a rack covered by what looked like a gauze umbrella to protect it from flies. The clock ticked softly on the kitchen wall and Rina let her gaze travel about the room. Beside the door was a large, framed poster of Rina in what had become her most famous and profitable role as Lydia Marchant in the television show *Lydia Marchant Investigates*. Lydia Marchant had paid for this house, and the ongoing fees from the popular series – it was estimated that Lydia Marchant investigated at least once every couple of hours somewhere in the world, dubbed into more than a dozen languages – still helped to pay the bills.

And now it had been revived. Rina still couldn't quite believe it. Nine years after the last series had been aired, Rina had just finished the filming of a new one.

And, frankly, she was exhausted.

They had done the Christmas special the previous year, just to test the water, and that had been hard if pleasurable work, but the pre-sell had been so good that a first series had been commissioned even before the taster aired. Now twelve new, hour-long episodes had been completed and Rina was relieved and tired and very, very happy.

She made tea and settled down to enjoy her cake in peace.

Life is good, Rina thought. Fred, I just wish you were here to share it with me. She smiled a little sadly. She and Fred had enjoyed just five years of marriage before his death and there had been no one else to take his place in Rina's life. But here, in her quiet kitchen in her beloved home, she could almost feel his arm around her shoulders and his gentle kiss as he welcomed her back.

THREE

'Is this her?' Mac asked, picking up a photograph from the dresser. It showed a smiling, blonde woman of, he guessed, about thirty-five and two children, a boy and a slightly younger girl. The girl wore a striped dress and a school cardigan with a stitched-on badge.

Frank looked at the picture and nodded. 'That would have been taken about a year ago I think. The kids look a little bit older now and in that photo Megan's still wearing her old school uniform. She joined Jeb at big school this term.'

'Jeb? Same name as his father?'

'Jebediah, yes. His dad and grandad were both Jebediahs. Some traditions just hang on round here.'

Mac nodded. He looked towards the body of Ellen Tailor. She had fallen backwards, away from the window, then hit what was left of her head on the edge of the kitchen table as she dropped.

She would not have felt that last injury, Mac thought.

'Her killer let her have both barrels at short range,' Frank said quietly.

The woman's face was unrecognizable. Glass from the window had blasted into her alongside the shotgun pellets and the face and neck were just a mess of pulp and blood.

'The kids?'

'Saw everything,' Frank confirmed. 'Jeb thought she might have fainted or fallen so they both ran over to her.'

Poor little sods, Mac thought. 'Any particular reason for them thinking that? I mean had she fainted before?'

'Jeb said she'd had a really bad inner ear problem a few months back. Very bad vertigo. She fell over a couple of times.'

'And no signs of robbery or' – Or what?

Frank shook his head. 'No, whoever killed her seems to have just fired the shots and then walked away.'

Rina's family had descended en masse just after five. She had busied herself getting the evening meal ready – a job the Montmorencys usually undertook but one which felt pleasant to be doing after so long away.

'Rina, Rina darling. It's so good to have you home.' Bethany and Eliza embraced her excitedly.

'Happy to see you, my dear.' Matthew Montmorency kissed her cheek, his long grey mane of hair brushing her neck as he bent his head. Stephen Montmorency, the shorter of the two and, unlike his supposed brother now getting a little bald on top, grasped her hand and kissed her other cheek. 'Have you enjoyed yourself, Rina, dear?'

'I have, Stephen, but I'm very glad to be home.'

The front door opened and closed again and two pairs of footsteps could be heard in the hall.

'Ah,' Matthew said. 'Here they are. Give me that spoon, Rina darling. I'll take over with the cooking. Girls, will you lay the table for me and Stephen, perhaps you'll get the kettle on.'

Tim Brandon stalked into the kitchen, dressed in his usual black, his fiancée Joy at his side. Joy let Tim get his hug in first and then grabbed Rina. 'It's so good to have you home. You've got to come and see what we've done to the cottage and Mum says she'll come for a visit next week and she's looking forward to seeing everyone.'

She turned to the Montmorencys. 'Anything I can do, boys?'

Rina shook her head in amusement and joined Tim at the kitchen table. 'You look well,' she said. 'Now what do you have to tell me? How are the jobs? And have any of you seen Mac?'

Mac reckoned that his reversing had been honed almost to perfection since moving down to the south coast, but backing all the way down the narrow lane leading to the farmhouse and on to what Frank ironically called the main road tested even his skills.

Avoiding the hedge, the ditch and the randomly parked police vehicles and the newly arrived mortuary ambulance did not add up to a whole lot of fun and he knew that the memory of the dead woman, seemingly burned on to his retinas, was not helping.

Ellen Tailor, he thought. Her name is Ellen Tailor and though he had never heard of her above an hour or so ago, she was now his responsibility.

Frank directed him to the Richardses' cottage. The kids, running to raise the alarm, would have cut across the next field, Frank told him, but they would have to go round by road. It was only about a mile, but seemed, to Mac to be a mile of long, sweeping, blind bend. He swore as he fluffed a gear change.

'You all right?' Frank asked him.

'I will be. Yes. But are you? I mean I didn't even know the woman.'

'Shocked,' Frank said simply. 'Violent death. It never gets any easier, does it.'

'Not that I've noticed.'

'I was out at the airfield last weekend. You know the de Freitases are setting up a bit of a museum in the old departure building?'

Mac nodded. He'd heard something about it. The de Freitases, Lydia and Edward, had moved back to the area a couple of years before. Edward had made money and wanted to reinvest in his old stomping ground. They'd started a software company, *Iconograph*, close to Frantham and also bought the old airfield and had been in the process of restoring it for the past year. They were preparing for the official opening later in the year. Although the little airfield would be open for business from early spring, the official relaunch had been scheduled to coincide with the Remembrance celebrations in November.

'I was helping Lydia go through the donations,' Frank went on. 'Box after box of stuff. Some of it on loan from local families and some just been given. All the young men, all going off to fight. Just kids, a lot of them. You think they ever got used to it? The man next to you getting blown to bits? I tell you, Mac, I'm not cut out for it, even now.'

'I don't know,' Mac said. 'I suppose when you have no choice. Is that the place?' A cottage, set a little back from the main road, hove into view.

'That's it, yes. Pull up on the verge.'

Mac parked up and got out of the car. The cottage was small and red brick. A shallow ramp led from the garden gate to the front door, a neatly tended garden on both sides. He caught a glimpse of a larger garden with small fruit trees behind. 'I'm surprised this hasn't gone to the holiday trade,' he commented.

'If the brother had his way, it would have done. He'd have sold off half the estate. That's why when the old man died, he left the running of the Breed Estate to Carrie and her husband. Paid the son off, or so they say. He's a bad lot.'

Mac would have asked more but the front door opened as they reached the gate and a middle-aged woman, her greying hair tied back from her face came down the path to meet them.

'Frank, thank the Lord you're here. The poor little mites, they can't stop crying and I don't know how to get hold of their auntie. I've tried phoning their nan, but she's not home and they don't know her mobile. The number's back at the house.'

Frank laid a soothing hand on the woman's arm. 'We'll take care of it, Hilly. Now don't you fret. This here is DI MacGregor, but he won't mind if you call him Mac like the rest of us do.'

Hilly looked at Mac distractedly as though not quite taking him in and then led the way inside.

The cottage was small, one room downstairs at the front with a kitchen diner behind it. The stairs led off a small hallway and Mac noted that a stair lift had been installed and a lightweight wheelchair stood on the landing.

'How long have you lived here?' he asked.

'What? Oh ten years or so. After the accident he didn't want to move so we – the Butlers and me – we found ways of adapting. It's not ideal, but I can't see him settling in town.'

'The Butlers. They own the Breed Estate.' Mac nodded, aware that Hilly thought his questions irrelevant and even insensitive given the bigger, present issues. The living room seemed crowded as he and Frank followed her in. A man in a wheelchair sat beside an armchair, shared by two very distressed children. Mac recalled that Frank had given their ages as eleven and thirteen, but at that moment they looked much younger. Pale, tear-stained and cold, snuggled beneath a thick blanket despite the warmth of the tiny room.

'Can I get you anything? Tea . . .'

'No, thank you Hilly, we're all right.' Frank told her. He grabbed a little stool set beside the chair and sat down in front of the two kids, taking Megan's hand and then Jeb's too. 'I'm so sorry,' he said. 'So very sorry.'

'Was it really Mum?' Megan asked him and Mac remembered the bloody mess that had once been Ellen Tailor's face.

'I'm sorry, Megan, but yes, it's her.'

Megan buried her face in her brother's shirt but, Mac noted, kept a tight hold of Frank Baker's hand. Mac was overwhelmingly grateful that his sergeant was there, that he was known to the family. That his big, friendly presence would have helped even had he not been familiar.

'You've got an auntie, up in York, if I remember, and your nan's just down the coast, isn't she? How about if we get hold of them for you?'

'We've been trying.' Toby Richards spoke for the first time. 'They think their nan might still be on holiday, she's due back later today or tomorrow. We don't have her mobile number and the aunt isn't answering her phone and the kids don't know where she works or—'

Frank nodded. It was clear that the Richardses were at a loss as to how to cope with this particular crisis.

'We'll make some calls,' Mac said. 'Get an appropriate adult down here and find Megan and Jeb somewhere to stay until we can get them to their family.'

He could see the relief in the Richardses' eyes. 'If you can just hold the fort for say, another hour? We'll get someone to take over.'

'You could phone Uncle Bill,' Jeb said quietly. 'He lives near here.'

It was the first time the boy had spoken and his voice trembled and almost failed.

'Uncle Bill?' Frank asked.

'He means Bill Trent, lives over at Stone End, edge of the Breed land. It's one of the places Carrie Butler sold off a couple of years back?'

'I know it,' Frank said. 'But would he . . . I mean?'

'We like him,' Jeb said. 'Mum liked him. We'd rather . . . I mean we don't want to be more trouble.'

'Oh, you're no bother,' Hilly said, and Mac could see she was frowning. It seemed that the idea of handing the kids over to this Bill Trent upset her more than dealing with them for a bit longer. He wondered why and made a mental note to find out later.

'Mum's phone book is in the kitchen,' Megan offered. 'We should have got it but—'

Frank patted her hand. 'We'll get it,' he said. 'And we'll get you picked up very soon, I promise. And we'll find your nan and your auntie and they'll come and look after you.' He stood up and looked from Hilly to Toby Richards. 'We'll be quick as we can, OK?'

Hilly nodded. 'I'll see you out,' she said.

Hilly Richards walked with them down the garden path. 'You don't want to let them have anything to do with that Trent man,' she said. 'He's not the sort. Not the sort at all.'

'The sort?' Mac queried.

'To take care of children, of course. Too grumpy by half, he is. Not a good word to say for anyone. I don't know why she encouraged him, I really don't.'

'The children seem to like him,' Mac commented.

'And can kids have that sort of opinion? What do they know?'

Usually quite a lot, Mac thought, but he kept his own counsel. 'We'll get a family liaison officer out to you,' he said. 'They'll be able to organize something for the children until their family can take them.'

Hilly Richards nodded, but she was still clearly bothered.

'Can you think of anyone who bore a grudge against Ellen Tailor?' he asked.

'Ellen? No. She wasn't from round here but she'd done her best to fit. There was something said by some when she sold off so much of the farm. Some said she was selling the inheritance, you know? But I thought it was probably for the best. She was never a farm girl. She did well, considering. There were a lot said Jebediah should not have married her. He should have married a local girl, one that knew what to expect, but the younger ones, they have different ideas, don't they?'

Have I just stepped back a century? Mac thought. He nodded absently and left Frank to make the final goodbyes.

FOUR

Mac and Frank Baker returned to the cottage where, they had been informed, DI Kendall awaited them. Mac had worked with Dave Kendall on a number of occasions. Based in Exeter, he had the resources that Mac lacked in his tiny Frantham outpost.

'Mac, Frank,' greeted Kendall, a blond, slightly heavy set man, who matched Mac for height, as he shook hands with his colleagues. 'This is a messy one. What do we know?'

'Not a lot,' Frank told him. 'We can narrow time of death to within about a half hour. One of our lads had the presence of mind to do a one-four-seven-one and call back the last number. She spoke on the phone to a Mrs Brigstock of the church flower committee in the village at ten past three. The school bus dropped the kids at the bottom of the lane at twenty to four. They found her dead when they got to the house.'

'And they saw no one unusual?'

'They saw no one full stop. But you'd have to know the area to *be* anywhere close by. There's a public footpath runs up on the ridge and joins the coastal path about three miles in that direction. You get on to it in Cranstock village, which is a couple of miles back that way.' Frank pointed back towards the main road. 'You probably came through it to get here.'

Kendall nodded. 'Hikers?' he asked hopefully.

'Not that we know of yet, but they'd have seen nothing. The farm is screened by the trees up there and if they heard a gunshot, well—'

'They'd have assumed someone after rabbits, I suppose.'

'More than likely. It's not such an unusual sound to hear round here.'

'So, how would the killer have left?'

Frank Baker shrugged. 'Could have gone back up on to the ridge or cut across the field in that direction towards the village. The locals tell me there's a gate back on to the main road. Or gone that way towards the Richardses' cottage, which is the route the kiddies took. Could even have gone back down the lane. The school bus didn't arrive until twenty to four, there'd probably have been time to walk down the lane and then cross the road into more fields. If you kept to the margins, close to the hedges, chances are no one would spot you whichever way you went.'

'Not even if you were carrying a shotgun?'

'Provided you weren't waving it about in a threatening manner.' Frank shrugged. 'Shotguns are part of the tool kit round here.'

Kendall scanned the ridge as Mac had done earlier and then turned back to the house. 'And you were first on scene.'

'I was, yes. I held the scene until the CSI arrived, then Mac got here and I handed off to Sergeant Conwell.'

'Yes, I spoke to him. He says it doesn't look as though the killer entered the house. Nothing seems to have been disturbed, nothing taken so far as anyone can tell. He's been going through the phone book, trying to get hold of family. I understand he managed to reach Mrs Tailor's sister just before you got back.'

'That's good,' Frank said. 'I'll go and have a word if you're done with me.'

Left alone, Kendall turned to Mac. 'I understand he knows the family. He really shouldn't—'

Mac stopped him with a wave of the hand. 'Frank Baker grew up not five miles from here, his entire police service, apart from the odd secondment or training course has been served round here. There's not many people Frank doesn't know. He wasn't a close friend, so there's no real conflict of interest and right now I think his local knowledge is going to be crucial.'

'Agreed,' Kendall said. 'I just felt I had to ask. How's Miriam doing, by the way?'

'Better,' Mac said. 'Enjoying her studies, though she's only just at the induction stage at the moment. I think she's relieved just to be looking at bones in the abstract for a while and not just in a mortuary.'

'And she's feeling better generally?' Kendall asked carefully.

'If you mean, is she over almost getting shot, then yes. Slowly. The dreams are down to every few nights now, so I suppose that's progress.'

Kendall nodded, accepting that Mac was probably still having a fair few of those himself and maybe still felt uncomfortable talking about it. Scenes like this one must bring back the reality of what might have happened. Miriam could have been killed just as cruelly as this Ellen Tailor had been.

'Dave, I'm fine,' Mac told him a little impatiently as though following Kendall's train of thought. 'It's the kids I feel sorry for. You can't unsee something like that.'

At Rina's house the radio was tuned to one of the local channels, Stephen Montmorency enjoying the gossip and music while he cooked, even though tonight there were so many people in the kitchen that they almost drowned it out. But a headline on the local news bulletin had him calling for silence.

A sudden quiet fell in the kitchen.

'Oh, what is it, dear?' Eliza asked anxiously.

'The news. Something about a shooting.'

'Here, oh that's . . .'

'Hush, dear, just listen.'

The fatal shooting of a woman close to the village of Cranstock. The shooting is believed to have taken place at a remote farmhouse, a few miles from the village. The police have not confirmed the identity of the victim, but she is believed to be a mother of two who lived at the farm. In other news . . .

'Well, we know where Mac will be,' Tim commented. 'A domestic incident or whatever they call it?'

'Possibly,' Rina agreed.

'Oh, Rina.' Stephen looked fondly in her direction. 'What a nasty piece of news to come home to. And it's been so quiet while you've been away.'

'Stephen, you sound as though Rina was responsible,' Eliza scolded.

'Oh, I'm sure he didn't mean that,' Bethany intervened. 'It's sad though, isn't it? A mother with little children.'

Tim met Rina's gaze and smiled conspiratorially. 'I know Mac hoped to call in tonight,' he said. 'I don't think that will happen now.'

'Probably not,' she agreed and felt oddly put out and then guilty for feeling put out. A woman had died, that took vast precedence over a mere social visit. She refilled the teapot and carried it through to the dining room, setting it with the second pot of hot water on the sideboard. Joy followed her in.

'Tim's missed you terribly,' she said.

'And I've missed him. I've missed everyone but . . . Well, you know.'

'I know.' Joy was fully aware that Rina regarded Tim very much as the son she had never had. She leaned over and kissed Rina gently on the cheek. 'And you know that you will always be welcome in our house, don't you?'

'Thank you, Joy. That means a great deal.'

But it won't be the same, Rina thought. For all that she wished the young couple happiness, she still grieved in a way. And for all Joy's assurance of welcome, Rina knew that she would never intrude on them uninvited, even though she hoped they would continue to just drop into Peverill Lodge as and when they wished. She remembered her precious time with her husband Fred. How wonderful it had been just to close the door and be alone. How they had treasured their privacy and she wished Tim and Joy the same precious time and hoped, fervently, that for them it would not come to so swift an end.

A family liaison officer came to collect the children just after seven and told them that their aunt was coming down from York and their nan was now at home. She got their grandmother on the phone to talk to them and there were more tears. Hilly Richards stood on the doorstep and waved them off. Toby watched from the window, his face grave and anxious. He knew what his wife was going to say before she came back into the living room.

'I know,' he told her. 'Maybe we should have said something.'

'There's no maybe about it!'

'Then why didn't you? Why don't you now?'

She frowned and closed her lips in a tight, tense line.

'The Inspector left his card,' Toby pointed out.

He watched as his wife stalked, stiff-shouldered into the kitchen, then looked back at the tiny scrap of card left on the telephone table beside the window. He wheeled his chair over and picked it up. For a full minute, he stared at the phone, listening to his wife clattering about in the kitchen behind him. She seemed to be making far more noise than was necessary for a bit of tea and sandwich making and he guessed that she was crying and didn't want him to hear.

She had cried a lot since his accident but she seemed never to want him to hear and so he always tried not to listen.

Sighing, he lay the card back down beside the phone. Yes, they probably should have said something, but would it make a difference? Or would it just cast suspicion in the wrong direction and waste police time? Ellen hadn't been specific in her accusations after all.

He really didn't know, but soothing himself with that possibility, Toby wheeled away from the phone and retrieved the remote control from where it had slipped down beside the seat cushion of his favourite chair. He transferred awkwardly from wheelchair to armchair, terribly aware that this was where Ellen Tailor's children had huddled beneath the plaid blanket not a half hour before.

Poor little sods, Toby thought. Both parents gone now. Then he put them from his mind and pressed the on button on the remote control.

FIVE

Day after Ellen's death

Mac had left his car parked at the police station the night before and walked home around the headland. It was something he often did. There was a small space, enough for three cars if you knew just how to arrange them, behind the station and it was about a ten-minute walk to work from the tiny flat above the boathouse that he shared with Miriam. Frantham old town, unlike the Victorian creation that had become Frantham New, had no vehicle access. It was a fairly sizeable settlement, scrambling down the hill from the main road to the tiny harbour. Still predominantly occupied by locals and fiercely resisting development it had largely escaped the holiday and second home brigade because, as Mac well knew, it was so damned awkward to get into.

A small car park had been established at the top of the hill a few years before he had arrived but a lot of people, like Mac, parked somewhere in Frantham New Town and made their way back and forth along the headland path, at least when the weather permitted.

Mac loved his walk to work; it gave him time to think and to get ready for the day. The old boathouse had once been the lifeboat store and the slipway was still in place. The first part of his walk ran down past the slipway, along by the harbour wall and then across a bit of beach. The wooden walkway that led around the cliff, suddenly rising up from the beach and separating old settlement from new, was treacherous in winter but for the rest of the year, Mac considered it a joy. Looking down through the slats he could see the ocean roiling and bubbling beneath, eating away at the rocks that footed the cliff. Looking out, leaning on the wooden handrail, he could take in the full expanse of Frantham bay. He was, Mac realized, somewhat in love with this little backwater, with its peace and its people and when violence intruded he became quite unreasonably resentful.

The walk to work ended on Frantham beach and then a few brief steps along the promenade. He was unsurprised to see Rina Martin leaning against the rail and looking out at the quiet sea.

Mac kissed her cheek and then took a good look at her. 'You're looking well. A bit tired though?'

'A lot tired. But I've enjoyed myself more than I thought I would.'

Mac leaned beside her on the railing. 'I'm sorry I didn't manage to come round last night. By the time we'd finished up the initial interviews and the paperwork and had time to talk to the family it was well after nine and, well—'

'I don't suppose you were in any mood for social chit-chat by then either.' She clasped his arm. 'I didn't expect you, but I thought it would be nice to catch you before work. I've missed my early morning walks. And our conversations.'

'Me too,' Mac admitted. Rina had become part of his routine and it had seemed strange when a hole had appeared in the daily fabric.

'I'm going to see what Joy and Tim have done with their house, later. Joy is very excited.'

They turned together and wandered along the promenade

towards the coffee shop halfway down. 'I went over last week,' Mac told her. 'Joy has been having a hard time keeping Bridie in check. Someone had told her there was a West Country tradition of painting cottages pink . . . well you can imagine . . .'

'Oh, Lord. Can I! Bridie is a wonderful woman but she does have her own distinctive style. I take it Joy won that one?'

'She did, yes. But Bridie did come up trumps in the end. She went to an auction and bought a scrubbed pine table, a smaller version of the one you've got in your kitchen. Lovely old Victorian thing with a little drawer. Joy was delighted.'

Rina smiled. 'I heard on the news,' she said, 'about the poor woman at the farm.'

'The kids found her, Rina. When they came home from school. I talked to them yesterday . . . or rather, when Frank talked to them yesterday. I must admit, I let him get on with it. I just stood around looking useless.'

'We each have our skills, Mac. Frank is a people person. Folk trust him instinctively. They also trust *you* to get the job done.'

'Well, anyway. The poor little buggers, they were in bits. Just utterly shattered. Can you imagine what this is going to do to them? They lost their father to cancer a few years back and now this.'

'Any leads?'

Mac shook his head. 'Not as yet. No one would have heard or seen anything. The farmhouse is right back from the road and pretty much hidden from view. On the face of it, though, it looks to have been a *cold* crime. Whoever it was came over the fence, shot her through the window and then walked away. There was no theft, no obvious motive.'

They had arrived at the coffee shop and Mac ordered his usual morning takeaway. When he had first arrived in Frantham, his predecessor, Inspector Eden, had still been a few months off retiring. Like Mac, he'd ended up in this backwater after a series of personal and then professional tragedies had knocked him for six. Frantham had been viewed as a place he could safely and quietly work out his final years. Eden had always started the day with a morning briefing and gallons of very strong, very black coffee. Since Mac had taken over he had maintained the morning ritual of coffee, but purchased from Tonino's on the promenade.

'I'd best be off, then,' Rina said. 'The family will be wanting breakfast.'

'Who cooked it when you weren't there?' Mac smiled.

'Apparently, they had a rota.' Rina rolled her eyes. 'None of them are morning birds, so I don't dare ask how that one worked out. Do try and come round, won't you? And Miriam. I've not asked how she is.'

'Doing well,' Mac said. 'Not so many bad dreams, and she's started her doctorate so the boathouse is full of books. But I think it's helping.'

'Good.' Rina patted his arm and turned back along the promenade, heading towards the little general stores at the end.

Mac watched her for a moment and then began to walk back in the other direction, carrying his holder and three cups of coffee. He was due to return to the farm later that morning and then go on and join the team interviewing friends and neighbours. DI Kendall would hold a briefing late afternoon and Mac hoped something would have broken by then. Something he could tell the family. Some reason he could give the children for why their mother had to die. Though the truth was that Mac could think of nothing that could excuse such an act. Nothing that could ever make it right.

'You think you can scare me? You're even more pathetic than I thought.'

He turned his back on me then and that's when I did it. I don't think I went out with the intention of killing him, but then, you never know what you're really capable of until it's done. But I just wanted some acknowledgement. Some consideration. Some sense that the bloody man actually understood what he was going to do to people if he carried on. To good people, honourable people. Not like him. He was not a man who even understood the concept of honourable.

So I killed him.

And I'm not sorry.

And I'm not going to give myself up.

SIX

'She was a lovely woman. Always willing to help out.'

Martha Brigstock had spoken to Ellen Tailor just before she had died. That fact, Mac decided had heightened her sense of shock, made it personal.

'And she said nothing to indicate that she was worried. She'd not mentioned anything. No strangers hanging about. No strange telephone calls or letters. Nothing out of the ordinary?'

Mrs Brigstock shook her head emphatically. She wore elephant earrings with crystal beads suspended from the feet. They jangled each time she moved her head. 'She was just normal. Just her usual self. She told me the children had been auditioning for the Christmas performance at the school. Jeb plays the clarinet and Megan is in the choir but she wanted an acting part. We just chatted. You know?'

Mac nodded. 'I'm asking people to make a list of anyone Mrs Tailor was close to or that she saw regularly. Any groups or clubs she was a member of, any hobbies. Her family don't live close by and the children are finding it hard to answer questions at the moment.'

The earrings jangled again and Mrs Brigstock pulled a large white handkerchief from her sleeve and rubbed at her already reddened eyes.

'Finding her like that. Can you imagine anything more terrible? What's going to happen to them now? The family have farmed here for generations. That will all be gone now. Jeb and Megan, they'll lose the farm as well. Oh, the poor children.'

Mac looked over at the young officer he had brought with him. She had been lent to him by DI Kendall but, to be frank, wasn't proving to be any better at comforting and soothing than Mac himself. She looked back, helpless. Mac sighed and leaned forward, patted Mrs Brigstock's hand. 'We all feel sorry for them,' he said quietly. 'All we can do now is try and find the person responsible.'

She sniffed loudly, but the handkerchief disappeared back up the sleeve and Mac was relieved to find that he had said the right thing. He got up, ready to leave. 'So, a list of anyone or anything would be really useful,' he reiterated.

'I'll get right on to it. And I'll call Julia Howell. She's on the flower committee too. Have you spoken to her?'

She was on the list, Mac assured her. Someone else was doing that interview.

Yolanda, the PC Mac had been assigned, slid into the front passenger seat with a great sigh of relief. 'Sorry, sir. I'm not much good with old ladies. Not much good with kids either. I never know what to say.'

Mac sighed. Tried to be patient. 'You'll learn,' he said. 'Just be sympathetic. Say you are sorry for their loss and how terrible it must be, that sort of thing.' He tried to remember how it had been for him, starting out and if he had been so pathetic. Was that being fair, he wondered? For the moment, Mac gave up and focused on the issue at hand. 'OK, who's next on the list?'

'Someone called William Trent. At some place called Stone End. Shall I programme the satnav?'

Mac shook his head. 'It would just tell you to go to the middle of a field,' he said. 'Don't worry, I've got directions and there's a map in the glove compartment, already marked up.'

'A map?'

'Yes, big paper thing with roads and rivers and fields marked on it.'

'I know what a map is. I just never . . . I'm just—'

'Let me guess. Not very good with them.'

He saw her blush and regretted his harshness. Then reminded himself that she was a serving officer, not a school kid. 'Give me the map,' he said. 'I'll show you where we're going. You never know, you might find it a useful skill.'

For the next few minutes he talked Yolanda through the route they were going to take and tried to curb his sense of irritation. The trouble was, he decided, he'd been working in such a small team for this past eighteen months or so – not counting a brief while on secondment to his old beat – that he had grown unused to having to explain or interact with anyone who didn't know what he was thinking almost before he thought it. Besides, Frank Baker and Andy Nevins, the young PC also based at Frantham, were born and bred in these parts. They knew the people, knew the area. Yolanda, from her accent, was another blow-in as Frank would call it.

'Where were you based before you came down here?' he asked as they drove away.

'Nottingham, guv. I'm aiming to go back there eventually. All my family are up there and—'

She glanced across at Mac, a faintly embarrassed expression on her face.

'And it's more you?' He smiled.

'Yeah, I guess so. I grew up there . . . did you . . . how long have you been here?'

'Not that long,' Mac said. 'But I've been lucky. It felt like home very quickly.'

Yolanda nodded. 'I hoped I'd like it down here,' she said. 'I came down on holiday for a couple of weeks, but that's not like working here, is it. I mean, there are just too many bloody cows for a start.'

Mac laughed. 'Why did you come down?' he asked.

Yolanda rolled her eyes. 'Boyfriend,' she said. 'We broke up three weeks after I got here.'

'Tough.'

'Believe it! Teach me, won't it. My mum said I was an idiot, but you know how it is?' She peered down at the map. 'We take the next left, I think, then a sharp right and then . . . then the road stops.'

'There's a bit of a farm track,' Mac told her. 'Then we walk the last bit.'

'There's bound to be cows,' Yolanda said. 'I'll just bet there are cows.'

Martha Brigstock had barely shut the door on the inspector before she was on the phone. Her first call was brief and left her with ruffled feathers. The man should be grateful she had thought to call him before the police arrived.

Her second was to Vera Courtney who, Martha knew, would be far more grateful for her call.

'I've just had he police here,' she announced. 'Yes, about poor,

poor Ellen. Oh, makes me sick to my stomach, just thinking about it. And you. You were so much closer to the poor girl than the rest of us. Are you sure you're all right?'

Martha listened to her friend's reassurances but she was unconvinced by them.

'Vera, dear, you don't sound all right, really you don't. Look, we had a meeting planned for today, didn't we, all of us. I think we should keep to our plans. Ellen would have wanted that and she certainly wouldn't have wanted you to be alone to brood. I'll pick up Julia and Celia will make her own way as usual. Do you need a lift?'

'Yes, I'm sure Celia said she'd try to come.' Celia Marsden was not the most active participant in their little group, but she was chief donor of the more expensive flowers and so Martha was always careful to keep on the right side of her. 'I'll give her a call, Vera. If she can't make it, then the rest of us will have a nice cup of tea and a chat. You shouldn't be sitting there on your own, really you shouldn't.'

Martha smiled as Vera reluctantly agreed. 'You know I'm right, dear. We old 'uns should stick together, especially at a time like this.'

As she put the phone back on its cradle, Martha reflected that perhaps that last comment was not as sensitive as it might have been. Ellen, after all, hadn't had the chance to grow old.

Vera Courtney stared at the phone, in two minds whether or not to call back and tell Martha that she couldn't face an afternoon of tea and talk; but in her heart she knew that her friend was right. If she stayed here by herself, she'd only spend the afternoon crying and Vera really couldn't face that idea. Better to be with people, to have to exercise the self-control that being in a public place demanded, better to talk to those who had known Ellen and had liked and cared about her than to stay alone to grieve.

Martha had commented on how close Vera had been to the younger woman but Vera doubted even Ellen herself had realized just what Vera felt about her. In the ten years she had known Ellen Tailor, ever since she volunteered to help out with the flowers, the two had been friends. It had been such an easy relationship, right from the start, Vera thought, and as time went on Ellen had begun to confide in her, talk about the family she had married into and the conflicts that were blighting an otherwise happy marriage.

Vera, who had lived in the village all her life, knew Daphne Tailor and the rest of the family and was fully aware of what Ellen had married into.

'You never got married?' Ellen asked her.

'Sadly, no. I had a young man, but things didn't work out. It was hard for us, I suppose. I was five when the war ended and after my father didn't come back, my mother married again and that didn't last. Or rather, it lasted, but it was never happy. I suppose it made me cautious and when my young man proposed, I should have said yes but I didn't and after a while he found someone else and that was that.'

Vera hadn't spoken about him for years. Bobby had been such a lovely boy and she should have trusted him, but that was a long time ago.

'That's sad,' Ellen had said and Vera remembered the sympathy in the younger woman's eyes. 'When my mother died, my father fell apart. He killed himself. Vera, I'm never sure if I should feel pity for him because he loved her so much or just feel angry with him for deserting us. Do you think that's a bad thing to feel?'

'No,' Vera told her. 'Right or wrong doesn't enter into it. We feel what we feel. My mother never stopped loving my father, but I know a small part of her was furious with him for not coming home to her, even though she knew there was nothing he could do about it.'

We feel what we feel, Vera thought now. Ellen had understood what she meant by that. She had understood a great many things about Vera and Vera felt she had understood a great many things about Ellen. Vera had loved her like the daughter she had never had. She cherished the time they spent together and now, she felt utterly and completely bereft, the more so because no one else knew how she had felt about Ellen and so no one could possibly understand the depth of her grief.

SEVEN

William Trent opened the door and then ushered them inside. 'That Brigstock woman phoned me,' he said. 'Informed me that I'd be getting a visit.'

He gestured towards a couple of chairs set either side of the window and took a third, set by the fire. It wasn't lit, but already laid for later. Mac glanced around. The cottage was very small. This living room, and a tiny room off that was lined with books. A kitchen on the other side of the narrow hall and Mac guessed there'd be two bedrooms and a bathroom upstairs at the very most. It had been an estate cottage, Frank had told him. For the farm workers on the Breed Estate. This and three others had been sold off a few years earlier, being right on the edge of the estate and, Frank had informed him, needing a lot of work and expense to bring them up to modern specifications. Two had been sold off as holiday lets, and William Trent had purchased this cottage, Stone End, with its very pretty garden.

'So, you want to ask me what?' William Trent leaned back in the chair and clasped his hands across his slight pot belly. He had ignored Yolanda since she sat down, focused all of his attention on Mac.

'You were a friend of Ellen Tailor, I believe.'

'Obviously. If I hadn't known the woman, you'd not be here.'

'Did you know her well?'

'Do any of us know anyone well?'

Mac bit down on his irritation. 'When did you last see her? And incidentally, I am assuming the answer to that last question would be yes. The children referred to you as Uncle Bill.'

'Then why ask it?' Trent demanded. 'If you can't ask anything sensible then I suggest you go. I can't abide fools, Inspector. Not at any price.'

'So Ellen Tailor wasn't a fool,' Yolanda said.

William Trent scowled at her.

'And I'm assuming you didn't think the children were fools

either. I can't see you tolerating them calling you Uncle Bill if you thought they were idiots.'

The scowl deepened, but Yolanda seemed untroubled by it. Mac watched curiously, the young woman suddenly going up a notch in his estimation.

'How are they?' Trent asked abruptly. 'I heard they found her,' he added and Mac was surprised to see the genuine concern in his eyes.

'They'd just walked up the lane from the school bus,' he said. 'They walked into the kitchen and saw her on the floor and thought she'd hurt herself or fainted. So they ran to help her. Whoever shot her had used both barrels at close range. Shot her in the face.'

William Trent closed his eyes for a moment and Mac was both gladdened by his response and angry with himself for saying so much; for wanting to shock.

'She was a bright woman,' he said. 'In both senses of the word. Intelligent and—'

Yolanda opened her mouth to say something more and then shut it again, a slight frown creasing her forehead. Mac wondered at it.

'And the children?' he asked.

'She'd raised them to be curious. Not to be puddings. I can't abide pudding people. There are too many of them these days. Content just to sit there and let life happen to them. Ellen wasn't like that and neither are her children.'

'Did you know her husband?'

'No. He'd died before I came to live here.'

'Did Mrs Tailor talk about him much? Did the children?'

'Of course they did. He'd been a good husband and father. Ellen loved him. You don't stop loving someone just because they've passed away. Her husband was still a tangible presence in that house, in all the decisions she made.'

'Even when she sold off part of the farm?'

'Especially then. What her relatives couldn't accept was that they'd been planning the sale even before he became ill.'

'And did she say why?'

'I'd have thought that was obvious?'

'I'm sorry, but no. It's not.'

William Trent sighed and leant back in his chair. 'Farming has always been a tough business,' he said. 'The Tailors ran a big dairy herd. It was taking them all their time just to keep heads above water. Ellen told me if it hadn't been for those tax credit things she'd not have been able to feed the kids sometimes. So they wanted to downsize, to release some capital so they could fix up the farmhouse and have a cushion in case of bad times to come. The family blamed Ellen, said she should never have married Jebediah if she couldn't cope with the farming. When they found out he was ill they put pressure on him to leave the farm to the brother and his wife. But she's not the kind of woman to be pushed around like that and Jebediah left the whole kit and caboodle to her and the kids and wrapped it up so tight they couldn't challenge a word of the will.'

William Trent tapped the arm of his chair as though to emphasize the point. 'As it should be,' he said. 'Ellen had a good head on her shoulders and she could see a damn sight more clearly than any of that lot.'

He shook his head. 'And now she's gone. Looks like they'll get what they were after, doesn't it?'

'You think the family might have been involved in Ellen's murder?' Yolanda sounded sceptical and Trent's glance in her direction was withering.

'Who else?' he said. 'Bloody inbreds and halfwits the whole lot of them.'

'Did Ellen run the place single-handed?' Mac asked.

'No, no not entirely. She had a man come in most days. Terry . . . something. He'd worked for her husband and he stayed on to help her out. I mean, she paid him for it, of course. But he seemed loyal to her. Not that I had a lot to do with him.'

'Another halfwit?' Yolanda asked.

'My dear,' Trent said with heavy emphasis, 'there are few people who are not.'

Mac could see Yolanda start to bristle. 'When did you last see Ellen Tailor?' he asked.

Trent turned his attention back to Mac. 'Tuesday afternoon,' he said. 'I saw her two days ago. I walked over. The footpath that runs at the back of her place, you can pick it up at the end of the lane, here. You'll see the stile and the sign as you walk back to your car. And yes, she was fine and no, she didn't seem worried about anything.'

Trent pushed himself out of the deep armchair and waited for Mac and Yolanda to do the same. Mac waited for a moment or two before he obliged; long enough for Trent to become irritated. Then he took a card from his pocket and laid it on the arm of Trent's chair. He tapped it for emphasis, as Trent had done earlier. 'My card, should you think of anything,' he said.

'Where next?' Yolanda asked as they arrived back at the car.

Mac fished the map from the glove compartment and laid it out on the bonnet.

'We're not going to walk anywhere are we?'

'You don't like walking?'

'Oh, sure, when there are people and shops and footpaths. I'm not one for hiking. I'm really not.'

'What did you notice in the cottage?' he asked. 'There was a moment when you looked as though you wanted to say something and then you stopped yourself.'

She frowned. The moment had clearly slipped from her mind.

'Trent talked about Ellen being a bright woman,' Mac recalled. 'Intelligent and—'

'Oh. Yes. I suppose I was about to ask him if he'd fancied her. Then I thought maybe I'd better not. Then I saw the picture on the bookcase and it threw me a bit.'

'Picture?'

'Oh, you couldn't see if from where you were sitting. It was in that little ante room. Study or whatever, next to the sitting room.'

Mac nodded. 'And it was a picture of?'

'Old grumpy guts,' she said. 'Him and a woman. But the way he was looking at her, it was like there was no one else like her in the whole damned world. Made me wish someone had looked at me like that, you know. So I thought, maybe, I wouldn't ask if he fancied Ellen Tailor.'

'Interesting,' Mac said. 'Well, we'll be checking out our Mr Trent. Look,' he said, pointing at the map. 'This is where we are now, just down from the stile and footpath he mentioned. If you follow the track along, it comes out here, on the main road just past the farm. How long do you reckon it would take to walk there?'

She shrugged. 'What's the scale . . . so maybe twenty minutes?'

She looked suspiciously at Mac. 'Oh, no. We are going to walk it, aren't we?'

Mac shook his head. 'I thought I'd leave that to you,' he said. 'I'll drive back and pick you up. It you're right we should arrive at about the same time. Your route is much more direct than going back by road.'

He left her glaring at him.

EIGHT

From his bedroom window William Trent watched the two police officers walk back up the lane. He could just see the back of their car but after that the lane turned and he lost sight of the two figures. He was surprised to see the woman return. Trent frowned, assuming she must have forgotten to ask him something. He prepared for a knock at the door but instead she paused next to the stile that led on to the footpath he had told them about.

From his vantage point he could see her clearly, tell by the set of her shoulders that she wasn't pleased. He heard the car engine start and heard the sound of it pulling away. The woman heard it too and turned to look. William Trent could imagine her glare. He chuckled to himself. 'So he's left you to walk to the farm, has he? Well, it'll do you good, burn some of that fat off.'

He watched as she climbed the stile and lowered herself carefully down on to the path. To be fair, Bill thought, she wasn't really fat, just carrying a bit too much around the arse for his liking. But then again, he didn't really feel like being fair. Life wasn't fair so why the hell should he bother?

He watched for long enough to satisfy himself that she really had taken the path and wasn't about to come back and bother him and then he went back down the stairs and into his tiny little study. I should be working, he thought, but the idea of writing up the notes he had made over the past few days and transcribing the interviews he had done the week before just defeated him.

Instead, he put on his walking boots and followed the police officer down the path that led to Ellen's farm.

So, how long did it take you?' Mac asked. As he'd suspected she might, Yolanda had reached the farm ahead of him and was sipping at a cup of tea kindly provided by her colleagues still on duty there.

She glared at him. 'Twenty-three minutes exactly. What took you so long?'

Mac ignored the tone. He'd taken his time on the drive and pulled into a lay-by, he knew where he could get a decent phone signal and spent fifteen minutes making phone calls to arrange their next set of interviews.

'What can you see from the ridge?'

Yolanda groaned.

'Come on, you can show me. You can bring your tea.'

The path the killer was believed to have taken was still cordoned. Yolanda had climbed the fence a little further on and now Mac followed her back the way she had come. He knew he'd have to make the walk himself at some point; but not today. Later, when he could either do it alone or with Frank Baker. Mac would welcome the older man's observations and local knowledge.

'Is it an easy walk?'

'Well, it's pretty flat, I suppose. A couple of stiles and a field full of cows. I knew there'd be cows. To be honest there's not much to see for a lot of it. Just a load of trees and hedges but you get a good view about halfway along and there are other connecting paths going off too. One leads to the coast, apparently. But you needn't think I'm walking that one, Sir.'

Mac found himself wondering if Rina Martin had walked those particular footpaths. Rina was a great walker and, much to Tim's dismay, often tried to drag her youngest lodger along on her excursions. More recently, she'd included Joy in her invitations and poor Tim had been most put out to discover that his fiancée actually enjoyed country rambles.

Mac, well Mac was pretty sanguine about the whole idea, but he had learnt quickly on moving down here that road was often the longest way between A and B and that he'd better get to know the alternatives.

Yolanda was slightly breathless as they reached the ridge, but she'd held on to her mug of tea and Mac, slightly envious now, watched as she drank it. 'You get a good view of the farm,' she said. 'And I bet you could hide really well up here. There's plenty of cover. The CSI think the killer waited somewhere about there.' She pointed to a small cordoned area beneath what Mac thought might be a beech tree. In front of the tree a thicket of bramble and nettle formed a natural screen. As he moved closer he could see where a gap had been created in the brambles and squatting down to look through it, Mac got a good view of the farmyard and the kitchen window and even a little of the kitchen.

'It's a perfect spot,' he said, 'and I suspect a well-used one. Look, you can see a narrow trail leading from the path down to the tree.'

'Looks like a rabbit trail to me,' Yolanda said. 'Doesn't look wide enough for a person.'

'It's only grass,' Mac pointed out. 'There's no foliage to push through, nothing to leave your mark on. You walk carefully enough it's plenty wide enough and to the rest of the world, yes, it's just another rabbit trail.'

'So the killer watched her before today.'

'Of course he did. He knew her habits, her routines. Could probably count on the fact that she'd be in the kitchen in the middle of the afternoon. Whoever did it must have known Ellen Tailor and her family.'

'Or they must have known the path. Maybe just chanced on the farm. Maybe just paused here one day, saw a potential victim, came back often enough to establish a pattern and then took a chance.'

Mac frowned, conceded she did have a point.

'But you're not convinced?'

He shook his head. 'No. But I'm prepared to keep an open mind. The one mitigation against your theory is that a stranger would stand out.'

'A stranger might stand out if anyone saw them. Look, I was on that blasted path for almost half an hour. I saw no one, not even a farmer in the field. Chances are you could walk this way ten days in a row and not have anyone see you and if they did? Well, the locals would just think 'tourist' and blank them. So long as they dressed the part, no one would think anything of it, and this time of year, even if they didn't dress the part, anyone noticing a stranger in shorts and flip flops would just assume it was some stupid townie strayed too far from the beach.'

Mac nodded. 'True,' he said.

'But?'

'But the victim must have stood by the window and seen her killer walk down from the ridge and across the field and over the fence and into her garden.'

'You're assuming she hadn't just gone over to the window.'

'She'd been peeling vegetables at the sink, so it seems likely that's where she was standing.'

'And if she had seen whoever it was, isn't she more likely to assume it's someone who's a bit lost and wants directions? Has just come down off the path to ask where the hell they are?'

'Carrying a shotgun? Ramblers are more likely to be carrying those ski pole things or walking sticks than they are a shotgun.'

'She might not have seen it?'

'Or she might be so used to whoever it was carrying one that it wasn't unusual.'

Yolanda shrugged. 'When do you reckon she realized he was going to shoot her?' she asked, her tone suddenly more sombre.

'From the way the body fell, right at the last minute, I'd guess. She didn't try to run or turn, she didn't even raise her hands – and people do, even when there's no logical way they can defend themselves.'

'So, we have to hope she didn't have long to be afraid, then.'

Mac looked curiously at the young officer. He nodded. 'Let's go down,' he said.

Back along the path, William Trent had listened to their conversation. They had no idea he was there, but then William Trent was good at going unnoticed. He'd had a lot of practice over the years.

When he was certain they had gone he stood in the shadows of one of the tall trees that topped the bank and looked down at the farm. The two who had come to his house were speaking with two other officers and after a few minutes they turned to go. As he passed through the farm gate, Mac turned and looked back at

the ridge and for a moment William Trent was sure the officer had
seen him. Then Mac closed the gate and returned to his car.

'You don't have a clue, do you,' William Trent asked softly as
Mac and Yolanda drove away. 'You don't have a bloody clue.'

NINE

Frank Baker could be said to have drawn the short straw in
that he'd been assigned to go and speak with the dead
woman's family. The truth was, he had been the obvious
choice. He knew them slightly, and also he felt oddly responsible,
having been the first on scene and also the first to speak with the
children. He wanted to give them some sense of continuity, a
familiar face.

He was met at the door by Sally Clarke, a liaison officer from
Exeter and someone Frank had known since she was ten years
old. She'd been at school with Frank's daughter. Frank had
requested that DI Kendall send her.

'Sally, love. How are you? Who have we got?'

'The kids, the sister and the grandmother. They're holding it
together but . . .'

Frank nodded and allowed Sally to lead him through into the
living room and introduce him. Ellen's sister looked a lot like her,
and the grandmother, Ellen's mother-in-law, a good deal like the
child, Jebediah. The two women sat on a small sofa. They were
holding hands, very tightly, the children on cushions at their feet
as though they wanted at all costs to display a united front against
this horror. Frank took a chair opposite, immediately feeling as
though he was facing an interview panel for a particularly difficult
job – one for which he hadn't even seen the advert or the
description.

'Have you found anything?' Daphne Tailor, Ellen's mother-in-
law, was the first to speak.

'Nothing yet. I'm sorry.'

'Who could do something like this? Ellen was—

'A lovely girl,' Daphne finished. 'I've got to admit, I had my doubts about her to start with. When my Jeb said he was going to marry her, when he could have the pick of any girl round here, I gave it six months. I think we all did. But we were wrong and she proved that.'

'And then your son died.'

'And Ellen nursed him to the end and ran the farm and he never wanted for anything. We all pitched in, of course. All helped out, but she was the one there twenty-four-seven. She got a cancer nurse to come and sit for the last few nights, give her a bit of respite, but Jeb was scared of going away. He hated hospitals, always had, and Ellen told him she'd be there for him no matter what. And she was.'

'And afterwards, when she decided to sell part of the farm. I heard there was some friction?'

Daphne nodded. 'I wasn't happy but I could follow her reasoning. Ray, my other son, wanted to take it over. He said Jeb had always promised the farm to him and he was mad as hell that Jeb left everything to Ellen including control of the farm and his permission to do what she thought best. He had that written into his will, just to make certain we all knew.'

'And that caused friction?'

'Caused World War Three for a while,' Daphne said. 'Then when the farm came up for sale, Ray wanted to buy it. Thought he would get it cheap. Put all sorts of pressure on the girl.'

'Pressure?'

'Emotional blackmail mostly. Then he took to harassing her. Phoning and calling at all times of the day and night. Finally she came and told me what he was up to and I had a word.'

'And did that stop him?'

'For a while. Ray always was a stubborn bastard.' She seemed, Frank thought, to have almost forgotten the children were there. He wondered if he should suggest they left the room, then thought better of it. He doubted anyone would agree with him.

'Did he ever threaten Ellen directly?'

'He didn't kill her,' Daphne said. 'He and that wife of his are halfway round the world.'

'They emigrated.' Diane, Ellen's sister spoke for the first time. 'New Zealand. They needed money to do it, and a job to go to. He found a job and we, as a family, Ellen included, raised the

money. She gave him a share when she sold the land. Most of the
rest went into trust for the kids and she kept some back as a
cushion against hard times. Daphne contributed too and so did I.'

'So, effectively you paid him to go?'

'He's an arsehole, pure and simple,' Daphne said. 'It pains me
to say that about my own flesh and blood, but there you go. When
his dad passed, the land I'd brought in when I got married, that
went to our Ray. He ran it into the ground. My dad would have
been spinning in his grave. He trusted me with that land and I
agreed it should go to Ray. Worst thing I ever did. And now there's
none of it left from either family except the ten or so acres Ellen
hung on to and the farmhouse. But we'll make damned sure we
keep hold of that. Won't we kids?'

Frank looked at the children. They had made no response and
he wondered how they'd all actually feel about returning to a place
where they'd seen their mother's body; their mother's blood. He
made no comment about that. Instead he asked, 'And the land Ray
owned – was that sold before he left?'

'Long before. He let the Breed Estate have it for a song just to
pay off his debts. I couldn't afford to buy him out, neither could
his brother. Ran it into the ground, he did. That place had been
in my family for four generations, did you know that? Four generations of Baxters. When I married a Tailor my dad thought the
place would be safe. The Tailors were good land managers. I feel
like I've let him down. I feel like we've let them all down. Both
families.'

Frank noticed Diane clasp the other woman's hand even harder.
Noticed the pressure returned. He asked. 'Did Ellen mention any
worries? Anything out of the ordinary?'

Diane shook her head. 'We were close,' she said. 'Even though
we lived miles apart. We'd speak on the phone a couple of times
a week, chat on Facebook nearly every day, even if it was just a
quick comment. Ellen was happy. Happier than she'd been since
Jeb died.'

'And did she say why?'

Diane shrugged. 'She just said she was finally getting over it.
Getting her head back together. Felt she was making some headway.
She loved Jeb so much. It took her a long time to just believe he'd
really gone, I think. Then when she sold the land and she managed

to sell it all as a going concern, I think she felt relieved. Like she'd done the right thing and not just for her and the kids but for the herd and the land as well. After that she seemed to get better, slowly. This last few months I think she'd almost got back to her old self.'

Daphne nodded in agreement. 'No one would want to hurt Ellen,' she said. 'No one that knew her. It's got to have been someone from outside. You hear about these things, don't you? Serial killers that travel from place to place. People released from mental hospitals. People who are just not right in the head. Someone saw her and just decided they were going to . . . to do it. That's what I think. No one that knew Ellen would hurt a hair of her head. Not even that blasted son of mine.'

'So what do we have?' DI Kendall asked. The afternoon briefing was supposed to have begun at four thirty but an RTA on the coast road had delayed the return of Frank and a couple of the others. It was now well after five.

'Nothing out of the ordinary in her financials,' an officer Mac did not know told them. 'I spent the afternoon with her bank manager going over her account and there's nothing that can't be accounted for. No unusual payments going in and none out. She was methodical. Had everything she could on direct debit and had a separate account for those bills that she topped up at the start of each month. She had the account her wages were paid into, and the bit of tax credit she got and what was left over from the sale of the land a few years ago was in there. She drew house-keeping money every week so presumably paid for most things in cash. Then there was the trust fund she started for the kids. Most of what was left from the farm sale seems to have gone into that. The manager told me she started it up just after the sale. He arranged for her to see a financial advisor at the time. We had a good look at the finances from that period because it's the last time there was any unusual activity. There was a payment of five thousand to a man called Ray Tailor. Apparently he was her brother-in-law and a further two thousand six months after. The last three years she's had a part-time job, a bit of income from the market garden at the farm and some tax credits.'

'No insurance policy when the husband died?' Kendall asked.

'Not that we could see.'

'She's on the PTA at her kids' school,' someone else picked up. 'Active on other local groups like the flower-arranging committee, helps out at the youth group that meets in the church hall. And another at the Breed Estate, run by someone called Dan Marsden. From the people I talked to I got the impression that she was visible and active but not keen on being on the committees or anything like that.'

'Apart from church flowers?'

'Church flowers is five women. Or was, with Ellen Tailor. They're all on the committee.'

'And the children?'

'The head teacher describes Megan as very bright and Jeb as good at sports and very kind. Megan's class teacher says she tends to daydream but she does her homework and gets good marks. She's got a couple of close friends she has sleepovers with and goes riding with.'

'Riding?' Kendall asked. 'Expensive hobby for a woman without many resources.'

'That's what I thought. But one of Megan's friends . . . um Stacy Ashdown, she lives up on the Breed Estate. Her dad is in charge of the stables. The girls get to ride the estate ponies.'

'Anyone been up to the Breed Estate yet?' Mac asked.

'I have, sir.' A young woman raised her hand and then opened her notebook. 'Ellen Tailor worked two days a week in the farm shop and they took most of what she produced in the market garden for the hotel.'

'Hotel?'

'The big house on the estate. Breed Manor, got turned into an upmarket hotel and wedding venue about ten years ago,' Kendall explained. 'Carrie Butler lives in what used to be the Dower House. Or in part of it anyway. It's divided in half. The estate manager and his family have the other half.'

'I spoke to Carrie Butler and to Mark Jones, the estate manager,' the young woman continued. 'Ellen Tailor was well liked and efficient. Good with the public, they said, and she sometimes helped out in the hotel too. Carrie Butler said she'd like to give her more hours but that Ellen still had what was left of the farm to run and the kids to look after.'

'And any strangers in the area, anything inconsistent? Anyone who didn't seem to like Ellen Tailor?'

Mac leaned back against one of the many filing cabinets lined up along the back wall and sipped the tea he had been given when he arrived and watched and listened as the picture of Ellen Tailor's life was reconstructed. Frank Baker, having delivered his own account, sidled over to him. 'Strikes me this is going to be a slow one,' he said quietly.

Mac nodded. 'No enemies, no one who wants to speak ill of the dead. No financial irregularities, unless someone turned up a tin box under the bed and hasn't declared it. No motive, just plenty of opportunity and what looks like a fair bit of planning. This wasn't an impulse. This was personal, I'm sure of it.'

Kendall was winding up the meeting.

'Heading straight for home?' he asked Frank.

'I am. Our youngest and her fiancé are coming over.'

'They set a date yet?'

'Have they hell. Still saving, they say. Want it to be perfect, they say, though our Sal reckons they'll get some sense and plough their money into a deposit eventually. Fortunately, they've both got decent jobs but even so . . .'

Mac nodded. Property was getting more expensive by the day. No way he and Miriam could think of buying anywhere at least not until she was working again. Tim and Joy had only managed it because Bridie, Joy's mother, was a woman of means, and these days most of it was even legally obtained.

'I'm going to call in and see Rina on my way back,' he said.

'Ah, the redoubtable Mrs Martin.' Frank smiled. 'Give her my best, won't you? And I'll give Andy a call, see how he's been, holding the fort.'

'He'll have been fine,' Mac predicted. PC Andy Nevins had only been a probationer when Mac had arrived in Frantham. Now a fully fledged PC he was the last bastion of law and order in Frantham while Mac and Frank Baker were busy elsewhere, but the full flood of the tourist season was over now and Andy, Mac knew, was well capable of dealing with anything that might arise. Though he was a little resentful at missing out on the murder investigation this time around.

'See you in the morning then,' Mac said.

He paused to catch a quick word with DI Kendall before he left. 'Any background on William Trent?' he asked.

'No, not as yet. Any reason for asking?'

'Maybe, maybe not. As you know, I got Yolanda to walk back to the farm from Trent's place.'

'She mentioned it,' said Kendall with a grin. 'And?'

'And when I got back to the farm we went up on to the ridge, just where it meets the path. We stood up there and talked things through. Our Yolanda has an aptitude for playing devil's advocate, doesn't she?'

Kendall laughed. 'It has been remarked upon,' he agreed. 'Not a bad trait in a young officer though.'

'True. But the thing is, I looked back once we were down at the farm and he was there, standing on the ridge. He was standing in the shadow of the trees and when he saw me looking back he dodged out of sight but he must have followed Yolanda along the path. Now why would he do that?'

'Curiosity? People are, you know? Why didn't you challenge him?'

'He was up on the ridge; I was standing by the gate. Frankly, I didn't much fancy running up that damned great hill. And what would I have said when I got there? Always supposing I'd have caught him? And, more to the point, I didn't want to freak Yolanda out. But I *will* ask the question. I just want to go in armed with more knowledge of the target, if you know what I mean. The Tailor kids regarded him as a friend, so it might as you say be down to pure curiosity, or to a feeling of impotence. His friend has been killed and he can do nothing but—'

'But he's well worth another look. I'll give it priority in the morning. God knows we've got nothing else. Nothing that even looks like a lead.'

'Early days,' Mac soothed, but Kendall's words echoed his own thoughts earlier. As Frank had said, this was going to be a slow one.

Tim met him at the door to Peverill Lodge and ushered him inside. 'We laid an extra place at the table just in case,' he said. 'Rina had a feeling you might drop in. She called Miriam but—'

'She's having a drink with new friends at the university,' said

Mac, nodding. 'She took a bit of persuading, but I'm going to pick her up and drive her home, so she should be fine. How's the house coming on?'

Tim rolled his eyes. 'We're trying to get the furniture in before Bridie comes down next week. Joy figures if there's no room for her to fit in any more furniture then she won't be able to go out and buy it and we won't have to deal with telling her it isn't quite what we want. Though, to be fair, the table and dresser she got us are just brilliant.'

'No giant sideboards, then,' Mac joked. Bridie loved auctions and on one occasion had bought the biggest Georgian buffet Mac had ever encountered. He had to admit that it was beautifully made but the original owners would probably have owned a stately home. Bridie's house was large but they'd still had to remove the patio doors to get it inside.

'I'm not complaining, though,' Tim added. 'She's been amazing.'

A chorus of welcome greeted Mac as he entered the dining room and took what had become his usual seat at the table. Matthew was already filling a plate for him and Stephen handed him a glass of wine and placed a tumbler of water beside his plate. 'Lovely to see you,' Matthew intoned. 'We've been following your case on the radio news.'

'Now Matthew,' Bethany chided. 'No business at mealtimes and especially no murders. You have to wait until at least dessert is served and preferably until coffee.'

Mac glanced across at Rina who smiled back at him and then settled to enjoy his meal among those who had become his extended family over the past couple of years. A little eccentric they might all be, but Mac had come to feel part of the Peverill Lodge household; to love being a part of it and a more loyal group of friends he doubted he would ever meet.

Afterwards, over coffee, talk inevitably turned back to the murder. Bethany, it seemed, had known the Tailor family slightly. 'I've been helping out at the airfield. You know that Lydia de Freitas is setting up that exhibition in the old reception area?'

Mac nodded. 'Well, it's not really Eliza's sort of thing, is it, dear, but I've always enjoyed history and when Lydia was asking for volunteers to help her sort and curate, well, I jumped at it. Well, Ellen Tailor brought us a whole load of stuff. They'd gone round the local villages, her and . . . oh I don't know, some other woman. Someone from the church, I think . . . Vera, something or other . . . and asked people to lend or contribute anything from the war. Lydia is hoping to change the exhibition several times a year, sort of keep up with what was happening, you know?'

Mac nodded. 'So, did you get to chat to her at all?'

'Oh yes. She came the first time to drop stuff off, then came back three or four times when I was there. She brought the children with her once and they played on the grass outside. Sweet little things they seemed. Especially the little girl.'

'I felt a bit sorry for the boy.' Eliza might not have been there, but she wasn't going to be left out. 'Who on earth calls their child Jebediah in this day and age?'

'Apparently it's a family tradition,' Mac said.

'Well, I'm all for traditions, but some of them are best forgotten about, don't you think?'

'Well, anyway,' Bethany continued, 'yes, I chatted to her on several occasions. I liked her very much. Who on earth would want to kill a nice young woman like that?'

'Is it true she was shot?' Matthew asked.

Mac nodded. 'Bethany, did you get the impression she was happy, or worried, or—'

Bethany shook her head, the carefully arranged white hair bouncing a little as she moved her head. 'No, dear, I didn't. We spent a lot of our time chatting about the things we were sorting through. You'd be amazed at what's come in. Be shocked at what some people are prepared to just donate. I mean, family photos and personal letters and all sorts.'

'And did Ellen Tailor bring anything from her family?' Not that it was likely to be relevant if she had, he thought. But he was curious about her and about her family. The family she had married into particularly. Some gut feeling niggled at him that the answers may lie there.

'She brought old photographs and ration books and various bits and pieces from her husband's family. Lydia could let you see, I'm sure. I don't remember there being anything particularly unusual.'

Mac nodded but it was clear Bethany had thought about something else. 'She brought a man with her one day,' she said.

'Introduced him to Lydia and they all went off to that little back room Lydia uses as her office. I don't know what they talked about, but Lydia seemed very pleased about something when they came out. Ellen didn't stop that day, she left with the man. I think he was driving.'

'Did you happen to catch his name?' Mac asked.

She closed her eyes as though picturing the scene, then opened them again and smiled happily at Mac. 'Oh, yes, as it happens I did. Lydia said, "Goodbye Mr Trent," and he said, "Oh, call me William."'

William Trent, again, Mac thought. Interesting. The man certainly deserved another visit.

'Is that helpful?' Bethany asked.

Mac nodded. 'I've met Mr Trent,' he said. 'I think he's a historian of some kind. Thank you, Bethany. Well remembered.'

Bethany preened herself and so, Mac noted, did Eliza. Mac had long since regarded the sisters as two parts of the same whole. It had probably taken him the best part of a year to remember consistently which one was which.

'A historian,' Rina said. 'Tim, didn't you tell me that *Iconograph* are working on a new series of games?'

Tim nodded. 'Edward wants to bring the first of them out next summer, I think. They're not like all the *Call of Duty* stuff that's around; these focus on some of the small stories he's dug up. To be honest, Rina, I don't know a lot. I've only been involved on the periphery. It's all still a bit hush-hush, you know. He found some bits of research about the camouflage and misdirection that went on in World War Two and that there had been people from the magic circle involved, and I was able to point him in the direction of the research that had been done recently on that, but I've been so busy with the new *Magician's Quest* that's out next spring that I've not taken a lot of notice of what everyone else is doing.' Tim, a skilled stage magician, had acted as consultant for the *Iconograph* series for about eighteen months now in addition to his performance career.

Mac thanked them all again and the conversation drifted off elsewhere. He wasn't really surprised that the Peverill Lodge crowd had crossed paths with Ellen or William Trent. It was only a few miles up the road to the murder scene and the occupants of Peverill

Lodge, though more blow-ins as Frank would have put it, had been in Frantham for almost a decade now and made a real effort to become integral parts of the local community.

But the William Trent link was interesting and he wondered if Lydia or Edward would be able to tell him anything useful about William Trent before he returned to poke the lion in his own den again.

TEN

Two days after Ellen's death

Vera Courtney was up early as always, watering the plants in her conservatory and feeding the cat almost before it was light. She found it hard to sleep. Ellen was there, whenever she closed her eyes. Point-blank range, the rumour was. She'd been unrecognizable. It was more than Vera could bear to think about. That pretty face blasted and the blonde hair stained and matted with blood. Vera knew the damage a shotgun could do and it wasn't an image she wanted in her head but it was there regardless. She couldn't stop thinking about Ellen.

Vera had promised to go out to the airfield that morning and meet the rest of the flower committee. They had taken it upon themselves to assist Lydia de Freitas at the airfield. Vera had mixed feelings about it all, though she enjoyed the company and the sorting and collating was interesting – and she had a liking for Lydia too. She still felt uncomfortable about the public display of personal objects. It felt un-British, somehow and, more than that, it felt like a betrayal of secrets. Especially in the case of individuals like her father. Even the family weren't supposed to know what he had been doing and she had heard that some of the operations that he and his colleagues had been involved in were still secret.

William Trent had told her that and he should know, she supposed. Though that didn't stop him from wanting her to tell him all the details she could recall. From him trying to persuade her to hand over her memories and those little bits and pieces that her mother had cherished.

Nora, Vera's mother had kept these scraps and scrats of souvenirs. The letters he had sent, the little journal he had kept. The will he had written for the time sure to come, when he never came back.

'Yugoslavia, Crete, Mitilini,' Vera whispered. Places she had never visited and only looked at on maps – or more lately on the Internet. Ellen had showed her how to access sites that showed her pictures and even video of the places where her father had been posted. She had looked on Google Earth and followed with her finger the paths he had taken. She had been barely five years old when her mother got the news she had been dreading and expecting. That her father was gone. But the sadness of it all, the real sadness, was that he had died not in distant Yugoslavia, as it had then been called, or a Greek island or North Africa. No, it had been a scant five miles from where he had been born.

Mac left Miriam still sleeping when he left the boathouse the following morning. She didn't have to be at uni that day and had made a rather late night of it. When Mac had picked her up, she'd actually been a little drunk – and very giggly and more relaxed than he'd seen her in a good while and he'd felt a pang of jealousy that he'd not been the one responsible for that.

'I love you. You know that, don't you?' he had told her as they had lain together in their bed and she had been drifting off to sleep.

'You'd better,' Miriam told him, snuggling her body closer to the curve of his. 'I'm not going anywhere.'

This morning there was no Rina waiting for him on the promenade and he didn't make his usual stop for coffee. Instead, he walked on out of Frantham and towards the airfield, about a mile beyond the perimeter of the town. Lydia de Freitas had to drive to Oxford later that morning but she had promised to give him an hour first thing to sort through what Ellen Tailor had brought in for the exhibition and to talk about William Trent. He found her in the tiny office that she had made her own at the back of the main airport building. The restorers were already busy as he walked through the reception. The art deco building coming back to life after years of near dereliction was a fine thing to see, he thought, and the de Freitases had brought a fair number of jobs to Frantham too.

Lydia greeted him with a kiss on the cheek. 'Pull up a chair,' she said. 'I've sorted out the boxes of family stuff that she brought in. Think I've found everything but I will do another check when I get a minute. Won't be today, I'm afraid, lord knows what time I'll get back tonight. But I don't see what—'

'Truthfully, neither do I. But neither can anyone come up with a decent motive for anyone shooting her, so I'm quite prepared to look at anything just now.'

Lydia nodded. 'Ah, so it's clutching at straws time, is it? Tough. You asked about William Trent?'

'I understand from Bethany that Ellen introduced him to you?'

'Um, yes. That's right. You want some coffee?' She had a large cafetière set up on the window sill.

She set his coffee down on the desk between them and passed him sugar and milk in a little carton. 'Next thing to get in here is a small fridge and a coffee machine,' she said, 'though I'm going to have to park them in reception. You couldn't swing a squirrel in the space I have left here, never mind a cat.'

'It's all coming together, though isn't it?'

'Oh, very well considering, though I don't think we realized quite what a major job it was going to be. Let's buy that old airfield, Edward said. Then it was, "let's get that old airfield functioning again."' She shook her head, fondly. 'Then it was "do you think you can project manage it for me."'

'And you're enjoying every minute,' Mac said.

Lydia chuckled. 'I am,' she admitted. '*Iconograph* has needed me less and less this past year. We've built a good team and I've been easing out of a lot of the executive stuff. Looking for a new direction, I suppose. This really has become my baby.'

Mac nodded and sipped his coffee. Lydia looked well. She had healed, he thought. It gave him hope for Miriam's healing process. 'William Trent?' he asked.

'Ah, William Trent. Hmm. Where to begin? I'd met Ellen a few times when she brought exhibits in and stopped to help out. We got chatting and she said she'd seen the call we put out for local stories, especially from nineteen forty and forty-one. Edward and the team wanted background to add depth to the storylines he's using. The latest project is called *Speculatrix*. It's apparently an Elizabethan word for a female spy and it's an open world gaming experience. That means that in addition to following the main quest or mission lines, you can, if you want, just explore the world, make up your own missions, do what the hell you like, really. So we need additional material, as much as we can get, to make the experience as detailed as possible.'

'And that's where the local stories come in?'

Lydia nodded. 'It's hoped that . . . well you know the *Magician's Quest* games that Tim's been advising on?'

Mac nodded.

'Well, I don't know if you understand much about it, but there's a facility for inserting your own magical character into the world, adding extra features, developing illusions, even building extra theatres and landscape and so on?'

'Tim told me about that.' Mac nodded. 'Mods?'

'That's right. These days the proof you have a successful game is when the community takes it to their hearts and starts building modifications and add-ons to it. In the past, we've actually recruited from the pool of modders that we've found through the games – or who have found us, I suppose.'

'And William Trent is a historian—'

'Who is writing a book – a second book, actually – in a series called *Hidden Histories*. It focuses on capturing the little stories, makes use of a lot of primary sources that don't usually surface. Letters, diaries, oral history—'

'So a lot of overlap with what you're doing here.'

Lydia nodded. 'Ellen realized that and thought we might have something to offer one another.' She frowned. 'It was an odd friendship,' she said. 'Between her and Bill Trent – sorry, I should call him William.' She grinned mischievously at Mac.

'I take it he doesn't like "Bill".'

'No, not much. He's a pompous man. That's why it was so odd. William obviously thought a lot of Ellen and her kids for that matter. The kids called him Uncle Bill, but I think they are the only people who could get away with using the diminutive. Ellen clearly liked him and yet two more opposite people would be hard to imagine. Ellen was so relaxed, so laid back. Friendly . . . you know?'

'Some people have a gift for friendship,' Mac observed. 'They draw others out of themselves, bring unexpected groups of people together.'

She laughed. 'You mean like our Rina? Well, yes, you do have a point.' She set down her cup and smoothed the already smooth skirt. Then snagged her suit jacket from the back of her chair and slipped it on. 'I must be off,' she said. 'Take the boxes if you like and I'll have another check around for anything else.'

'I walked here,' Mac told her.

'Ah, right. Look, I'll have a word with Don, the foreman, on the way out. Get him to give you a lift back if you need it. Must go.' She bent and kissed him on the cheek again. 'I'm really sorry about Ellen,' she added. 'Violent death is an appalling thing to happen in any family.'

And she should know, Mac thought as he heard her walk away.

An hour later, having skimmed the contents of the boxes, he took Lydia up on her offer and got Don to drive him back to Frantham. Don helped him carry the boxes along the pedestrian promenade to the tiny police station and dump them on Mac's desk.

'DI Kendall's here,' PC Andy Nevins told him as they passed through the reception area. 'He's just gone for coffee, I told him you were heading back.'

Don left and Frank Baker mooched through into Mac's office. 'What's all this then?'

'Probably nothing. Ellen Tailor took this lot to the airfield for their World War Two exhibition. I just thought I'd take a look and it seems that she introduced the de Freitases to William Trent about a month ago. They're employing him as a technical adviser apparently. Kendall say what he wanted?'

'He just wants to bring you up to speed on overnight developments.' The man himself came into the already overcrowded office and Mac hastily moved a box so he could set the coffee down.

'Developments?' Mac asked.

'Small developments.'

Andy Nevins leaned against the door, the bright sunlight streaming into the reception area setting his red hair aflame. Frank and Kendall squeezed chairs into the tiny space. Mac explained about Ellen and William Trent and then waited for Kendall to give his information over.

'It may be something, may be nothing,' Kendall said. 'At first glance, Ellen Tailor's financials looked clean. Then the sister told us about a second bank account. They'd set it up between them after the sale of the farm. Started a bit of a trust fund off for the kids. Ellen had seeded it with a couple of thousand, presumably from the sale, then both women added regular amounts on a pretty regular basis. We're not talking big amounts here. Ten pounds, twenty, occasionally a hundred, but it was in both their names and it was, Diane Emmet said, good to be doing something that was just *their* family. Nothing to do with the Tailor's.'

'Friction?'

'She said not. She was quite emphatic about that. She said Ellen may not have totally liked her in-laws but she made a real effort to get along well with them. She said there were what she expected – the usual conflicts between close families.'

'What she expected? That sounds a little vague.'

'The sisters were orphaned when they were fifteen and seventeen, spent a couple of years shunted around relatives and then when Ellen went off to uni, she took her little sister with her. After that, they shifted for themselves. It can't have been easy, but you can see how it would have made them very close. Diane finished school, also applied to university in York and got in. She stayed up there when Ellen moved south but when Ellen was widowed, it seems they wanted to do something to safeguard the kids' future themselves, however small and symbolic.'

'And now the kids are orphaned too. How did Ellen's parents die?'

'Well that's pretty tragic too. Cancer took one, depression the other. The father committed suicide. Threw himself under a train. Nasty way to go. Nasty thing to make someone else responsible for.'

Mac nodded. 'So this bank account?'

'Either sister could pay in or withdraw. About four months ago, larger amounts started to be paid in. Five hundred, a thousand on one occasion. In total nearly seven thousand pounds. Ellen apparently said she's sold off a bit more land and some redundant farm machinery, but when Diane mentioned that to Daphne Tailor, she didn't know anything about it. So she came to me and showed me the account.'

'How was the money paid in?'

'Cash and at several different branches.'

Mac frowned. 'So, where was she getting it?'

'It's the first anomaly we've found. It might be innocent. She might have been selling stuff off and not telling the in-laws. From what I've seen of the Tailor's they are quite a controlling bunch. I've arranged to speak to Terry Bridger, the farm worker who comes in part time to help out. We interviewed him yesterday but this information about the bank account didn't come in until last night. Thought you might want to tag along. I figure if anyone might notice missing equipment or more land being sold, it'll be him.'

'*From the summer of 1939,*' William Trent wrote, '*the government began to recruit hundreds of amateur radio enthusiasts to listen out for German transmission. Most of them were drawn from the ranks of The Radio Society of Great Britain, headed by a man called Arthur Watts. They were organized into cells by the Radio Security Service and dubbed Voluntary Interceptors . . .*'

William broke off, unable to think how to finish the sentence or even if it required more words. He couldn't seem to concentrate this morning.

He looked across his desk at the scatter of journals and hand-written notes and World War Two publications. The Penrose, *Home Guard Manual of Camouflage* and *The Partisan Leader's Handbook* by Major Colonel Gubbins, all original editions and made even more extraordinary by the marginal notes made by their original owners. On any other day he would have been excited by just being able to handle such authenticity. To read and touch such genuine history, but today he couldn't seem to concentrate.

He knew it was useless to go on today and so he put down his pen and picked up the telephone.

She answered on the fourth ring. 'Vera,' he said. 'I'm so glad to have caught you. How are you today?'

She told him that she was fine, but he could hear that her voice was flat and tired. He knew she was grieving for Ellen, much as he was – perhaps even more, William thought.

'Vera, I'm so sorry. I miss her too. I wish . . .'

What did he wish? That time could be turned back? That he could stop it in its tracks and take the gun away?

'I wondered,' he said, 'if you'd maybe changed your mind. If—'

Her response was cold. No, she told him. The answer is still no. She would not allow him, as she put it, to trade upon the lives and deaths of others. He'd already had more than she'd been happy to provide and she would do no more.

William sighed, was about to try again when the phone went dead and he realized she had cut him off.

'Damn. Stupid, stubborn bloody woman.' He replaced the receiver on his side of the conversation and thought about what he should do. Hopefully, she'd come round. If not, well, he would have to see.

William Trent grabbed his coat and set out for his usual walk. Although it pained him now, carrying such memories as it did, he couldn't seem to break the habit. He took with him one of the journals he was currently reading and annotating. This one had been a real find, unusual and significant in amongst the mess of soppy letters and auntie's hedgerow jam recipes he'd been working through so far, though he'd done so just as assiduously, knowing that such anecdotes sold books as surely as the more dramatic discoveries he hoped this little diary would lead him on to. Vera too, if only she would play ball. It was one thing having this journal and the other odds and ends Ellen had quietly borrowed for him, but unless he had formal permission to make use of them, his research would be all for nothing.

William resented that. Enormously.

He hoped, actually that this material might be the substance for a second book, one much more focused on the secrets and lies and misdirection perpetrated in 1940 and '41 which so fascinated him.

The morning was cool and William was grateful for his heavier jacket. His habitual Harris tweed, thornproof and windproof and the colours of earth and moss. She had so loved natural things, William thought, recalling the giver of this particular jacket. Both of the important women in his life had been like that though. Feeling an affinity with the natural world that William himself sought but never quite succeeded in emulating. And both were now gone.

William paused ten minutes or so into his walk and leant upon a farm gate looking into a field where he'd seen hares on a few previous occasions. Ellen had loved the harum-scarum flighty creatures and they'd watched them together on several occasions. There were sheep in the field now, no sign of anything even vaguely hare-like. But then, he'd never been the first to spot them, that had always been Ellen. She'd seemed to have an affinity for them, feeling for where they might be even before they became visible and little Megan seemed to have inherited her mother's gift.

He felt sorry for the children. Sorry for himself. He wasn't sure if he felt sorry for Ellen. William found that he'd not yet decided about that one and he knew himself well enough to know that his sympathy for Megan and Jebediah would also fade until only the regret for his own loss would remain. William had few illusions about his own capacity for love in the long term.

Giving up on the hares, he opened the journal and read a now familiar entry. It seemed to William that the writer had William's own struggle. That desire to connect and yet that inability to do so. Lodged in the countryside, the writer sought to use the language of his location. It sounded awkward, to William. Forced. He guessed perhaps that was because the man was uncomfortable with what he had to do and was also acutely aware that he should not have been making a record of any of it. Vera had no idea he had this book, though it was only a matter of time before she realized, he supposed. He knew Ellen had felt bad about borrowing it and the last time he had seen her she had begged him to give it back to her so she could return it, secretly, to Vera.

'I have sown the seeds,' the writer stated. *'I doubt I will be here when they are ready for harvest. I doubt I will even hear of the outcome and have no way of knowing if the harvest will be a good one or one worthy of burning. But it is done, now. The lies will spread like blight and I just have to hope that it will have all been worthwhile.'*

We all have those moments, William thought. When you look at what you've done and pray, even if you don't believe in any kind of god, that you've not completely fouled things up. That your judgement was sound.

He walked on until he came to that point on the ridge that looked down on the farmhouse. So familiar to him now from all the times he'd sat up there. He sat now and watched the somewhat desultory activity in the yard below. He guessed the forensic teams would have finished their prodding and scraping and prying and the two officers he glimpsed as they walked across the gravel were all that remained of the police presence. Soon, they too would leave and the house would settle into a passive and unsatisfactory silence. It was not a house that was made for silence; it should, he thought, be filled with noise and bustle and activity. He had been oddly aware, when he'd visited Ellen, especially when the children had been absent, of that odd, hollow feeling to the place. As though the house craved the big families and the cook and the gangs of farm workers that the old land would have supported when this had been the main house on the Glebe Farm. He'd done some research and found that the farmhouse, as it existed now, was just one wing of a much larger structure. That what was now an outbuilding used for storage had once been attached to the main shell of the house. He suspected that the holding of land once related to this farm would have been at least equal to that of the Breed Estate, though there'd been no time to follow up on his theories, all his research time currently being devoted to the books and now to the consultancy work he was doing for the de Freitases. Work he had Ellen to thank for.

The day had still not warmed and the air had an autumnal sharpness to it. The ground beneath him began to feel uncomfortably damp as the chill worked its way through his clothes. Awkwardly, feeling his age in his joints and bones, William struggled to his feet and stretched, then moved back on to the main path.

'It's a bad business, that.'

William turned sharply, startled by the voice, recognition following only seconds after. He nodded. The farmer stood on the path, dog at his side, shotgun broken over his arm. They had spoken a couple of times before when William had met him on the path.

'It is,' he agreed. 'Very sad. I hear the children found her.'

The other man nodded. 'Not something they'll forget in a hurry. If the Tailors have any sense left in their heads, they'll sell up and get rid.'

'You think so?'

'Wouldn't have said it if I didn't. Times change, there's no one left to carry on so they should give it best. No shame in that.'

William decided that the easiest thing was to nod. He couldn't see Ellen's mother-in-law agreeing to that. She was a tough old bird and not likely to give in to anything, no matter how sensible, that she didn't want to.

The farmer wished him a good morning, called the dog to heel and moved on. William stood and watched them walk away, deciding that he would cut his walk short and turn back towards the cottage in part because his knees were now chilled and stiff from sitting and in part because should he start to walk in the same direction as the farmer, he might have to make conversation. William was in no mood for that.

ELEVEN

Terry Bridger was somehow younger than Mac had imagined. He'd assumed the man who had also worked for Ellen's husband would be older, more experienced. Instead, he found himself confronted by a very nervous young man in his mid-twenties who still lived with his parents and sister in what looked like another farm cottage.

'You found anything yet,' Terry asked. 'Like, who killed her?'

'Nothing yet,' Kendall told him. 'But we've got a few questions to ask you.'

'I told you all I know. I saw her two days ago, was due to go over again today. I work on the Breed Estate Mondays and Wednesdays and do a bit here and there on the weekends down the Lamb.'

'The Lamb?' Mac asked.

'The pub down the village. Can't get anything full time for love nor money. Not in farming. No one can afford full-time help.'

'Terry, did Ellen sell any more of the land off lately? Any extra equipment? Any machinery?'

Terry stared at him as though processing the words and not quite getting to grips with the meaning. 'Lately?' he said finally.

'This past year.'

Terry frowned. 'Not that I know about. Not that she'd said to me.'

'And you'd have known?'

Terry laughed suddenly. 'She'd got a dozen showy-looking sheep and that market garden and some chickens, just what kind of equipment you think she needs for that? Biggest thing we got left was a petrol-driven rotavator we used to prep the land for sowing. She used that green manure stuff over winter and then straw and chicken shit. We left it out to weather over winter and rotavated it in come spring. We did a four-way rotation she'd found in some old book somewhere. Worked though, didn't it. For all they told her she was a stupid idiot who didn't know nothing about growing. She bloody well made it work.'

'Who said she was an idiot?' Mac asked.

Terry looked uncomfortable. 'Some of the locals,' he said finally 'and that family of Jeb's. Daphne Tailor was always on at her, expecting her to fail.'

'You heard this for yourself?' Mac asked. 'Or is it just local gossip?'

Terry laughed harshly. 'I saw that old witch arguing with her. Heard her too. Daphne and the brother, they thought the land was theirs and the house too. You should have heard them at it.'

Interesting, Mac thought. The opposite of what Frank had been told, it seemed. 'What did the Tailors want her to do, then?'

'Clear off back to where she came from,' Terry said. 'But Daphne didn't want her to take the kids away with her. Said she was the grandmother and the kids were part of her family. Well, you can imagine what Ellen said to that!' He laughed at the memory of it. 'I reckon Daphne didn't know what hit her by the time Ellen had done.'

'And did the animosity continue?' Mac asked.

Terry frowned. 'I reckon this last year or so it settled. Ray and his wife emigrated and that took some of the pressure off. Daphne saw Ellen was determined to make a go of things and was actually making a success and so she got off her back most of the time. So I reckon it settled.'

He frowned and Mac got the impression that he was close to tears. 'I liked her a lot,' Terry said. 'She was a good person. Kind, you know?'

'And did she happen to mention maybe coming into some money? Maybe a lottery win or something?' Kendall asked.

Terry looked surprised. 'She thought the lottery was a mug's game,' he said. 'Said she didn't have money to waste on that sort of thing. She never mentioned anything else.'

He was clearly curious about the line of questioning and looked from one to the other, waiting for an explanation. He was to be disappointed. Mac and Kendall left shortly after.

'Interesting what he said about the family,' Kendall said as they drove away.

'It is, but someone listening in to a family argument can often get the wrong end of the stick. Worth talking to Daphne Tailor again though at some point. Although it's a bit of a stretch from believing your daughter-in-law might not be capable of running a farm and wanting to blow her head off.'

'True,' Kendall agreed. 'So on to our Mr Trent, next, I suppose.'

They arrived at Stone End just as William Trent was crossing the stile from the footpath. He didn't look happy to see them.

'Been for a walk, Mr Trent?'

'It's not against the law, so far as I know, Inspector. I suppose you'd better come inside.'

He led them through to the room Mac and Yolanda had been in before. This time, Mac took more notice of his surroundings. He spotted the photograph that Yolanda had mentioned. William Trent, only a few years younger, standing beside a pretty woman. They were both dressed up as though for a wedding or some other special occasion and while the woman smiled straight out at the photographer, William Trent's gaze was fixed upon her and the expression on his face was, as Yolanda had said, utterly focused and utterly loving.

William Trent saw him looking and scowled. 'What do you want, Inspector?'

'Why did you follow my sergeant the other day? I saw you at the farm. You were standing up on the ridge.'

'What if I was? I went for a walk, that's all. The path leads that way.'

'There are several paths leading in several different directions,' Mac countered.

William Trent shrugged. 'I went for a walk,' he said. 'I like to walk that way. I do it a lot.'

'And did you go that way the day Ellen was killed?' Kendall asked.

'What are you suggesting?' William Trent's face flushed and then as swiftly paled.

'That you may have seen something, or someone,' Kendall said blandly. 'It's a possibility, don't you think?'

'I walked that way in the early morning. Long before she was killed. I saw no one.'

'And today?'

Trent scowled again. 'A farmer. I think his name is Jenkins or something. Farms down the way from Ellen's place. He was out with his dog, after rabbits I presume.'

'You presume?'

'Because he had his shotgun with him. Like half the population round here. I, on the other hand, don't own a gun.'

'Can you shoot?'

'Any fool can point and pull the trigger. What kind of damn stupid question is that?'

'How would you characterize your relationship with Ellen Tailor?' Mac questioned.

'A friend, a very dear friend. I shall miss her terribly. Satisfied?' Trent made a move towards the door as though to usher them out but neither Mac nor Kendall moved.

'Would she have confided in you?'

'About some things perhaps. Look, I have work to do. I'd like you to go.'

'About money, perhaps?'

'Money? I don't know. I know it was tight, but that's true for most of us.'

'For you too?'

'None of your dammed business. I have a decent pension and I top it up with writing and bits of other work.'

'Like consulting for the de Freitases at *Iconograph*. I understand Ellen introduced you.'

'Like that, yes. And yes, she did.'

'Had Ellen had any unusual expenses lately? Anything she might want extra money for?'

'I don't know.' Trent waved his hand impatiently. 'School uniforms and stuff for the children at the start of term, I suppose. She didn't say.'

'Did she say if she had plans for raising money? Maybe by selling more of the land, some other assets?'

'For the school uniforms?' Trent laughed. 'Inspector, I know these things are expensive, but—'

Mac abandoned that line of questioning and picked up on what Terry Bridger, the farm worker had told them. 'How would you say Ellen got along with her in-laws?'

Trent laughed then and for the first time there was no tension in either his laughter or his expression. This, it seemed was an easy one to answer.

'She couldn't stand Daphne or the rest of the clan,' he said. 'But she hid it well, said you had to go along to get along and that the children had the right to have a family and as she couldn't really offer one—'

'There was only Ellen and her sister.'

Trent nodded. 'They were very close. I think there's an aunt and a cousin or two, but Ellen didn't mention them much. She said that after her parents died the relatives helped out for a time but made it very clear that the girls would be on their own in the long term, so Ellen and Diane fended for themselves. They both worked and studied and got a bit of financial help from some government fund or something. When Ellen went to university she moved into a shared house and moved her sister in with her. She said it was stressful, but that they managed.'

Mac nodded. 'It demonstrates a certain determination,' he commented.

'It demonstrates character,' Trent said flatly. 'And Ellen had that in spades.'

Rina was finding life back in Frantham very quiet. For the past three months or so she had been on set from about eight and worked through with only brief breaks until early evening. It had been a gruelling schedule and she was secretly rather impressed with how she'd handled it. She had been looking forward to the long rest and lazy mornings that a return home would offer, but the truth was, she was now at a bit of a loose end.

The arrival of Joy mid-morning was, therefore, a very welcome relief.

'I thought you might want to come and look at the cottage,' Joy said. 'Then I thought we might have some lunch and then find ourselves a nice antique shop to rummage in this afternoon.'

'I'll get my bag,' Rina said.

They took Joy's little red car. She had passed her test that spring and was, as Matthew had once remarked, 'a good little driver'. The cottage was out on the coast road, with a bit of a sea view from the upstairs windows but mostly looked out on to the garden, an overgrown orchard and surrounding farmland. The front door opened straight on to the kitchen and a door led through to the living room at the back. The stairs had been concealed by what looked like a cupboard and were very steep and a nightmare, she imagined, for getting furniture up them. They reminded Rina of the Victorian terraced house she had grown up in, with the two small rooms and a kitchen downstairs and stairs leading from behind a door in the middle living room.

'It's really looking homely,' Rina said, surveying the rather large kitchen table, the small dresser decked out with an assortment of blue and white china. The small living room had a comfortable looking sofa and an armchair and a modest flat-screen television perched atop what Rina thought of as an aspidistra stand. Shelves ran all round the room at picture frame level and a bookcase had been tucked in beside the window.

'It's small,' Joy said. 'But I really love it, Rina.'

'And so you should. It's a sweet little place. You and Tim will be really happy.'

Joy beamed at her. 'Come and see the orchard,' she said. 'There's so much fruit it's broken one of the apple trees. Do you know of a good gardener? I mean, not to do the work but to come and show me how to do it? I'll pay the going rate for their time, of course, but I want it to be my garden, you know? Oh, and I've enrolled at college two days a week, starting next week.'

'Oh, good for you. Doing what?' Joy had taken a beauty therapy and massage course but Rina knew she was keen to do something else now that was finished. Something that actually challenged her.

'Um . . . I've enrolled on a silversmithing course,' she said and then blushed as though this was a somehow shameful revelation.

'Sounds wonderful,' Rina approved and saw Joy relax a little. 'That's a real departure, isn't it?'

'Well, yes. But I wanted to do something like that before, only no one . . . I mean, Rina, you know my family and how much I love them and I know they love me, but to my dad and I think to my mum too, I was always a bit of an airhead, you know? Mum suggested I enrol on the beauty course because she knew I wasn't academic or anything and I went along, but I'm not stupid, Rina, I managed the work standing on my head and I knew I wanted to do something else. And I'm good with my hands and I've got an eye for design and I went and did this taster day thing while you were away. In fact I did three, all different things. And I just loved the jewellery design day. So I enrolled. It's only a fairly basic course, but if I get on all right—'

'Joy, you will succeed at anything you set your mind to. We all know that.' Rina hugged her tightly. 'Your dad would be very proud of you,' she said quietly.

Joy laughed. 'Dad would have been proud whatever I did,' she said. 'But I don't think he'd set his expectations of me very high, bless him. I need to carve out something just for me, you know? Something new.'

Rina nodded.

'Especially now Tim is getting established. His career is getting off the ground . . . well, both of them really. The performance side and all the other stuff he's involved with and I'm not going to be one of those women who just defines herself by what her husband does, you know.'

Rina nodded again, but she was a little puzzled by Joy's sudden vehemence. 'Who's upset you, Joy? It's not like you to be so—'

'Angry?' Joy laughed suddenly. 'I'm not. Not really. Rina, it's just that everyone seems to have a purpose, a direction, and suddenly it feels important that I have one too, you know. I think it's getting this little house and moving down here and it suddenly just hit me like, wow, I'm not playing at this. This is real life. It's not like when I was still studying and travelling down to see Tim and he was coming up to see me and it was all kind of easy. This is for real.'

'Cold feet?' Rina asked gently.

'Oh, not about Tim! Never about Tim. About everything else, yes, bloody freezing.'

Rina hugged Joy close and kissed the soft strawberry blonde hair. 'You know how much you and Tim mean to me,' she said. 'I promise not to intrude, but I'll always be there for you both. You know that, don't you? I know your family must seem like they're a very long way away.'

Joy shook her head. She pulled away a little and looked Rina in the eye. 'I miss my mum and my brothers,' she said. 'But I have a family here too. Tim and you and all those mad people who live in your house and I'm going to be fine. It just hit me the other day that I'd moved into a situation where everyone already had their lives and their routines and their jobs and everything already set out and that I'd better do the same, carve out my own piece of turf as my dad used to say.'

Rina laughed. 'I'm guessing your dad had other things in mind when he said that,' she said.

'Oh, probably.' Joy smiled a little sadly. 'My dad was a right crook, we all know that. But he wanted the best for all of us and he was a great dad and I miss him a hell of a lot and coming to live close to where he died . . . it's a strange feeling, Rina. We drive past the spot all the time. Rina, does it ever stop hurting?'

'It gets better,' Rina said quietly. 'But if someone you love is gone, I don't know that you ever stop missing them, not completely. I still tell my Fred everything, talk to him as if he's still around and he's been gone for more years than I really want to count.'

'I talk to my dad,' Joy confessed. 'And sometimes, it feels like I get a reply. It feels like he's happy for us, Tim and me.'

Rina nodded. She wasn't an especially religious person, but where her beloved husband was concerned, Rina needed no convincing about survival. Fred had never really gone away. She could sense, though, that Joy was in need of a change of mood. 'Are you going to show me this orchard, then? I know a bit about pruning and I could give you a hand when the trees have gone dormant.'

'Oh, yes. Come and see and there's something else too. If it hadn't been for the way Tim likes to ferret about, I don't think we'd even have known it was there. It wasn't even on the house details.'

Intrigued, Rina followed Joy into the back garden and through a little gate into what, to Rina's eye, looked like a very old orchard. Gnarled trees, some finished cropping for the year, some still loaded down with fruit, stood in semi-straight rows circled by a low fence. What looked as though it might have been a good-sized kitchen garden lay beyond. 'Joy, this is lovely. But what are you going to do with all this fruit?'

'Gorgeous,' Joy agreed. 'But really, really daunting, you know. Mum's garden is all bedding plants and patio. I've no experience of anything like this. I just don't want to get it wrong.'

Rina laughed. 'You'll be fine, sweetheart. We'll all pitch in and help out.'

Joy reached out and squeezed Rina's hand. 'This is what I wanted to show you,' she said, leading the way to the very back of the orchard. 'Tim found it, we're hoping to clear it out and use it as storage if we can make it safe.'

A few bricks sticking out of the ground were the only initial clue but the long grass had been cut back and a bush hauled from the bit of all supporting wall that kept the garden at bay. Steps led down to a rotting wooden door.

'Oh, my goodness,' Rina said. 'It looks like an old air raid shelter.'

Joy nodded. 'That's what we thought. But would they really need one out here?' She tugged on the door and dragged it aside so Rina could look inside. The walls seemed to be a construction of brick and corrugated iron and a scent of rotting wood and leaf mould rose up to greet Rina as she prodded a toe into the damp earth just inside.

'Earth and turf on the roof,' she said. 'Must be quite a weight. I'm amazed it's not fallen in on itself. Be very careful when you start poking around, won't you?'

'Tim's found a local builder who's going to come and take a look, see if we can do anything with it. I'd hate to have to demolish. It's been here for so long. But we were really surprised, I mean, what is there round here to bomb?'

'Oh, a great many things,' Rina said. 'The airfield up the road, the harbours and bays all along the coast. There are memories of the war everywhere if you know where and how to look.'

Joy nodded. 'I suppose there are. Sobering, isn't it?'

Rina made her way back up the steps and took a proper look around. Now she knew it was there, it was possible to see the arch of the roof, the difference in the plants growing close to the shelter. Nettles, probably poppies too in their season, she guessed. Plants of disturbance, following closely wherever people built and dug.

'Have you been helping out at the airfield?' Rina asked. 'I thought I'd go and see if Lydia needs an extra pair of hands.'

'Oh, I think she can use all she can get,' Joy said. 'I've been going over a couple of times a week. It's fascinating, all the different stuff that's coming in. Funny, though, not everyone is pleased about what she's doing?'

'Oh?'

Joy laughed. 'Rina, I know that look! No, most people are really happy to help out and loan stuff or even give it to Lydia. People want their families to get credit for what they did and a lot of the older people especially think it's really important that the younger generation finds out what they all went through. Some people though, they've really been against it.'

'In what way?'

Joy thought about it. 'Well you get the "she's no right to do this because she's not local" brigade. Lydia's pretty good at winning them round, though. She usually just puts them in charge of something and gently reminds them of how many jobs *Iconograph* has brought to the area. Then there's those people who think some things in the past should stay . . . well not buried, exactly, but undisturbed, I suppose. One old woman came in and yelled at Lydia, accused her of muckraking, but I really don't know what that was about. I suppose people are bound to feel sensitive, if it's their relatives, their family history, you know? Even the old lady who came with Ellen Tailor, the woman who was killed? Well even she had her doubts about some things. And she'd been helping Ellen with the collections, too.'

They were back in the cottage now, Joy collecting her jacket and preparing to lock up and leave for their lunch date. 'You got everything, Rina?'

'Yes, all set. You met Ellen Tailor, then?'

Joy nodded. 'And the kids. They were a really close, really nice family. I liked her. It's a horrible thing to have happened.'

'It is indeed. Especially terrible that the children found her. And this Vera, what was she so bothered about?'

'Hard to say.' Joy shrugged. 'She was really enthusiastic about putting all the everyday stuff on display. She thought it was a great educational opportunity, I think, but Ellen mentioned some journals or personal papers from Vera's father and Vera got really upset. She said they were far too personal and . . . and this was a bit off, Rina . . . that there were still things that shouldn't be talked about.'

Rina nodded thoughtfully. 'There are still a great many people who stay silent about what they or their families did in the last war,' she said. 'We knew nothing about the code breakers at Bletchley Park until the mid-seventies and even then information was scanty. It's only been in the past decade or so that everything has started to come out. People can be surprisingly good at keeping secrets when they believe in the cause strongly enough.'

'I suppose so,' Joy agreed. 'But what can possibly matter after all this time?'

Rina had no clear response to that one. 'When do you plan to go over again? I'll meet you there.'

Tomorrow, Joy told her. In the morning. Conversation turned to other things then but Rina's mind kept drifting back to the old orchard and the shelter at the end of Joy's garden and she understood, too, Joy's feeling that she didn't want to get things wrong. Whoever had planted those trees, cared for that garden, had loved it. Intensely. You could feel that, Rina thought and, without being too fanciful, could feel that someone almost holding their breath to see what the new owner would think and do with their beloved trees.

It's all right, Rina found herself thinking. It's in the right hands now.

So I killed him.

And I'm not sorry.

And I'm not going to give myself up.

I bent down and used my sleeve to wipe the blade of the knife and then I walked away. Just like that. I was amazed, if I'm honest, at just how good it felt to know that he was no longer in the world. Could no longer torment and persecute and malign. If I'm honest I was almost proud of myself – though I didn't expect that feeling to last long. I'm a realist after all and I know that euphoria is the least real, least permanent of all emotions.

But, boy, did it feel good at the time.

What did I do then? Oh, I came back to the dance and bought a round of drinks. My own private little celebration. And then I danced what was left of the night away.

I wondered if that was what psychopaths felt like all of the time. That feeling of power, of lack of control and yet being in control all at the same time. If it is, then I can understand it totally, why they do what they do and yes, I do know how that sounds.

And how do I feel now?

Well, of course the emotion has cooled a little and I'm terribly conscious that there may be consequences, but I can't bring myself to worry about that at the moment, I have to behave normally, keep my life as it was before I did this momentous thing.

TWELVE

'I didn't sleep a wink last night.'

'Sorry, love. I know I was tossing and turning. I couldn't get myself comfortable.'

Hilly shook her head. 'It wasn't you, love. I just couldn't stop thinking about—'

'Hilly, there's nothing we could have done.'

'How can you be so sure of that? Toby love, she was in a right state the last time we saw her. She was scared, Toby.'

'Of nothing. Look, Ellen was a lovely girl but she wasn't from round here. She wasn't used to being alone in that barn of a place. She imagined it.'

'Did she? What about the letters. What about the phone calls?'

'We get strange phone calls all the time. You pick it up, there's no one on the end, then when we look the number up it's some company trying to sell us compensation or a PPI refund or some such. That's all it was.'

'Ellen wasn't stupid. She'd not mistake a cold caller for a threat.'

'And do you honestly believe that anyone in her own family,

or in Jeb's own family, would do something like that? Shoot her in the head with both barrels and then leave her for the kids to find. Do you really think they'd be as callous as all that?'

Hilly, reluctantly, shook her head. 'I just know the girl was scared,' she said. 'And we should have said so. Oh, not in front of the kids, maybe, but we could have called that inspector, told him about the time she came here. White as a sheet she was.'

'Hilly, it was late at night, she was on her own. The kids were across at their grandma's and she wasn't used to being alone. It was probably the first time she'd spent a night alone there in that old house, at least since her husband died. You know how an old house can make strange noises. How the night can crowd in on you.'

Hilly gnawed at her lower lip, clearly far from convinced. 'Look, even Ellen said that was probably all it was the next morning.' Involuntarily, he glanced over at the sofa where Ellen Tailor had spent that night, huddled under a spare quilt, the television on because she couldn't bear to be left in silence. 'Look,' he said finally, 'if it bothers you, then phone the bloody policeman. Or call Frank Baker. Better than talking to some stranger. He'll tell you it was nothing. Just a case of too much imagination. She was still grieving, after all, wasn't she?'

'I suppose so.' Hilly drew a deep breath and her husband knew she was close to tears. Though she'd seemed to be on the verge of tears most of the time since his accident. He reached out and patted her hand. 'Give Frank a ring later, if it'll make you feel better, eh?'

She nodded and, as so often, retreated to the kitchen. He could hear the clatter of pots and pans as she sorted and tidied and washed up their breakfast things and he wondered if she would actually call Frank Baker or if, now she had his permission, in a manner of speaking, she'd let it drop.

Toby wheeled himself over to the front window and stared out at the garden and the hedge and the road beyond that led down towards Ellen's farm. Hilly was right, of course, she had been terrified and at the time he had believed that something or someone really had come with the intention of scaring her witless. Afterwards it had been easier to just accept Ellen's assurances that she had been mistaken. That she had woken with a start and not been able to get over the shock and had scared herself half to death imagining things that weren't there. But he recalled watching her eyes as she had made her explanations and her excuses that morning before she left them and Toby had known that her protestations of stupidity and her apologies and forced laughter had all been a front. There'd still been the residue of fear in her eyes but there'd been determination too and Toby had gained the impression that during that long night on their living room couch, Ellen had come to realize something. That maybe she had realized who it was that had come to frighten and threaten her.

One truth was unassailable: less than two weeks after that incident, Ellen was dead.

Kendall had dropped Mac back at Frantham and then gone off to speak to Ellen Tailor's bank manager again. Mac walked back along the promenade. Not so many tourists this late in the season but those there were strolled slowly, enjoying the unexpected warmth in the September sunshine.

Andy Nevins looked up from the book he was reading as Mac came into reception.

'Afternoon, boss. Thought I'd make a start on those boxes you brought in. I've inventoried one and just started on the next.'

'Quiet morning then?'

'Boring. One lost purse, one person wanting directions to the de Barr Hotel.'

'Sorry, Andy, but someone has to hold the fort.'

Andy Nevins grimaced and then showed Mac what he was reading. 'This woman seems to have itemized every single thing she did for every single day of 1940. And I mean itemized. Look.'

Mac took the book. It was set out as a diary, but read more like a list of timed bullet points. 'Seven forty-five, changed the sheets and aired the beds. Eight fifteen fed the chickens.' Mac laughed. 'She was either very bored or she had OCD.'

'Did people have OCD back then?'

'What, back in the depths of pre-history. Well, pre-Andy, anyway. Does she say why her day has to be itemized?'

'Not that I've noticed, but I'm only flicking through, to be fair. There's some interesting stuff in those boxes, though. Letters and photos and another couple of journals. It's really moving, some of it.'

'I'll take a look,' Mac said. 'Meantime, how about you go and patrol the promenade for a bit, get us both some coffee and get yourself a few minutes break?'

Andy grinned and departed with alacrity. For himself, Mac would have welcomed a bit of quiet and a little less drama, but since he'd arrived and Andy had been part of his team, first for his probationary year and then as a fully fledged PC, Andy had been involved in the investigation of more serious crime than officers with many times his experience might have encountered and he was finding life as a 'normal' community policeman just a tad tedious – a feeling exacerbated by his relative lack of inclusion in this current murder enquiry.

Mac picked up the inventory list that Andy had compiled and glanced through it, then went to fetch the second box, planning to continue Andy's task and hoping that something routine and unpressured would free up his mind and help him to focus on the Ellen Tailor murder. On the whys and wherefores and the possible solutions.

He had a bad feeling about this one. A feeling that this case would be one of those that swiftly becalmed and stagnated. The only lead they had so far was the anomalous payments into the other bank account. It was possible that someone might recall who had paid those amounts into the account. Did five hundred or a thousand pounds paid in cash into an account constitute a memorable event? Mac thought he would probably recall such a thing, but, thinking about it, if a branch was used to receiving, say, takings at the end of a day or whatever, would that really stand out as strange? Had Ellen paid that money in herself? And why hadn't she mentioned it to her sister? That was, of course, if Diane was telling the truth about having just discovered the payments. Was that likely? How often would she have received a statement? Mac added that to his list of questions – he figured someone would have asked already and must have received some kind of satisfactory response as Kendall hadn't raised concerns but no harm in asking again – preferably when Diane was away from the influence of Daphne Tailor. Even though he'd not yet met the woman he was doubtful that anyone would say anything in front of her of which she did not approve.

He supposed he ought to meet Daphne Tailor too. Make a proper, personal assessment of the woman instead of relying on all of these conflicting statements of the kind of woman she was – to say nothing of the conflicting reports of her relationship with her daughter-in-law.

Sighing, Mac began to sort through the second box of documents and photographs that Ellen Tailor had taken to the airfield. It soon became obvious that Ellen might have delivered this stuff but that most of it had nothing to do with her husband's family. She had collected and collated, slipping related objects into clear, flimsy plastic wallets – the sort that were usually clipped into ring binders – and the name and address of the original donor had been stapled to the outside of each wallet.

Mac glanced at the list that Andy had compiled and realized that he had recorded this in his inventory. Listing by the name of the donor and then the contents. It was obvious that Lydia de Freitas hadn't got around to looking properly at these contributions yet, and had assumed that they all had something to do with the Tailors.

Mac picked out one of the wallets and added the name to Andy's list, flicking through quickly to see what it contained and recording the photographs, ration books and petrol coupons inside.

'This is stupid,' he told himself. 'There's going to be nothing here.'

Figuring that he'd leave the rest to Andy, he had a final check to see if anything in the box did, in fact, relate to Ellen's family and extracted three of the plastic wallets. One had a note attached, directed to Lydia, telling her that William Trent had another couple of items. A pack of letters and a diary. That Lydia should ask him for it directly.

'Looks like you'll be getting another visit, Mr Trent,' Mac said. Hearing footsteps, he looked up to see Frank Baker coming up the steps.

'I saw Andy on the way in,' Frank said. 'He's getting coffee and I've brought some fresh bacon cobs from the corner shop.'

Mac suddenly realized that he was hungry. He'd had nothing since breakfast.

That it was after three and he couldn't think of anything useful that had been achieved.

'Kendall suggests we phone in before making the trek to the late briefing,' he told Frank. 'He's gone back to talk to the bank manager but if nothing new comes up, there's not much point us being there.'

Frank handed him his bacon bap and Mac wolfed it hungrily, looking out at the quiet promenade. It was one of those still, becalmed, autumnal days when the world seemed to stop. When nothing could be bothered to move. Or maybe he was just projecting what he was feeling about the case. This was a murder. Surely he should be rushing about somewhere, finding clues? He thought about all the bodies Kendall had out doing just that, all the activity that was *actually* taking place. Door-to-door enquiries, fingertip searches of the surrounding fields and the Tailor farmhouse, officers dispatched to the various banks where money had been paid in to Ellen Tailor's other account and he felt oddly excluded from it all and very put out by that, even though he knew that he and his little team were doing all they could to contribute. It was a simple matter of allocation of resources but right now Mac felt decidedly under-allocated.

Frank was poking around in the boxes Mac had been looking through. 'Anything?' he said.

'Not that I can see. I've picked out the stuff that came from Ellen's in-laws and there's a note attached that says she's lent some stuff to William Trent.'

'Right,' Frank said, nodding. Andy arrived at that moment with coffee. As he deposited it on the desk the phone began to ring. He reached over the counter and picked it up. 'Frantham police station. PC Nevins speaking. Oh, yes, he's just come in. Right. Frank, it's for you.'

Mac picked up his coffee and moved out of the way so that Frank could get to the phone. He went over to the door and stood in the sunshine. Andy joined him.

'Find anything useful?'

'I sorted out the bits that actually belonged to the Tailors but, no. The only anomalous thing that's turned up so far is those payments into that bank account.'

'Follow the money, as they say.'

'Usually good advice,' Mac agreed. 'But we don't even know if Ellen paid the money in herself. Where it might have come from. If there's even anything to be suspicious of. No one seems to say she had more than her usual money worries and she doesn't seem to have done anything to raise extra – at least not openly.'

A young woman in the uniform of a Community Support Officer sauntered towards them up the promenade. 'What's this,' she said, 'a gathering of the clans? I expected only Andy to be here.'

She grinned at the young man and he blushed furiously. His cheeks suddenly matching his hair. Mac raised an eyebrow at Frank, but it seemed he had other things on his mind.

'That was Hilly Richards,' he said. 'She reckons there was something she should have told us the other night. Something that happened a couple of weeks back. So I'm off over there.'

'Take Andy with you,' Mac said. 'I'm going to take another look at the farmhouse. Stella,' he said to the CSO, 'you're OK doing the lock up?'

'Of course I am.'

'And I've got a bit of a job for you, while you're here.'

Andy and Frank left and Mac talked Stella through the little archive they had begun to process.

Then he collected his car from the rear of the police station and set off for the Tailor farm.

THIRTEEN

Frank and Andy were hustled into the living room and offered tea. Frank, recognizing a displacement activity when he encountered one, declined.

'Sit, down, Hilly. Tell me what you didn't before.'

He saw the anxious look she cast in Andy Nevin's direction and shook his head. 'Hilly, Andy here's a serving officer and a good one too. He'll have heard worse, young as he is, I can assure you of that.'

Hilly still looked doubtful. Toby coughed, clearing his throat. 'It's probably nothing,' he said. 'We've probably dragged you all the way out here for nothing.'

'We won't know unless you tell us, will we?' Frank said gently.

'Come on, lad, our kids grew up together, went to the same school. How long have I known you? I've never known you make a fuss where none was needed.'

Toby nodded. 'It was just over two weeks ago,' he said. 'We were in bed when we heard this almighty banging on the door. Hilly looked out of the window and saw Ellen standing there in her nightie and dressing gown. She'd shoved a pair of trainers on her feet and come racing across the fields to our place. White as a sheet she was, reckoned there was someone up at the house.'

'The kids were away,' Hilly said, picking up the story. 'Staying with their nan for the weekend. It was the first time they'd been away for a full weekend since . . . since their dad passed away. So she'd been on her own in that big house. We thought—'

'We thought she'd scared herself. Maybe had a bad dream or something.'

'When people have a bad dream, they usually just get up and make themselves a cup of tea and put the telly on,' Frank observed. 'They don't normally run half a mile across ploughed fields in their nightclothes.'

Hilly bit her lip and Toby coloured up at the criticism. 'Well, that was what we thought at the time,' he growled.

Frank nodded. 'OK, so she turned up on your doorstep. What time was that and what exact date, can you remember?'

'It was the Saturday,' Hilly said. 'Today is Monday, so . . . I could look it up if—' she half rose, pointing towards the kitchen where the calendar hung on the wall.'

'Sit yourself down, Hilly. Andy'll work it out on his phone. What time?'

'One thirty, maybe closer to two.'

'And what did she say when you let her in?'

'That she thought there was someone in the house,' Toby confessed.

'And you didn't call the police? You didn't think of summoning help?'

'First thing I said, wasn't it, Toby? But she said no. She just asked if she could sleep on the sofa, said she'd be gone by the time we woke up. We got . . . well we got the impression she was already a bit embarrassed about making a fuss. That she'd thought it through and realized she'd just been jumping at shadows. Maybe at the strange noises all old houses make, you know.'

'Wouldn't she recognize the sounds the house made?' Andy asked. 'She'd lived there for a while, hadn't she?'

'But she'd not been alone there before.' Hilly sounded offended that the young officer had dared to question her.

Andy looked away and began to fiddle with his phone, working out the date the incident had taken place.

'Hilly, no one is saying you did wrong, but that's twice now you've had someone from the Tailor family come to you for help and you've not called the police. When the kids came knocking at your door—'

'We called you, didn't we?' Toby retorted.

'As a friend, not as a police officer. You didn't think the kiddies understood what they were seeing.'

'They came here, telling us their mum was dead and someone had used a shotgun on her. What kind of a tale is that? Who'd believe that?'

'Did they say that exactly?' Andy was curious. 'They recognized what had caused her injuries?'

Toby shrugged. 'They know what a gun can do. Anyway, we called you, didn't we, Frank. You went out there and sorted it. No point in calling up the hue and cry if it's not necessary.'

'But it was necessary, wasn't it?' Frank insisted gently. 'So maybe if you'd taken Ellen a little more seriously—'

'You're saying we're responsible!' Hilly was outraged. 'Frank Baker, you'd better take yourself away now if that's what you're saying.'

'Mrs Richards, the person responsible is whoever pulled the triggers on the shotgun,' Andy said. 'Unless that was you, then that's not what Frank is saying.'

Hilly cast a scowling glance in Frank's direction and turned for the first time to the younger officer. 'Ellen was scared,' she said. 'But she settled down quick enough and seemed prepared to laugh it off. She insisted we didn't call anyone. Said she didn't want to look like a fool. She said she'd called the police once before and they'd found nothing and she'd felt like a right idiot.'

'She'd called us out before?' Frank asked. 'When was that, then?'

'About six months back, I think. The police decided the intruders were probably ramblers trespassing. Come down off the path, trying to find a road. They didn't seem to take it seriously, Ellen said, so she didn't want to look like a fool again.'

'This sounds like a more serious incident, though,' Frank said, earning himself another scowl.

'What exactly did she say had scared her?' Andy asked.

Hilly shrugged. 'She said she'd had a lot of silent calls that week, but we all get those, don't we. Bloody marketing companies cold calling and insurance and pensions and PPI and what have you. She said she'd had a load of them that night, which was a Saturday, so that seemed a bit odd. So she'd unplugged the phone and later she'd gone to bed. She said she heard someone knocking on the front door, soft like, just enough to wake her and when she looked out there was no one there. Then she reckoned they were tapping on the windows and then throwing stones. Broke her bedroom window, she said. But she could see no one. Then she said she heard someone in the house, in the kitchen, she thought. So she got really scared then. She couldn't call the police because the phone is in the kitchen, so she got herself down the stairs and went out the living room window and ran across to us.'

'And when did she go back home?'

'Early next morning.'

'She went back alone?'

Hilly and Toby exchanged a glance, then Toby nodded. 'Hilly drove her back in the car, took her to the end of the lane and dropped her off.'

'You didn't go up to the house?'

Hilly would not meet Frank's eyes. She looked away and shook her head.

'By that time we'd all decided it was a fuss over nothing,' Toby said. 'She phoned me once she'd got into the house and said there was no sign of anyone there.'

'And the broken bedroom window?'

'I don't know. I forgot to ask and she didn't say.'

'What are your impressions?' Frank asked Andy as they drove away.

'That they knew something was very wrong,' Andy said. 'But

that they didn't *want* to know. It's like they couldn't cope with knowing, if that makes sense.'

'It makes a kind of sense,' Frank said. 'They've been through a lot these past few years. There's Toby's accident, and they lost a daughter too, a couple or three years ago.'

'How?'

'She went off with friends one night, had too much to drink and three of them decided to go swimming. One of them managed to get back to shore and raise the alarm. Carol and her friend were washed up down the coast a few days after. One of those stupid, meaningless accidents, you know?'

'How old was she?'

'Eighteen, nineteen, maybe. My Gracie was at school with her elder sister, Poppy. She's the same age as Gracie and she moved off to London with her job last year. I don't think she comes back much.'

'So more trouble coming to their door would be met with a bit of resistance.'

'It would seem so. Let's go and take another look at the farmhouse. A fresh pair of eyes wouldn't hurt. And I'll look into the complaint Ellen Tailor made six months ago.'

'Why wouldn't it have shown up before now? Has no one done a background check?'

'Of course, so I don't know why that hasn't featured. We'd better find out, hadn't we?'

Andy nodded. 'Mac said he was going out to the farm. Think he'll still be there?'

Frank turned into the narrow lane leading to the farm. Mac's car was visible, parked up near the gate. 'Looks like it,' he said. 'I wonder if she got the bedroom window repaired.'

Hilly closed the front door and then stood in the hallway, listening to the sound of the car engine as the two officers left. She kept expecting the engine to be cut, to hear the footsteps coming back down the path. To hear Frank Baker's voice telling her, *Hilly, you've not told me everything, have you?*

But it didn't happen. The car drove away and there was silence in the lane once more.

She retreated to the living room. Toby, remote in hand, was busy flicking through channels.

'Put that damned thing down and talk to me.'

'About what?' He pressed another button, settled for a moment on a shopping channel selling boy's toys and then moved on.

'You know what about.'

Toby sighed and muted the television. He'd settled on some seventies cop show and kept his eyes fixed on the screen, avoiding hers.

Hilly sat down. 'Toby, you're not hearing me.'

'Of course I am. I just don't see what more we can do. She never said. Not really. I'd have put money on it being that brother-in-law of hers. That's what I said to her, wasn't it?'

'And she said that so far as she knew he was still halfway round the world in New Zealand. Toby, you saw her face that night. Terrified, she was.'

Her husband glanced sheepishly in her direction, then shook his head. 'I asked her who she thought it was, she didn't say.'

'She hinted, though. She didn't deny it when you said. We know she'd been seeing *him*. You should have told the police.'

'Told them what? That she'd hinted at trouble with a boyfriend but she'd laughed at me when I'd suggested . . . no Hilly, I'd be wasting their time. Let the police figure it out, that's what they're paid for. We did all we could and that's that.'

He unmuted the television and Hilly sighed, knowing he'd say no more about it. For a few moments she thought about picking up the phone herself and summoning Frank Baker. Then she let the idea slide. Instead, she took the tea tray through to the kitchen and set about clearing the dishes away.

FOURTEEN

Villiam Trent lifted his gaze from the book and removed his glasses. His eyes were sore and tired from trying to make out the small, crabbed script that covered every inch of the flimsy page. The writer had used an old, prewar diary, reusing the pages so that this new set of entries often overlapped with notes in another hand. *April 26th, Albert's Birthday.*

June 2nd, Ian and Ruby's wedding anniversary. The new writer had taken this little book, originally from some seven years earlier, so far as William could tell and had converted its discarded contents into a treasure trove of detail and commentary.

William had known from the moment he first noticed it that it was important. He'd not realized quite how important.

'Can I borrow this?' he'd asked.

She had shrugged. 'William, you know how she feels about this stuff. I shouldn't really have shown it to you. I had a hard enough time getting her to let me read it. I practically had to swear a blood oath!'

'Does she have to know? Ellen, I think this is something special. Something unusual.'

'I thought so too. I thought you'd be interested, but I still feel bad. She trusts me.'

'And I won't betray that trust. Look, she knows I've at least seen this stuff. I've asked her about it enough. I was here that day she brought it round. Ellen, it seems to me that Vera . . . secretly . . . despite what she says . . . wants someone to share all this with. She wants to share it with you. Given a bit more time and a little persuasion, I think she'll come round to sharing it all with the rest of the world. People deserve some acknowledgement for all they went through, don't you think?'

He remembered the way she had frowned, not totally convinced, but he had also understood that Ellen, despite her intelligence and her usual wisdom, had not really grasped the importance of this little diary and the scatter of other items that now lay on her kitchen table. To her they were simply curiosities; to him they were pure gold.

'Please, Ellen. Just for a few days.'

He remembered that she'd sighed and glanced up at the kitchen clock. The kids were due home from school any minute and she'd not want the added complication of their curiosity or the possibility that they might, inadvertently, say something to Vera about the book and the tape and the letters.

'Look,' she said, 'if you think it's worth taking up time with. Take anything you like but get it back to me by Friday. That's when I'm seeing her next. You know what she'll be like if she thinks something of the precious family history has gone missing.

It's been hard enough to get her to let me look at this stuff as it is.'

'I don't want to cause problems.'

She had laughed then, but he could hear she was still uneasy. 'What she doesn't know won't hurt her I suppose. Just keep it safe. I don't want any more upset.'

That had been on the Tuesday and Ellen had made him promise to bring everything back by the Friday morning. But that hadn't happened. By the Thursday afternoon Ellen had been dead.

William rubbed his eyes again and replaced his glasses. He'd moved his chair right up to the low window, making the most of the daylight and laying his notebook on the arm of the chair so he could annotate particular passages in the diary as he went along. It was slow work and he had this strange feeling that whatever he did was just scratching the surface. Trent read the scratchy, spider words: *'Three came back this time. For an operation like that, three is a good result. We raised a glass to those that had passed and then moved on to planning the next move, though I fear that Teddy, poor, poor Teddy will have to be retired this time. I see it in his eyes, even when he tried to laugh at Alfie's bad jokes. If I send him out again then I know beyond doubt that I'll be numbering him among the dead. Worse, he'd be a liability to his team. He will hesitate and there is no time for hesitation.'*

His eyes hurt. Reluctantly, William laid the journal and notebook aside and accepted that he had finished working for the day. He wondered who had been the last to read this diary. Vera obviously knew what it contained, but when had she last looked at it? Had she read it once and then tucked it away? A secret to keep, a link with a past she treasured because it linked her to a father she could hardly have known. This book that, in truth, should never have been written and certainly never have been kept. But he was beginning to get a feel for the man who had written it. Small references to place were exciting, though, and Trent was starting to have suspicions as to where these people, spoken about in the diary, had been based. If he was right, then it cast a whole new light on the airfield and so-called tin huts in Frantham.

He pottered through to the kitchen and made a cup of tea, glancing up at the clock and trying to decide whether or not to go for a walk, take another look at Ellen's farm and see if the police activity had ceased. He grimaced. It was only a matter of time before the police lost interest. He doubted they would progress with the investigation. He had little faith in the modern police force, for all their forensic resources and, he supposed, commitment.

'Oh, Ellen. The world may not miss you after a while, but I will.'

He supposed that her children would too . . . but they were young, William thought. They would survive and probably even heal.

Setting his tea cup down, William went back through to the tiny living room and slipped the diary into his jacket pocket. Not that he intended reading more of it today, but because now he had found such a treasure he liked – needed – to keep it close, though in more sober moments he reminded himself that there were unlikely to be more than a dozen or so people in the entire world who would be as excited as he was by its contents.

Then, donning his overcoat against the autumnal chill, William Trent set off again for Ellen's farm.

'The window wasn't properly repaired,' Andy noted. 'Someone's cut up a square of plastic and glued it in with what looks like car body filler. It's not putty, that's for sure.'

'Maybe she wanted to get it fixed up before the kids came home,' Frank speculated. 'You'd probably not notice it unless you were looking. The edge of the curtain would have hidden it most of the time.'

Andy nodded. He straightened up and followed Frank back down the stairs and into the living room. He surveyed the room thoughtfully. Frank waited. As he'd said earlier, a fresh pair of eyes was a useful tool and Andy was observant. The room had been searched and the photographs of the room as it had been before the forensic teams disturbed it had been laid out on the window sill and a small table. Items had been replaced more or less where they had come from but Andy now picked up a couple of the photographs and compared them to the present scene. Following the younger man's gaze, he noted the photographs on the mantelpiece, the books and cheap ornaments on bookshelves. Children's drawings propped up on display and a couple of pretty, handmade bowls. A basket of beach pebbles. The sofas were old but prettied up with cushions and bright throws. It was a comfortable, homely room. Nothing expensive or even new – even the television was a heavy, ancient looking thing set on a pine stand which also housed a video recorder and DVD player. The family computer had been set on a small deal table in the corner behind the television stand. Only the screen remained, the tower unit having been removed and taken for forensic examination, but as far as Frank knew, nothing interesting had turned up.

'Internet?' Andy asked.

'Village down the road got cable about three years ago. Not sure if it got this far. The Richardses are still on dial up. We know Ellen and her sister emailed regularly and the kids used it for homework. There are some bits and bobs printed out from websites in the drawer. Just school projects from the look of it.'

Andy nodded and, picking up another set of photographs, wandered over to the bookcase. Mostly, the shelves housed cheap paperbacks and a stack of hardbacks that looked as though they'd been there for generations and a part set of encyclopedias that Frank knew dated back to the nineteen fifties. The contents of the shelves tracked the history of the Tailor family, accreted over time and undisturbed.

'It's like it's a veneer,' Andy said thoughtfully. 'Like she put a veneer of hers and the kids stuff over the top, but couldn't quite manage to put all the past stuff aside, you know?'

Frank nodded. He'd not thought about it before, but now he saw that Andy had a point. What was the point of leaving Victorian novels and useless, out-of-date encyclopedias on a shelf that could have been used for new, more personally relevant items? He noticed now that the children's drawings were propped against these older items as though to impose a new structure; a new veneer, as Andy put it, over the established. The ornaments and pebbles and knick-knacks that this new family had acquired were similarly placed in front of older photographs, a mantle clock with frozen hands, green vases, decorated with elaborate flowers.

'Like she was on holiday,' Andy said. 'A long holiday, so you wanted your own stuff around, but you didn't like to disturb anything that belonged to the real owners, you know?'

Frank nodded. 'I'd not thought of it, but maybe you have a point.'

Andy laughed. 'And maybe I'm letting my imagination run a bit too much, I don't know. How long had she lived here?'

'The boy, Jeb, he's thirteen. So at least that. Her husband died five, no, nearly six years back .'

'And she still knows she doesn't belong,' Andy said. 'It must be hard, moving into a family home when the family isn't yours.'

'And when they resent you being there,' Frank added. He nodded. 'My money's still on a family dispute,' he said.

'Some dispute. There are members of our family me mam can't stand, but I doubt she'd get a shotgun to solve the problem.'

Frank, who had known Mrs Nevins for longer than her son, wasn't so certain of that. She was, Frank reckoned, a tough cookie and capable of anything if one of hers was threatened. He was saved from the requirement of giving an opinion by Mac. He'd been making calls, following up on what the Richardses had told Frank and Andy about the two possible intruder incidents.

Mac perched on the arm of one of the sofas and flicked through his notes.

'Right. On August the twenty-third, a call was routed to a local patrol. A possible intruder had been reported at Low Ridge Farm – that's the official name of this place – and a request for a welfare check. The caller, who identified herself as Ellen Tailor, said she was alone and was sure she could hear someone creeping around outside. She made a second call about ten minutes later saying it was a false alarm. An old friend had come to call, couldn't find his way up the lane in the dark and had trouble trying to find the door.'

'Probably went round the front,' Frank commented. 'No one uses their front doors round here.'

'Well, the officers, one PC and one community support officer, decided that as they were on their way they'd take a look anyway. So they arrived about five minutes after the second call and found Ellen Tailor and a man called Philip Soames. According to their pocket books, the officers say that the man and Ellen both apologized profusely, said that Philip Soames was a friend who'd not been to the farm before and he'd fallen over some equipment in the yard, made a noise and scared Ellen.'

'And so—'

'The officers were satisfied, stopped for a cup of tea and a chat, just to make sure there was nothing untoward, then got a call to another location and that was that. They reported a false alarm to control, wrote it up in their pocket books but—'

'But no further action, so it disappeared into the system.'

'It wasn't flagged, certainly. It's on the system as a call from Low Ridge Farm. Like I say, that's the official name of the place, but as everyone and his wife calls this Tailor's farm or Tailor's patch . . .'

'When did it become Low Ridge?' Frank asked. 'I've never heard it called that.'

'Apparently, when Ellen sold up a big chunk of it just over two years ago. I spoke to the mother-in-law, Daphne Tailor, and she claimed to know nothing of the incident or of this Philip Soames and when I mentioned the name change, well let's say I got a very frosty response. She claimed that Ellen had no right to change the name. That this was family property.'

'And Ellen was not family,' Frank finished. 'So much for her protestations of affection for her daughter-in-law when I spoke to her.'

'The two officers that came here,' Andy began.

Mac was ahead of him. 'Were not local. They came to the address via the post code in their satnav. They wrote this up as an incident at Low Ridge Farm, so nothing showed up on the system until we cross-referenced the incident with a date and a time and managed to track it from there.'

'And this Philip Soames?'

'I'm hoping Ellen's sister might be able to throw some light. But I'm going to try and separate her from the herd, as they say. Get her away from the influence of Daphne Tailor. I think she might be a little more likely to give me a straight answer if Daphne Tailor isn't around. I'd also like to talk to the children without their grandmother being around.'

'That might be tougher to manage,' Frank said. 'Maybe the sister could take them out somewhere and we could arrange a meeting.'

'We'll have to see,' Mac said. 'I want to talk to them but I've no wish to cause more pain than I have to.'

'Nothing's going to hurt more than finding their mum like that,' Andy said.

And Mac nodded. He was probably right.

On the way out, Andy went into the kitchen to view the scene. Mac encouraged him to look around, see if he noticed anything new. Andy had no expectation of doing so, but he liked the fact that his boss thought he might.

The kitchen wasn't fitted. Old pine dressers and a nineteen fifties cabinet stood against the walls. The main work top was beside the sink and the big table probably served as another, Andy thought. The table was now stained with Ellen's blood and the floor had been marked to indicate where she had fallen.

The most modern things in the kitchen were the chest freezer and the fridge. Andy wandered over to look at the drawings and notes fixed by magnets to both surfaces. He opened the fridge. It was well stocked with milk and cheeses and veg and little pots of yogurt. The freezer contents were a mix of bought-in frozen and home-baked. Andy poked around, but he knew the freezer would already have been examined. He glanced at some of the labels on the pies and pasties.

'Anything strike you?' Mac asked.

'Not really. Um, rabbits,' he added. 'Bet they're a pain round here. She must have got someone to bag a few for her.'

Mac nodded. 'There was no shotgun here so she must have done.'

Andy closed the lid and scanned the kitchen for a last time.' I bet this was a lovely place,' he said. 'Homely, you know?'

Mac nodded. He wondered if anyone would ever live here again.

FIFTEEN

William Trent looked down at the farm from his vantage point on the ridge. That policeman, the inspector who had come to his cottage, he had returned and was prowling around again. William was careful to keep well out of sight; he had no wish for more awkward questions.

The inspector was accompanied, this time, by a young officer in uniform and an older man that Trent vaguely recognized from visits to Frantham. He watched them as they circled the farmhouse, inspecting windows and gesturing in the direction of the lane and the ridge and the little path that crossed the Tailor farmland and the fields beyond.

'Oh, Ellen,' William breathed. 'Sometimes life is not very fair, is it? Doing the right thing can just be an exercise in grief and pain.'

He pulled his coat more tightly across his chest, feeling suddenly cold now the sun was going down and the air and ground feeling damp and chill against his legs. He shoved his hands back into his pockets, feeling for the little notebook again. He was still not certain who had written it though he assumed it was probably Vera Courtney's father. He knew, obviously, the kind of man it had been. The position he must have held. He knew it was only a matter of time before someone – probably Vera – discovered he had it and demanded it back. William had made certain to copy everything, just in case, but that wouldn't be the same as handling the original material. He had already made up his mind not to return this journal or the little bundle of letters or the tape recording, not if it could be avoided. He still needed access to a reel to reel recorder on which to play that, but he'd phoned around old friends and one had promised to search his attic and let William know if he could help out. The idea of listening to the old recording excited him. It might be nothing, of course, but the diary had looked like nothing until he had taken a proper look.

'She doesn't deserve to get it back,' William told himself. 'No one has the right to keep this sort of thing to themselves. No one.'

With a bit of luck Vera Courtney would just believe that Lydia de Freitas or even Ellen had been careless with her possessions and they had gone missing. A woman like Vera Courtney had no right to own such valuable resources. She had no understanding. She was yet another pudding brain.

William watched as the inspector and his cohort got into their cars and drove away before hauling himself back on to his now very cold feet and stumbling back on to the path and heading for home.

*   *   *

At the evening briefing Kendall went through the list of friends and associates of Ellen's that Mrs Brigstock and her friends had put together. He split the list into sections and assigned interviews for the following day.

She was a busy lady, Kendall thought. Aloud, he said, 'As you can see, Ellen Tailor was a very active member of her community. She was well known and it seems well liked. Go and talk to these people. If you can't get them tomorrow, go back and try again, but I want everyone on that list interviewed and alibied. Use these contacts to generate new lists. Ellen's killer almost certainly either knew her or knew enough about her to be able to pick his moment. It's more than likely that he'll be here. Or that she'll be here. And we can't discount the idea that a woman might have shot her.'

He allowed his gaze to travel around the room. 'So far no one seems to have any clear or obvious motive so don't close your eyes or your minds to anything, however outlandish it might look or feel. We can't afford to let our preconceptions get in the way. Anything else?'

'Some background on William Trent, sir. I've left it on your desk.'

Kendall nodded his thanks. They went through the notes generated by the house to house and he added his interview with the bank manager about Ellen's other account.

'We're still checking branches for the days the deposits were made,' he was told. 'One teller thinks he remembers Ellen, but nothing definitive so far. Three more branches to check tomorrow.'

The briefing wound up shortly after that and Kendall paused to read through the notes on William Trent. Most of it was unremarkable. The man was sixty-five and had spent his career in academia, publishing regularly and specializing in the history and politics of the twentieth century. The history department at the last university he'd taught at had been called and an old colleague tracked down. From them, Kendall learnt that Trent had been married and had a son, but the marriage ended in divorce after only a few years and that he had lost contact with the wife and child. It was estimated that the son would be in his mid-thirties now.

There was a list of publications, and bits and pieces about the lectures he had given since leaving the university. Nothing stood out as far as Kendall could see.

Kendall flicked through the rest of the folder and then paused. There were several news reports, obviously downloaded from the Internet. They dated from seven years before.

'Woman Killed in Suspected Carjacking.'

Kendall sat down and skimmed through the articles. Her name had been Maria Renshaw and she was an editor at one of the publishing houses that dealt with Trent's books. It seemed they had been engaged. One night she had been driving home and stopped at traffic lights. Witnesses saw a man open the passenger door and get inside. Some said he had a knife and one other that he held a gun. All agreed that he was armed and that the woman tried to get out of the car. That the car then drove off at speed.

Maria Renshaw was found a mile down the road. She had been stabbed to death. Her car turned up a week after and although there were suspects, including an ex-boyfriend, no one was ever charged. The car had been used in the commission of an armed robbery two days after it had been taken and Maria Renshaw killed. The assumption was that she had fought back and things had gone too far.

Frowning, Kendall closed the folder. He remembered Yolanda talking about a photo she had noticed at Trent's cottage. Presumably, that was the woman who had died.

Bad luck? Coincidence? Of course that was the most likely explanation. There seemed no logical link between this death and Ellen Tailor's except for one unlucky former professor.

It was getting dark and had begun to drizzle with rain but despite their grandmother calling them to come inside, neither Jeb nor Megan had moved. Megan sat on the swing and Jeb leaned on the frame that held it up. Neither had spoken for a while. Megan stared at the ground and Jeb stared at Megan.

'I want to go home with Auntie Diane,' Megan said at last. 'I don't want to stay here and I don't want to go back *there*.'

Jeb knew that 'there' was the farm. The home they had both loved until . . .

'Auntie Diane can't look after us,' he said. 'She's only got a tiny flat. And anyway—'

'Anyway, *she* won't let us.' Megan said. Jeb wasn't used to hearing such fury from his little sister. Megan was quiet, happy. Easy going. Jeb had always been what their mother called the 'intense one'. He knew full well who *she* was. Their nan, Daphne, she was adamant that they would be staying with her and that they would be, as she had put it, reclaiming the farm.

Jeb hated the idea and he knew that Megan did too. The thought of going back to where . . . He didn't even have to close his eyes to see what their mother had looked like. Bits of bone and brain and blood. He'd tried to grab Megan before she saw, but he hadn't been quick enough. Now, they both had that image stuck in their heads and Jeb knew it would never go away.

The back door opened and light flooded into the garden but didn't quite reach the swing. Jeb scowled, expecting their nan to be coming to demand they went back inside. Instead, it was their auntie Diane. She held their coats and silently handed them over before taking up a position that echoed Jeb's on the other side of the swing. 'She's gone to get fish and chips,' Diane said.

'Can't we just get in your car and go?' Jeb asked 'We could be miles away before she gets back.'

'And then what?' Diane asked. 'Things have to be done properly, you know? If they're going to be right.'

Jeb shrugged. 'You'll be going away soon.'

'Not soon, no. I called my boss. He's a nice guy. Says they'll cover for me as long as I need. I'm not running out on you, Jeb.'

'I hate her,' Jeb said.

'Hate is a bad word, sweetie.'

'I don't care. I do. The way she talks about Mum. I can't stand it.'

'She and your mum didn't get along,' Diane said, trying to keep her tone reasonable. 'I'm sure she doesn't say anything bad in front of either of you.'

'We can still hear her,' Jeb argued. 'When she's on the phone to Uncle Ray—'

'Uncle Ray? When did she talk to him? Did she phone all the way to New Zealand?'

'She can't have done,' Jeb said. 'She was arranging to go and have coffee with him.'

'Was she now? She kept that quiet.' Diane frowned. 'Not that

I'm encouraging either of you to go round listening to other people's conversations, but did you happen to hear when?'

'Tomorrow?' Jeb looked at Megan, who nodded.

'In the afternoon,' she said.

Diane nodded. 'Right.'

'So can we leave then?' Megan asked. 'She'll be out for a while. She likes Uncle Ray.'

'Sorry, loves, but we can't go chasing across the country. Like I said, these things have to be done right. We might take the opportunity to go out for a bit, though. I've had a text from that policeman that came to talk to us. His boss would like a word. He's based over at Frantham, sooo.'

'That's by the sea,' Megan said. 'Mum liked it there.'

'I know she did, love. Ah, looks like your nan's back. So keep this quiet, OK? I'd rather she didn't suddenly decide to tag along.'

The back door opened again and Daphne appeared. 'You're not all still out there, surely. Diane, I thought you'd have had more sense. Get yourselves in here and eat your fish and chips. Megan, I got you a fish cake. I know you don't like the batter very much.'

Silently, the children followed their aunt back inside, little Megan bringing up the rear. She allowed her nan to give her a quick hug as she passed through the door, tolerated the kiss planted on the top of her head. 'Mum used to share a fish with me,' she said. 'She used to take the batter off my half so I could just eat the fish.'

She felt her grandmother stiffen and draw away. Megan looked up at the woman's face and saw her try to smile. 'Well,' Daphne said, mustering cheerfulness. 'That is a bit wasteful, don't you think? And you're a bit too old now for people to go pandering to your fussiness, now aren't you? Get the plates, Jeb, and I'll find the knives and forks.'

Extract from the diary of Bob Courtney. Feb 4th 1943:

> *I walked into town today, then along the promenade and towards the old town. The path is blocked, of course, barbed wire strung across their walkway just before it turns on the headland. Some fool must have fancied himself clever, blocking the way, but whoever made the decision had never*

been in a boat, not if they imagined even for a moment that there was any kind of landfall there. I stood for a little while and watched the sea boil at the foot of the cliffs and I wondered if life would ever be normal ever again. Then I wondered if I would ever be and I think the answer to that one, my darling girl, is a resounding negative.

The truth is, my darling, I see their faces. I catch sight of them in the mirror when I'm shaving. Reflected in the glass door in the hall. And it catches me off guard every time. They look so young, just as I remember them, each and every one, and I, my sweet love, I am starting to look so very old.

I think we all are. And there are moments when I envy them, even though I know that is a terrible thing to say.

Yesterday, I had a drink with Alan, we met for a beer in a little pub just up the coast and he told me that he was the only one who'd made it back. You know, I think that man has more lives than your old cat. He joked about making a pact with the devil and we drank to lost friends. A year ago, six months ago even, we would have named them all, but the losses have been too high and neither of us had the stomach for it. My darling, I know in this we are no different to anyone else in this damned business. No one has been untouched. By the end of it many will have been touched many times. When he left, I stood there, watching him walking away and I wondered if and when he would go back and then I knew he would. Alan is one of those rare animals who is most alive when he is looking his own demise in the face. I'm not sure he cares one way or another, if he makes it through or if he doesn't, and he and I both know how dangerous that makes him.

And I wonder sometimes, if that's why he's the only one to have made it back. Three times now. Three bloody times.

And I know damned well that I'll send him out again, in a heartbeat, because what he's learnt by surviving is of the utmost and rarest value. He gets the job done.

SIXTEEN

Dan Marsden read his children a bedtime story about owl babies and the night time sounds of the forest. Sitting between them on Becky's bed, little Chloe leaning into him and sucking her thumb as she always did when she was really tired.

Afterwards, he lifted a half asleep Chloe into her bed and smoothed down the covers then kissed both of his daughters good-night, dimming the light on the landing just the way they liked it.

'Night, daddy.'

'Good night, pumpkin. Sleep tight.'

As he went back downstairs he found himself thinking about *her* children. Ellen's children. They were older, of course, but they were still only children. He could have met them off the bus. He could easily have said that he was on his way to their house and run into them by chance after they got off the school bus. He poked at the memory, rather as he might have poked at a sore tooth or a mouth ulcer, knowing that would increase the pain, but unable to resist and, to his surprise, he found that the memory itself caused no additional grief.

A little guilt, perhaps; knowing that should anyone have treated his own children with such disregard then he would not have held himself responsible for his reactions.

Perhaps one day someone might, he thought. Perhaps someone would have a grudge sufficient that they took their revenge against him and his little girls might find themselves in such a place as Ellen's children had.

He poked at that particular thought and found, with a degree of satisfaction, that it did in fact genuinely hurt. That was good to know. That he could, genuinely, hurt.

Holly was on her hands and knees piling toys back into the toy box. He bent to help her and she smiled at him. 'Food's ready, just needs serving.'

'You want me to do that while you finish up here?'

'Thanks. That would be good.'

He went through to the kitchen, set plates on trays, ladled casserole and vegetables on to them, poured two glasses of wine. By the time he returned to the living room the floor was cleared and the television on.

He smiled. 'Had a good day, baby?'

She nodded. 'You?'

'Oh, I think so.' He set her tray on her lap and her wine glass on the little table beside her chair. Ellen and her children now far from his mind.

Lydia de Freitas twisted the phone cord between her fingers and Edward could see she was imagining what it would be like to twist it tight around the caller's neck.

'Mrs Langton, yes, yes . . . I do understand, believe me and if items have been donated in error, I—'

'No. Loaned. Of course I meant that.'

'Mrs Langton, please, I'm sure . . . Look, I'll be there from ten tomorrow. Come then and we'll . . . No, Mrs Langton, I can't be there earlier.'

'I'll see you tomorrow,' Lydia finished firmly. She set the receiver down.

'There's always one,' Edward observed. 'Now, put the answer phone on and come and have your dinner before it gets completely cold.'

'More than one,' Lydia said as she took her seat. 'Most people have been absolutely wonderful, but that Langton woman seems to have taken it upon herself to stir up trouble and there's, what, three of them that are now on the rampage. Don't want their personal possessions being on display for all and sundry to see.'

'So why donate in the first place?'

'Well, I think that's the whole point. I think the Langton woman's daughter brought a box of stuff in. Mrs Langton, however, I think she's just changed her mind.'

'So, she could just say so. She doesn't have to get nasty about it. Will it affect your display?'

'Fortunately, no.' Lydia told him. 'I've got plenty of material and most of it much more impressive than the Langton contribution.'

Edward laughed. 'I must come over and have a proper look. You're all set for the grand opening, then?'

'Will be. Rina and Joy are due to come over tomorrow and that's going to be a real bonus. Joy is so good at smoothing ruffled feathers and making everyone feel important and Rina's got organizational skills in spades, so I'm very grateful. I might be really wicked and get Joy to deal with the Langton cow tomorrow.'

Edward grinned at her. 'But you won't.'

'I'm tempted. How are you doing with William Trent? Didn't you have another meeting scheduled for today?'

'He called and said he couldn't make it. I don't think either of us was sorry about that.'

'This business with the woman at the farm,' Lydia said. 'I'm sure it's upset him a great deal. He was a good friend.'

'So I understand. It's a bad business all round, Lydia. This area has seen enough blood, enough sacrifice. I hope they get the bastard quickly.'

Lydia nodded. Silently, she raised her glass, thinking about Edward's brother and their own sense of loss. William Trent might be a royal pain, but if he cared for this Ellen Tailor woman then Lydia had a lot of sympathy for him regardless.

Mac called round at Peverill Lodge on the way home and spent a half-hour in the embrace of his strange extended family. He felt in need of the off kilter sanity that came with tea and cake and casual conversation and, most of all, affection and concern.

'It's a bad business,' Eliza said. 'Are you any further forward, Mac?'

He shook his head. 'Not so far, Eliza. Though I can't say much, you know that.'

She patted his hand absently and then cut more cake and put it on his plate. 'I'll get more tea.'

'Not for me, thank you,' Mac said. 'I'm going to get home and see if Miriam's back yet.'

Eliza nodded absently and left to make more tea anyway. Rina laughed. 'She worries about you,' she said. 'They all do. I went to the airfield today and had a chat to Lydia about helping with the exhibit. She's very cut up about Ellen. She said that Ellen Tailor had been very persuasive with the locals. That she didn't think she'd have such a range of exhibits without her help.'

'Everyone you talk to seems to have liked her,' Mac said. 'She seems to have been a genuinely nice woman.'

'Just a case of no one wanting to speak ill of the dead?' Rina asked.

'No, I don't think so. But you know the thing that keeps nagging at me? She must have known or at least been familiar with her killer. From the kitchen window you could see anyone coming off the ridge and towards the farm. True, anyone that wanted to stay hidden could have done until they were almost at the fence, but once they'd reached the boundary, they'd have been in clear view. She'd have seen them. Recognized a threat, even had time to run.'

'But she didn't.'

'No. She must have been standing by the sink, beside the window as they came across the yard. She would have had a clear view of them. Them and the gun. It has to have been someone she knew. Someone she'd no reason to be afraid of.'

'And everyone that you speak to says how much they liked her,' Rina said.

'Yes,' Mac said quietly. 'Yes they do.'

SEVENTEEN

Day three after the murder

In the end, it was Rina who dealt with Mrs Langton, who arrived prepared for a fight, along with her daughter, embarrassed and looking guilty, in tow. Lydia had already sorted out her ration books and photographs and petrol coupons and had found the list that, as it happened, Ellen Tailor had made of the Langton possessions.

'Don't worry, I'll deal with her,' Rina told Lydia. 'You go and get on with something useful.'

'I'd better at least say hello,' Lydia grimaced.

'Mrs Langton, Janet, good to see you both. I've got everything ready for you, and Mrs Martin here will get you sorted out.'

Rina stepped forward with a smile. 'If you'd like to check the list, everything should be ready for you to collect.' she said. 'And would you like a cup of tea?'

'I shouldn't be having to collect anything,' Mrs Langton said. 'But Janet, here seemed to think I wouldn't mind. And she was wrong,' she added, staring hard at her daughter.

Janet was clearly becoming irritated with her mother's blame game. 'Mum, it was just a few pictures and bits. They'd all have come back home after the exhibition. Half the people in the pictures aren't even family. I'll bet you can't even name them.'

Rina smiled. 'Ladies, if you'd like to check?'

Mrs Langton poked at the documents on the table and then examined the list, critically. 'It looks all right,' she said grudgingly.

Rina slid everything into a large manilla envelope. 'I hope you'll come and see the exhibition when it opens,' she said.

'I will,' Janet told her. 'I think it's a brilliant idea.'

Rina watched the women go and wondered idly how long they could keep the argument going. Three other women came in through the double doors as the Langtons left and Joy, coming out from the back room, greeted them with a smile.

'Hi Vera, Martha, Julia. Is Celia with you today?'

'No, she won't be able to make it. How are you today, dear?'

'I'm fine thank you, Martha. How are you all? I've heard about poor Ellen.'

Rina's ears pricked up. Ellen's friends? The three newcomers and Joy drifted off to find Lydia and Rina crossed the foyer and trailed along at the rear so that Joy could introduce her.

Vera, Rina noted, said the least of the three. They were full of talk about Ellen Tailor and the wider family and how terrible it all was. It was natural, in Rina's experience, for people to deal with the shock of violent death by discussing the horror of it – provided they weren't too close to the victim. Death at a slight distance, however much it genuinely horrified, was also just a tiny bit glamorous; a little bit exciting. These women were on the border-line, Rina guessed, still close enough to be genuinely horrified but also distant enough from the victim that they would handle their shock by being just a tiny bit excited and stimulated by it. Rina wasn't judging when she thought this; simply acknowledging what she had observed as true.

Vera, on the other hand, was clearly in pain.

'Would you like some more tea,' Rina asked her quietly when the other two women were involved with yet another box.

'No, I think I've had enough, thank you. I just can't seem to settle to the task today.' She tried to laugh but it didn't happen. Instead it sounded almost like a sob.

'You knew her well, didn't you,' Rina asked gently. 'She sounds like a very special woman.'

'Oh, she was,' Vera nodded. 'She was gentle and funny and a brilliant mother. I enjoyed her company and I shall miss her terribly. I can't believe she's really gone.'

Rina nodded. She could have suggested that time would heal, that the feeling of loss would diminish and so would the pain, but Rina knew that was only partly true. Instead she asked. 'Are any of the exhibits yours?'

Vera shook her head. 'No, I did sort some things out, but then I didn't feel right about bringing them over. Or rather, I let Ellen bring them over. I said she could have a look through first. She was interested, you know? I thought I'd feel all right about it all. But then . . . it felt all wrong and I changed my mind, you know. I'll collect them and take things back before the exhibition opens. Ellen was going to sort things out for me but—'

'Maybe I could help? We could go and look in the storeroom,' Rina suggested.

Vera shook her head. 'Thank you, but I don't think I could cope with anything else just now, if you don't mind. My brain feels like it's full of cotton wool.'

Rina nodded. Lydia called her over to check that the Langtons had found everything in order and when she looked again the three women were preparing to leave.

'Who's Celia?' Rina asked Joy.

'Oh, Celia Marsden. She's sort of part of the flower-arranging committee at St Peter's church, where the other ladies come from, but she only turns up when she thinks it's going to make an impression.' Joy grinned. 'She's something big in local charity work, as is her son, Dan, and everyone makes a big fuss over her. Except Lydia, of course, I don't think she's that keen. I saw you talking to Vera?'

'Ellen's death has hit her very hard.'

Joy nodded. 'They got on like a house on fire,' she said. 'I think Vera is a very lonely woman. It's going to be tough to pick herself up after this I think.'

A little later curiosity got the better of Rina Martin and she wandered into the storeroom. Boxes marked up alphabetically sat on wide shelves and Rina, remembering Vera's name was Courtney, looked for C. There were two and she lifted the first one down and examined the contents. No Courtney to be seen, despite the fact that everything had been carefully labelled and annotated. She tried the second, still no Courtney. Puzzled, Rina looked around the room to see if anything had been stored elsewhere. If there was some sort of overspill area, but she spotted nothing.

Rina wandered out again and went to find Joy. No, Joy told her, so far as she knew everything was in there though if Vera had told Lydia she no longer wanted her stuff used, Lydia might well have separated it from the rest.

That was a possibility, Rina thought. For the moment, she put the puzzle aside.

EIGHTEEN

Mac leaned on the promenade rail and watched the children running on the beach. Diane stood next to him, coffee in one hand, the other clutching at her long hair as it blew about in the stiff breeze.

'It's good to see them behaving something like normally,' she said as Megan, shoes clutched in her hand, squealed as the waves lapped her bare feet.

'That sea is cold,' Mac said. 'How are they? Or is that a silly question?'

'It is, but it's one that has to be asked, I suppose. They are miserable and lost and mourning and waking up at night with the most terrible dreams and not getting on very well with Daphne and . . . oh well, you can guess, I suppose. How would you be?'

'Glad of a little normality,' Mac said. 'Even if that is on a windy beach, playing in a freezing cold sea.' He paused and sipped his coffee. 'Not getting on with Daphne?'

'Woman's a control freak. Won't let them out of her sight most of the time. She's going to play merry hell when she discovers we've been out this afternoon.'

Mac raised a sceptical eyebrow.

'Oh, you don't know her. Jeb and Megan overheard a phone conversation she was having. She was calling their mother all sorts. They were really upset.'

'I can imagine. All sorts?'

'Oh,' Diane shrugged. 'Ellen was never good enough for her son. She was saying Ellen was a bitch and that she was running round with other men, not raising the children properly. Properly according to the rules of the blessed Daphne. That she was running the farm into the ground—'

'That's not what I heard. I heard she was making a go of it.'

'And she was. Not that she could earn a proper living from it, not yet, but she was managing and the kids were happy and she was there for them, you know? What more could she have done? When her Jeb fell ill, she nursed him day and night. Daphne wanted him to go and stay with her. Said he should be "at home" as she put it, or in the hospital. He hated the hospital. But nothing Ellen could do was ever right for that bitch.'

Mac waited, but Diane's anger seemed to have burned out for the moment. 'And where is she this afternoon. How did you manage to escape with the children?' He was smiling, trying to break the tension but looking at Diane's face he realized he'd hit a nerve.

'That's what the kids want to do,' she said. 'They want to just get in my car and clear off somewhere. Anywhere. They don't want to be with Daphne.'

'Not a good idea,' Mac cautioned.

'Being their grandmother doesn't give her an automatic right to take care of them, you know?'

'No, it doesn't. But until guardianship is established . . . Diane, did Ellen leave a will?'

For the first time she smiled properly. She nodded. 'After Jeb was told he wouldn't make it, they both made wills. You know how much resentment his caused, I'm sure.'

'I have some idea, yes.'

'Well, that's going to be nothing to the upset Ellen's is going to create. I've not said anything to the kids yet. I've got the solicitor going over it, making sure nothing can be challenged, and that we're ready to counter anything if she tries. Ellen was careful, though and so far it all looks absolutely watertight.'

'And the will says?' Mac asked. But he thought he could guess.

'The farm is left to the kids. Equal shares. Daphne gets first refusal if they want to sell. They get the rents and the solicitor takes an admin fee if they want to keep it on and rent it out. And I get guardianship of Ellen's children. And there's not a damned thing she can do about it.'

'Does the name Philip Soames mean anything to you?'

The self-congratulatory mood was broken. Diane rounded on him. 'What about him?' she demanded.

'I understand he was an old boyfriend.'

'Understand this. That bastard was a creep. Big time. She tried to break up with him, so he stalked her. Phone calls, letters, waiting outside the flat, outside where she worked. Making a scene.'

'Well, it seems he came to see her a few months ago.'

'Hope he got himself arrested.'

'Ellen reported an intruder. Then she called back a few minutes later to say it was a false alarm.'

'That bastard. He made her!'

'Officers did a welfare check, stayed for a while. They left, satisfied that all was well.'

Diane laughed, mirthlessly. 'Oh, he was good at twisting a situation, was Philip. He'd seem all sweetness and concern, but he was a right bastard.'

'Did he hurt her?'

'Physically? No. He just tried to control her. To stop her seeing her friends, to stop her seeing me. Didn't want her to work or study or do anything except be where he could be in control of her.'

'A bit like Daphne then?'

She scowled at Mac. 'Beside him, Daphne is an amateur. He threatened her, though. What he'd do if she left him. He threatened violence. He threatened to kill her once.'

'And she went to the police?'

'Eventually. Got a court order. I heard he'd been arrested for something else, got out, but I'm not sure how long for. Ellen left and moved away while he was inside. She came down here, met Jebediah and the rest—'

'As they say, is history.' Mac nodded. 'Do you have an address? Know which prison he was in? Where he was sentenced?'

'I can give you his last address. That's all I know.'

Mac nodded. 'You never told me where Daphne was this afternoon.'

'Ah, that's another story, isn't it? Another conversation the kids overheard. It seems her lovely son, Ray, is back in the country. She's apparently meeting him this afternoon.' She laughed. 'She kept that one quiet, didn't she?'

NINETEEN

Day four after the murder

Philip Soames tapped his fingers against the plastic table top and shifted uncomfortably in his chair. Mac watched him for a few moments on the video link and then glanced over at Kendall. 'You're lead on this, of course, but I'd like to sit in.'

Kendall shook his head. 'I'd rather you watched from here. I want Yolanda in with me. She could use the experience and, besides, I'd like to keep you in reserve for now.'

'Yolanda,' Mac said. Then nodded. 'She needs something, that's for sure. I suppose you could call it experience.'

'From what I've heard she could do with a pair of walking boots too,' Kendall said. He grinned at Mac. 'She's a pain in the arse,' he agreed, 'but I think she's got potential.'

'For? Well, if you're not going to let me play then I'll spectate for a bit and then I'm going off for a word with Daphne Tailor. See what she has to say about her son being back and where he was the day Ellen Tailor died.'

'Lucky us,' Kendall's voice was heavy with sarcasm. 'Two solid leads.'

'Best we've got at the moment. Better than we had at any rate. I still think William Trent is worth another prodding too.'

'Because you don't like the man or because you think he's got
something to offer?'

Mac shrugged. 'Because I've got a feeling,' he said. 'An itch I
can't scratch, if you like. And it's probably nothing, but.'

'You want to take Yolanda back with you after I've done with
her?'

Mac actually thought about it for a full minute. Yolanda,
annoying though he found her, had noticed something that Mac
had missed. He'd not seen the photo of Trent and the woman. But
did that amount to anything? And what about the material he had
borrowed from Ellen Tailor? Could that possibly, in any small way
have significance? It seemed unlikely that Ellen had been killed
because she'd loaned a historian some old papers but – 'I'll take
her out with me next time. You'd better get in to see our man
Soames, before he wears a hole in that table or thinks he'd better
call on the services of a lawyer.'

'He's just here for a little chat,' Kendall said airily. 'If that
worries him, then all the better for us.'

Mac watched as Kendall and Yolanda took their seats and
announced their presence for the tape. Soames was thirty-six,
according to his file. Muscular, but without being obviously heavy,
and a shade over six feet. Had Mac been asked, he would have
speculated about him being a swimmer; the broad shoulders and
slim waist seemed to fit that sport. Good-looking, Mac supposed,
with very blue eyes and very dark hair and the sort of square jaw
that he had been told a lot of women went for. He thought of the
pictures he had seen of Ellen Tailor and decided that they would
have made what his mother would have called a handsome couple.
It was a phrase she used when she was at a loss to explain why
on earth else two people might be together, as though the fact that
they looked well together might provide an explanation of sorts.
But then, Mac thought, he was also guilty of making assumptions
on the basis of appearance. He hadn't known Ellen. Everything
he knew about her was second-hand and, when he actually thought
about it, pretty vague.

'I want to ask you about February third of this year. You went
to see Ellen Tailor. We had a call out about an intruder—'

'Which she explained was a mistake. Look, I'm sorry I spooked

Ellen but I got a bit lost. There are no lights in that lane and I was looking for a front door. Something with a bell, as you do.'

He was trying to look bored. Insouciant, Mac thought, and not quite pulling it off. Mac could see the tension in the man's shoulders.

'She went to court to stop you from stalking her, I understand.'

'Stalking?' Soames laughed. 'Look, what Ellen and I had was special. I just didn't want to lose her, so maybe you could say I came over a bit heavy-handed. A bit too intense. But, Inspector Kendall, when you've got something special, you really don't want to let it go, do you?'

'You obviously frightened her,' Yolanda said. 'No woman wants to go through the courts, all that hassle, all that pain, just because someone is a bit intense.'

'So, she misread what I wanted. Look, that was a long time ago and I've learnt sense. When she got the police and the courts involved, well I backed off, didn't I.'

'Or you backed off because you'd been locked up,' Kendall said flatly. He consulted the folder on the table in front of him. 'GBH, wasn't it? Because someone dared come on to your girlfriend, according to the reports.'

That was news to Mac. He'd not yet seen Soames' sheet.

'Look,' Soames was saying. 'He got drunk. I'd had a bit too much. Ellen was flirting, trying to make me jealous the way women do.' He gestured towards Yolanda. Good job there's a table between them, Mac thought. She looked ready for a bit of GBH herself.

Kendall read from the file. 'Dale Ritchie. Required thirty-eight stitches to his face, was unconscious for three days, ruptured spleen . . . need I go on. I don't wonder Ellen was scared of you and wanted out.'

'I never laid a finger on Ellen.'

'You don't need to hit someone for them to live in fear of you,' Yolanda said firmly. 'You can intimidate and undermine another person without resorting to outright violence.'

'So she waited until you were safely locked away and then did a runner,' Kendall said.

'No, she left before it came to trial. And I let her go. I never followed her, never bothered her again.'

'Is that because you knew you were in enough trouble without breaking the terms of a court order? Wouldn't have looked good at the trial, would it.'

'And it seems that Ellen applied for the order only days after the fight with Dale Ritchie. That she'd tried to break up with you weeks before that. In fact this Mr Ritchie had been her date for that particular evening and not you. That you saw them together in the Black Horse pub and as one witness puts it "went ballistic".'

Soames shrugged, but Mac was again aware of the tension and the anger he was trying to control. 'Like I said, she was trying to make me jealous. Anyway. Like I also said, that was a long, long time ago.'

'Odd, though, that you suddenly turn up down here and Ellen Tailor suddenly winds up dead. What are you doing in this neck of the woods, Mr Soames?'

'Working,' Soames said flatly. 'Like you well know seeing as how you dragged me out of my place of employment.'

'We called your employer and requested your presence, if that's what you mean. And it's not as though Marsden is ignorant of your past, is it, Mr Soames. They've taken a fair few ex-cons in their time. Mr Marsden works closely with the probation service.'

'Is that what you call it? I call it cheap labour at the minimum wage.'

'Which is more than you'd get in a lot of places. I understand you told Marsden that you wanted to work down here to be close to family. What family is that, Mr Soames?'

Silence for a moment or two, then Yolanda took up the questions once again. 'What did you talk about that night, when you made your unexpected visit?'

'Who said it was unexpected?'

You could practically see the man preening, Mac thought.

'You're suggesting she invited you to come and see her.'

Soames shrugged. 'A woman on her own, you know what that's like I'm sure.' He smiled at Yolanda.

Dangerous ground, Mac thought, hiding a smile of his own, even though he knew she could not see him.

'Really?' Yolanda returned. 'It's been what, fourteen, fifteen years since you saw her. She's been married, had two kids, been widowed and suddenly she wants to catch up with the man she ran away from? Pull the other one, Soames.'

'I can prove it,' Soames said quietly. He opened his jacket and felt in the inside pocket. Produced what looked like a note-card and an envelope and lay them down on the table. He paused, hand resting lightly on the card and then pushed them over to Kendall.

Mac craned to see. The card had a bird on the front of it and some kind of company logo on the back.

'I hear you're down this way. Come and have a chat sometime. I might have some work for you. Ellen.'

'And if you notice, the address and mobile number are written on the other side.' Soames leant back in his seat, evidently satisfied.

'So, if she knew you were coming, why did she call the police and report an intruder?'

'Because I didn't tell her I would be. I wanted to scope the place out first, see what I might be getting into.'

'In the dark?'

'Only time I could borrow a car, wasn't it.'

'And when you got there, what work was she going to offer you?'

'Don't know, do I. Your lot interrupted and she seemed distracted after that. Said she'd talk about that later.'

'And so? You left? You stayed? You talked about . . .'

'Old times. You know, like old friends do when they're catching up? Though, no. I don't suppose either of you do know about that, do you.'

'And how did she know you were working locally?' Yolanda demanded.

Soames shrugged. 'She didn't say, I didn't ask.'

'Not curious?' Kendall asked.

'Just glad to see her again, I suppose. I didn't stop long, though. She seemed eager to get shot of me after your colleagues had showed up. That boy of hers came downstairs and wanted to know what was going on. She said I should go, she didn't want to upset the kids.'

'So?'

'So I went. And I never went back. She said she'd be in touch but I thought at the time I wouldn't be holding my breath. She always was one to blow hot and blow cold, you know? And I had enough of that the last time. She's not worth going back inside for.'

'And why would you think that anything to do with Ellen Tailor would put you back inside?'

'Let's just say I'm the cautious type these days. A feeling I had.'

'Even though she never discussed what work she might have had in mind. You think it was something illegal?'

'How would I know? I never went back.'

Yolanda had picked up the notecard and envelope and was examining both closely. 'Must have been a surprise, hearing from her?' she said. 'An envelope lands on your front door mat and you recognize the handwriting of someone who used to be so important in your life. Someone you ended up doing time over? Me, I'd have dumped it straight in the bin.'

'Well, we're not all that cold, are we? Anyway, I didn't recognize the writing. Like we said before. It was a long time ago.'

Nice question, Yolanda, Mac thought.

'And she's signed it Ellen Tailor, like you'd need telling which Ellen it was – though I'm forgetting, she wasn't Ellen Tailor back then, was she? How did you know who it was, sending you a mysterious message like that?'

'Because I called her. I'm not that stupid. I called her, recognized her voice right off. Then I asked her. Had she been Ellen Emmet when I knew her and she said yes. Mystery solved.' Soames shrugged. 'I rang off as soon as she'd confirmed who she was.'

'Why was that then?' Yolanda asked.

'Because I didn't know how I felt about it, that's why. This was a woman who'd caused me nothing but trouble back in the day. She'd done a runner, I'd gone inside.'

'Hardly Ellen's fault was it?'

'I never said it was, but it was the start of bad things happening. I got into a bad place. It's taken a long time to climb back out again.'

'My heart goes out to you,' Yolanda said, coldly. 'The second spell inside was nothing to do with Ellen though, was it? Seems you got into another fight, over another woman, more stitches, more time inside.'

'Like I said. I was in a bad place.'

'So you called this woman you'd not seen in a decade and a half and you asked if she was the woman you thought she might be and then you rang off before she'd got a chance to say anything else. Can you imagine how that might have made her feel? How vulnerable?'

'Look, so far as I was concerned. So far as I *am* concerned. She sent me that card. She opened the conversations. I thought she'd realize it was me. I figured I was just returning a call she'd already made, so to speak. But I still wasn't sure I wanted to get involved again. In whatever she had in mind.'

'So you thought you'd just go out there and take a look.'

'Like I said. I'm cautious these days; I want to know what I'm getting into.'

'Wanted to see if there was likely to be money involved,' Kendall put in. 'One look at the farm would have told you she was just getting by. Nothing to spare for the likes of you. Nothing to make it worthwhile anyway. And I have to ask. Did it ever occur to you that Ellen might not have been the one to send you the card? That someone might have been setting you up?'

'Like who?' Soames shrugged. He scraped his chair back and stood up. 'Are we done now? I came in here to set you straight so unless you've got something to charge me with, in which case I want a solicitor, then I'm off back to work.' He held out a hand for the envelope and card. 'My property, please.'

Mac saw Yolanda hesitate and then look at Kendall.

'I'm sure you won't mind if my constable takes a copy,' Kendall said. He nodded at Yolanda who rose and left the room, Kendall announcing the fact for the tape. Soames did not sit down again. He waited in silence, staring at the door until Yolanda returned and handed his letter back. He snatched it from her hand and made for the door. Yolanda skipped aside.

'Mr Soames has now left the interview room,' Kendall intoned for the tape.

TWENTY

'**W**hat do you want, Inspector?' William Trent stood aside and allowed Mac inside. 'You'd better sit down.'

'I'm sorry to bother you, Mr Trent, but I need to follow up on a couple of things.'

'I'm waiting.' Trent flopped down in his favourite chair and looked intently at Mac. 'But I know nothing about Ellen's death. I know very little about Ellen's life.'

'Did you ever meet her sister or her mother-in-law?'

Trent sighed impatiently. 'The sister, no. Ellen talked about her a lot but we never met. Daphne Tailor, yes. Twice. I didn't fancy a third encounter.'

'Why was that?'

'Because in addition to a lack of intelligence, she struck me as a shallow, spiteful woman who didn't consider Ellen good enough for that dolt of a son of hers.'

'Dolt? You never met Ellen's husband, did you? Isn't that a little harsh?'

Trent shrugged. 'I'm making assumptions based on evidence,' he said. 'As you yourself do all the time. Anyway, what about them? Daphne and Diane?'

'I'm trying to get the measure of their relationships with Ellen,' Mac said.

Trent laughed. 'And you consider me a good source of information? Inspector either you are seeking to flatter me or you are clutching at straws. Look, Ellen disliked Daphne. Daphne interfered. A not unusual situation in families I believe.'

'You never wanted to find out?' Mac asked. 'You never married?'

Trent's gaze skittered over to the photograph on the bookshelf, then back to Mac. 'I was engaged,' he said. 'She died. The rest is not your concern. I believe Ellen was very close to the sister but beyond random gossip, she told me very little of consequence.'

'And what *would* be of consequence?'

Trent gestured his impatience.

'Did she ever mention a man called Philip Soames?'

Trent frowned and narrowed his eyes as though trying to access a memory and finding it a physical strain. 'Ex-boyfriend,' he said at last. 'She mentioned him once, a few months before she . . . before she was killed. Said he'd suddenly reappeared in her life and she didn't seem too happy about it.'

'So, if I suggested that she'd invited him back into her life?'

'I'd say you were mistaken. Grossly so.'

'How did she seem when she spoke about him. Did she give any details?'

Trent looked closely at Mac. 'Is he a suspect? No, you wouldn't tell me even if he was, of course. I'd say she was shaken by him. Uneasy. Not scared, exactly, but certainly not happy to think he was close by and might come visiting.'

'And did she give any impression that he had? Come visiting I mean.'

Trent thought about it. 'I got the impression that she'd seen him and that he'd seen her. Beyond that, I really couldn't say.'

Mac nodded thoughtfully. 'A couple of weeks ago the children stayed over at Daphne's house and Ellen was alone. Something frightened her enough to make her run out of her house and across the fields to the Richardses' cottage. Do you know the Richardses?'

Trent nodded. 'Frightened her? What frightened her?'

'She never mentioned this? According to the Richardses she arrived at their door in a very distressed state.'

'Never. She never told me anything about that.'

He seemed, Mac thought, very put out. 'She was scared, they said. But didn't want them to call the police. The thing is, this incident happened only a couple of weeks before someone killed her.'

'Did the Richardses say what frightened her?'

'Silent phone calls, then someone prowling around the house. A window was broken and she was almost certain that someone got inside.'

'And the Richardses never called the police? Ellen didn't summon help?'

'The phone was in the kitchen. She thought she heard someone in there so she got out through the living room window and ran.'

'And she never told me. Why didn't she tell me? I thought she

counted me as a friend. Why didn't she come to me that night?
I'm as close as the Richardses.'

'But the route across the fields is easier in the dark,' Mac said.
Trent nodded but didn't seem much mollified.

'She didn't seem disturbed. She didn't mention this at all?'

William Trent thought about it. He seemed truly upset, Mac
thought, as though he'd somehow let Ellen down. 'She seemed a
little down that last week or so,' he said. 'Not quite herself, but
nothing I could put my finger on. I asked if she was all right on
several occasions and she just said that it was coming up for the
anniversary of her husband's death and as I understood what that
felt like, I didn't press. I should have done. I should have asked more
questions. I should have been a better friend.'

Mac had left just a little later. He had asked for the letters and
notebook itemized in Ellen's list of loaned artefacts and Trent had
handed them over without comment. He seemed utterly distracted.

A little later, Mac got a call from Kendall asking him to talk
to Soames' probation officer and his employer. Soames had offered
no alibi for the night Ellen had fled from her house and on the
day she was killed he claimed he must have been in work.

Mac was intrigued. This was normally the sort of routine check
carried out by uniform.

'Marsden, Soames' employer, he's an important man round
here, supports a lot of ex-cons as part of his back to work and
rehabilitation scheme. Does a lot of work with young offenders
too and we've just turned up a link to Ellen Tailor.'

'Oh?'

'Seems she volunteered for a group called Youth Scape.
Youngsters at risk of offending and a few that have already found
themselves in the system for drugs-related or petty offences. The
Breed Estate lets them use one of their old farm buildings to camp
out in and as a base for orienteering and whatever.'

'So it's possible Soames might have had contact through that?'

'Possible if unlikely but as a courtesy to Marsden and because
it's possible, I'd like you to have a chat. There's a second, more
direct link to Ellen through Marsden's mother, Celia. It seems
she's part of the church flower-arranging committee, but I can't
see Soames having anything to do with that. But it's possible Ellen

might have said something relevant to one or the other of them. Oh, and Mac, Marsden is, shall we say, a little intense about his projects.'

'Thanks,' Mac said drily. 'And the probation officer?'

'You've got an appointment with him at four fifty. He can give you ten minutes, apparently.'

Mac laughed. 'Good of him,' he said. 'I'll make sure to be on time.'

TWENTY-ONE

Still day four after the murder

Dan Marsden wasn't what Mac had been expecting. After Kendall's comments about Marsden being a little intense about his projects, he'd anticipated an older man in some posh office, pontificating about his duty to society. Instead, the room he was shown into, at the back of a large warehouse, was a hasty looking construction of stud wall and plastic panels housing furniture that had once been cheap flat pack and looked about set to revert to that state. The most solid looking things in the room were a couple of steel filing cabinets and an old pine table on which were set an equally robust looking all in one printer and copier and a kettle and mugs.

'Inspector MacGregor? Pleased to meet you. Dan Marsden.' He held out a hand, which Mac took. The palm was calloused and dry as though Dan Marsden was as used to manual labour as he was to executive office. He guessed Marsden was in his mid-thirties.

'Please, sit down and have a coffee, it'll give me an excuse. I don't seem to have stopped today. You're here about Philip Soames, I understand.'

Mac agreed that he was. He accepted the mug of instant coffee and was relieved to see that a tiny fridge had been tucked beneath the table and he would be spared the synthetic creamer.

Dan set the mug down on the table. 'I've checked his work records. He was working on the day Ellen Tailor was killed. I've also checked that he was actually here and he shows up on the CCTV for the hour between three and four so . . .'

'So, on the face of it, he's off the hook for the murder. Did DI Kendall ask you to check for the evening of the twenty-third August?'

'He did, but Phil wasn't on the night shift that week, so I've no idea about that one. Sorry. I've got the CCTV records for you and you're welcome to talk to his work colleagues, but—'

'Thanks,' Mac sipped his coffee. 'I'm surprised you keep your recordings for so long. Most companies overwrite after a week or a month at most.'

Dan shook his head. 'All stored on a hard drive. Inspector, I may be more than happy to employ ex-cons, and very happy to give anyone deserving of it the chance to start over, but I'm not stupid. There's always going to be someone who tries to take advantage. They all know that there are cameras and I don't take any shit from them. If they do good work they'll get the rewards, otherwise . . .'

Mac nodded. 'I'm told Marsden's has been working with the probation service for quite some time?'

Dan Marsden nodded. 'My parents started the ball rolling about twenty years ago. I took over the day-to-day running of things about five years ago and I've just carried on. I've broadened things out a bit, I suppose, started up the Youth Scape project for young offenders and those considered at risk. Carrie Butler over at the Breed Estate has helped out with accommodation. I can't say Carrie is a big fan of the project, but one thing I learnt from my mother was how to twist arms,' – he laughed – 'and I think she's coming round to my way of thinking.'

'And you worked with Ellen Tailor?'

Dan nodded. 'I did. I liked her a lot. Carrie let me borrow her and a couple of other members of staff when I was trying to get things set up. Ellen continued to help out. The kids loved her.'

'Were you close?' Mac asked.

'Close . . .? No, not really. We worked together, had the odd drink at the end of a long weekend of wrangling teenagers and I went to the farm a couple of times. Once for dinner and one time I just happened to be passing the end of the lane and I dropped in.' He paused as though considering carefully then said, 'I should probably tell you now that I was close by the farm on the afternoon she died. I'd been driving back from Carrie's. I even thought about dropping in.'

'And what time would that have been?'

'I'm not sure. Two thirty, maybe. You could check with Carrie what time I left, but I doubt it would have been much later than that. I was back in the office just after four. I expect our CCTV could confirm that for you.'

He's providing himself with an alibi, Mac thought. Guilt or just the sudden need many people experience to account for their movements when the police come calling.

'I liked her a lot,' Dan added. 'We got along fine but I'm not sure I ever knew her that well.'

'What makes you say that?'

'Ellen was like . . . I don't know, like a lot of people who are hurt by life. They learn to keep a bit of themselves kind of private. Closed off, if you know what I mean. I felt I caught glimpses of Ellen, the real Ellen, especially when she was with her own kids.'

'Would you have liked to know her better?'

Dan Marsden laughed. 'Inspector, she was in love with her husband. Even after he died, she was still in love with her husband. There was never a chance of anyone getting to know Ellen better, not while that was true, so, let's say, I didn't give it any thought. I enjoyed working with her and I enjoyed her company. I believe she thought of me as a friend. That was all. Besides, I'm a married man.'

Which means nothing, Mac thought. He waited, but Dan had said all he was going to say on the subject. Mac, on the other hand, was certain there was more.

'Anyway,' Dan said. 'You came here to ask me about Philip Soames.'

Mac nodded. 'How come he worked here? As I understand it, he served his time in the Midlands.'

'That's right. Two terms. The first for GBH, twelve months I believe, though he was out in eight. The second time, he served three years. Wounding with intent. I checked his file when I knew you'd be coming over. I don't have all the details, of course. The probation service only tells me what they consider I need to know.

It was, Mac reflected, more than *he* knew, but he made no comment. 'What do you think of him?'

Dan shrugged. 'He does his job, doesn't make trouble. I think he goes for an occasional drink with some of the others but beyond that, not much.'

'How come he's here,' Mac said, returning to his earlier question.

'That's not so unusual. Word gets around and schemes like this are rare. Proper jobs at the end of a prison term are like hen's teeth. He applied, got through the interview, came down and stayed in a hostel until he found a bedsit. The probation service helped with that, I believe.'

'But you know nothing more than that. He never said anything?'

'I can't say I ever asked. Inspector, I manage the warehouse. I manage our other projects, but the day-to-day interaction with the employees is handled by Jake Partick. I thought you might want a word, so I've asked him to drop by. He should be here in a few minutes.'

Mac thanked him. 'And do you think Philip Soames had any contact with Ellen Tailor as a result of them both working for you?'

'Strictly speaking, Ellen was a volunteer. Granted, I gave her some paid hours recently. Got her on a training course, so she got a basic youth work qualification too. But there's no reason they should have met. This side of the business is kept strictly away from the youth work. It wouldn't be either wise or proper to connect the two. Ah, here's Jake. If there's nothing else, Inspector, I'll leave the two of you to talk. Help yourself to coffee.'

Dan Marsden breezed out before Mac had time to say a word. He saw Jake try to hide a grin. 'Is he always like that?'

'What, in his own little world? Oh yes. You want some more of this very average coffee?'

Mac handed Jake his mug.

'But he's a good man to work for,' Jake added. 'Takes care of his people. And he genuinely believes he has a moral obligation to do good, I think . . . which can be a right pain, as I tell him from time to time.'

Jake set the coffee down on the table and settled into his boss's chair. He looked quite at home there, Mac thought.

'So, Philip Soames,' Mac said.

Jake nodded. 'He works hard enough to not be noticed, not so hard as to be considered an arse-licker. He's intelligent, got a bit of a short fuse, doesn't like being made fun of but he's got the sense not to let that show generally speaking.'

'Does he ever talk about his past?'

'Not so I've noticed. But most don't.'

'And is it unusual for your employees not to be local?'

'Not unusual at all. No. Like I said, most don't talk about their past and a good number are trying to get as far away from that past as possible. It's easier to make a fresh start where no one knows you or has any preconceptions or any demands. I'm sure I don't need to tell you that one of the biggest causes of reoffending is getting drawn back into your old circle of friends. The other biggest cause is not having the basics in life. A job, a place to stay, a sense of self-worth.' Jake grinned again. 'I'm starting to sound like the boss,' he said.

'You're starting to sound like a social worker.'

This time the grin turned into a laugh. 'Guilty,' he said. 'To make it worse, I actually studied sociology at university, but I'm told it's not an arrestable offence. Not yet, anyway.'

'And you've worked here for?'

'Five years, now. Since Dan took over. He made some changes, brought in some new staff and I was one of them. I'd been looking for a new direction for a while and this seemed like a good opening.'

'And do you get involved with the youth work?'

Jake shook his head. 'No, Dan is very strict about keeping the two interests separate. No crossover of staff, and he's careful not to allow any of the ex-offenders have contact with the youth outreach side. He treads a very careful line.'

Mac nodded and then checked his watch. 'I'd better be off,' he said. 'If you think of anything I should know, here's my card. And a second one for the boss.'

He was aware of many eyes watching him as he walked back through the warehouse. He knew they would recognize him as a cop from a mile off and know also that speculation would be rife about Soames' police interview earlier that afternoon. Glancing back as he opened the small door set into the massive warehouse shutters he saw Jake speaking to one of the men. Jake seemed to be telling him to calm down, his hand gestures and general demeanour suggested he was dealing with quite a major upset. He was in half a mind to go back and ask what was wrong. Did it have a bearing on Mac's visit? Then he looked again at his watch and realized he was only just going to make his slot with the probation officer, so he let it go but, on impulse, Mac took his phone from his pocket as though responding to a call and, surreptitiously, he took a picture of the two men.

'Carrie, hi, it's Dan Marsden here. Yes, thanks, I'm fine. You? Good, good. Carrie, I was wondering if the police have been to see you. About Ellen.'

He listened as Carrie told him that they had interviewed just about everyone on the estate.

'Yes, an Inspector MacGregor was just here. He asked what I assume was the usual stuff. If she'd got any worries, that sort of thing. I told him what I could. Carrie, you've not spotted anyone strange hanging around or anything? No, it's just that, well you know I keep the Kid Scape projects as far away from the work we do here as it's possible to be, but . . . well I worry, you know. What if—

'No, you're probably right. I'm probably worrying about nothing. Yes, we'll all miss her. Any news on the funeral yet? No, I've heard nothing from the Tailors, but I didn't know them that well. I've just been telling the inspector, though, I was over that way the day Ellen died. Yes, it didn't strike me at first either. I must have been driving by the end of her lane at about two, two thirty.'

He laughed. 'Yes, I'm sure they will be checking that out. Right, thanks, Carrie. See you soon.'

He put down the receiver as Jake came into the office. 'I'm off then,' Jake said. 'Everything all right?'

Dan nodded. 'You give the policeman all the help he wanted?'

'I think so, yes. Not much I could tell him really. Tough on Phil, though. He's bound to be up there at the top of their list.'

'You've no worries on that score?'

Jake shook his head. 'From what I've seen, he's trying to get his life sorted. But I'll keep my eyes open and I'll have a word when he comes into work tomorrow.'

'Do that. Night, Jake.'

Dan Marsden walked out of his office and stood on the walkway looking down into the warehouse. Having the police come here was never a good thing. It unsettled the employees. Made them feel that the law wasn't giving them the second chance they thought they deserved. That some of them, Dan conceded, probably did deserve.

But unlike Jake, he wasn't so sure about Philip Soames or if he deserved anything at all.

TWENTY-TWO

William Trent walked along the footpath towards the farm. He paused, as always, to look down at the place where Ellen had lived.

Where Ellen had died.

It seemed to William Trent that anyone he had ever cared about had been taken from him one way or another. But to lose two women to violence seemed . . . unnatural.

There seemed to be no police activity today, though he assumed someone would still be watching over the place. William found that he was dreading the day when the last of the police cars drove away and the farmhouse would be left alone and uncared for. Open to anyone who cared to break the flimsy lock on the back door. To smash one of the thin panes of an ageing window and lift the catch.

Ellen had installed bolts and even window locks to those windows that would take them, but the house had never been built for defence from the outside world. It had been a home, a shelter, a sanctuary, but those security measures it did possess relied upon the occupants to implement them once they were safe inside. Once the final policeman left, the house would be alone, unprotected, helpless.

William turned away, finding the thought just too much to bear.

He walked further along the ridge and crossed the stile that led to the footpath across the fields of the neighbouring farm. In the distance he could see Jenkins, dog at his side, shotgun broken across his arm. William Trent wondered if the man slept like that. Dog at his side, gun close at hand. He wondered if the police had taken neighbours' guns for testing and then decided probably not. Unless they had a suspect, it was unlikely they'd go round, farm to farm and take away the everyday tools of the farming trade. It would be like seizing a tractor or a combined harvester.

The farmer watched Trent approach. 'Afternoon. Rain later, I reckon.'

Trent nodded. 'Looks that way,' he said.

'Off your usual route, then?'

'I suppose I am,' Trent agreed.

'Well, watch out for the cows in the next field down. They'll not hurt you, but they do get curious. And there's muck everywhere so don't you go slipping.'

Trent looked carefully at the man, wondering if he was having a laugh at William's expense, but he decided not. It was simply advice and observation. 'I will,' he said and decided that he'd probably walk back round by the road, at least to Ellen's farm. He could get back on to the ridge close to there and not have to risk the cows for a second time.

In the event, William had been so lost in his own thoughts that he traversed the cow field and the next without consciously realizing it and the next time he took account of his surroundings, he had reached the road and was only a hundred yards or so from the Richardses place.

Hilly Richards opened the door and greeted him with a puzzled frown. 'Can I help you? Oh,' she added, her frown relaxing. 'You're that historian fellow, aren't you? Ellen talked about you a lot.'

William acknowledged that he was and asked if she could spare him a few minutes. 'There are a couple of things I'd like to ask you. You and your husband if you've got the time.'

'Who is it, Hilly?' Toby called out from the other room.

'You'd best come in. But if you could take your shoes off first. Cow shit's a devil to get out of the carpets.'

William looked down at his feet. His walking boots were caked in mud and, as Hilly so accurately put it, cow shit. 'Of course,' he said. 'Thank you very much.'

'I'll get the kettle on then,' Hilly said, though Trent could hear the uncertainty in her voice now the invitation had been extended. 'You come in when you're ready.'

Trent sat down on the porch and began to untie his laces. The mud and muck smeared across his fingers and he wiped them on his pocket handkerchief, dropping that down beside his boots when he was done. Entering the Richardses' house, he could almost taste the near animosity drifting like fog from the living room. He wondered at it. He'd met Hilly Richards once, when she'd dropped by Ellen's to get some eggs, but they'd not spoken beyond introductions and he could think of no reason for dislike. Maybe he was just imagining it, William thought. But the feeling wouldn't go away; was intensified when he opened the living room door. Toby sat in a large armchair, his wheelchair set beside it. Hilly on the other side, her hands clasped in front of her as though they had decided they must present a united front.

Against what? William wondered.

Behind Hilly the kettle began to scream and the strange spell was broken. She unclasped her hands and moved off towards the kitchen. Toby directed William to take a seat.

William perceived the unspoken demand that he should get on and state his business.

So he did.

'The police came to see me today to ask more questions about Ellen Tailor's death,' he said. 'They told me something I didn't know. That Ellen came running to you for help one night. That she came here, scared out of her wits.'

And you didn't report it, he added silently, a surge of anger growing up from the pit of his stomach.

'She did. Yes. What about it?'

'I want to know what frightened her. I want to know why it took until two days after her death for anything to be said about it.' He drew a deep breath, but the words escaped anyway. 'I want to know who killed her.'

Toby Richards regarded him coldly. 'Are you accusing us of something?' he asked. 'Ellen arrived, late at night, in a right state. We were all for calling the authorities, but she wouldn't hear of it. Didn't want to make a fuss, she said. Was most likely just spooked because it was the first time she'd been in the house alone at night since her husband died. She let her imagination get the better of her.'

'Imagination doesn't break windows,' William observed.

'One of the kids might have done that and not said.'

'Is that likely?'

'As like as not. Look, we took her in, she slept the night, we fed her next morning and Hilly drove her home. What more could we have done? What more would you have done?'

I'd have gone to the house or at least called the police, William thought. 'Did your wife go in with Ellen when she drove her home?'

Toby sighed. 'Like I told the police, Ellen had Hilly drop her at the bottom of the lane and she walked up.'

'Why was that?'

'How the hell should I know? She felt embarrassed, maybe. Ellen was a sensible woman, most of the time. I suppose she felt bad about making that amount of fuss. Didn't want it getting around.'

'In case Daphne Tailor got wind of it?' William asked.

Toby seemed to relax. Just a tiny bit. 'She'd have had a field day,' he agreed. 'Had it in for the girl all along, has Daphne.'

'So Ellen said.'

Hilly had appeared in the kitchen doorway, carrying a tray laden with mugs and biscuits. 'I made coffee,' she said. 'It was quicker. I hope instant's OK?'

Quicker, William thought. Hilly must be hospitable, but she didn't have to encourage any length of stay.

She set the tray down on a low table and handed William a red mug. 'Sugar?'

'No thank you. Do you know Daphne well?'

'Their family have been our close neighbours since we moved here. But we've known them for years. Our kids went to the same school.'

'In very different years, though,' Toby said. 'Our eldest was starting at secondary when Daphne's were finishing.'

'Well, yes.' She eyed Trent warily. You're an outsider, the look said. We'll talk, but don't expect to find out much.

'And do you get along with Daphne?'

'Fortunately,' Hilly said, 'we don't have to. We're not family.

Daphne is protective of family and that can make her fierce at times. If she doesn't approve of what they're doing, she says so but I'm sure she'll look after the children now their parents are gone. Probably move back to the farm. I know she was put out at having to leave.'

'To leave?'

'Oh, for the Lord's sake, man.' Hilly was impatient now. 'Ellen and Jeb took over and Daphne was still living there. Well, I wouldn't want another woman in *my* kitchen. Neither did either of them. Jeb sold off some bits of land and a plot he'd got building consent for, set Daphne up with a house of her own. She didn't want to go and I know it nearly broke them doing it. You ask me, they should have got shot of the whole lot, divvied up the money and all gone their separate ways. Jeb was never a farmer, not at heart. He'd have loved to have just up sticks and gone, but Daphne wouldn't hear of it. And what Daphne says . . .'

Ellen loved the place, William thought. She was happy, with her husband and her children. Heartbroken when she lost him, of course, but determined to carry on.

'Did Ellen seem worried? Apart from that one night. Did she say anything?'

'Like we told the police, she said nothing to us. We could go weeks and barely see her. I'd pop in for eggs from time to time, but apart from that, we'd got no reason to see one another.'

She set her mug down on the tray and held out her hand for William's. 'If you've done with that?'

William had barely sipped his coffee, but he surrendered the mug anyway. He rose from the deep armchair that he guessed was usually Hilly's. 'The police say she left in a hurry, that night. That she was really frightened.'

Hilly frowned again and then nodded. 'She'd pulled her jeans on under her nightie and got her dressing gown on top and an old pair of trainers with the laces gone. Said she'd got out through the living room window and run across the back way. Fortunately it was a dry night, had been dry for weeks, or she'd have been muddied up to hell coming across the path that way.'

Trent nodded. Hilly was ushering him towards the door. He went out on to the porch and sat down to put on his shoes. The front door closed behind him, but he could feel Hilly's presence, still in the hall, standing guard until he should actually leave.

William retied his laces and then wiped the muck off his hands again. His boots would need scrubbing when he got home. He was used to picking up a fair bit of mud on the ridge, even when the weather had been fair. The trees created deep areas of shadow, wonderfully cool in the summer but rarely completely dry. Today the mud had been supplemented by muck of another kind that seemed to have a particular attraction to his laces.

He was back on the road, thinking about what Hilly and Toby had told him when it struck him. Old trainers without laces, they had said. He was certain he knew the pair they meant. She had kept them in the back porch, a covered area just off the kitchen, slipped them on when she had just little jobs to do outside, such as fetching in the washing or watering those great tubs of flowers she loved so much. She said she liked the fact that she could slip her feet into them quickly and then slip them off again before going back into the house. No laces to untie, no fuss.

But that policeman had said she had avoided the kitchen. So she couldn't have fetched them from the back porch.

William thought about it as he walked and the more he thought about it the more it bothered him. He tried to think of a reason why Ellen might have taken that old pair of shoes upstairs and therefore had access to them that night. Maybe she'd forgotten to remove them? Gone upstairs still wearing them and just left them in her room?

But no. That wasn't Ellen. Everyone knew you took off your shoes before going into the house. The kids did it automatically. Occasional visitors would be let off, provided they'd not tramped too much mud into the house, but regular visitors, like William, sat on the bench seat and removed their shoes.

He'd walked back along the road rather than trek back through the cow field. It was a longer route and it took him about twenty minutes to get to Ellen's farm. He turned up the lane intending to cross the stile that led across the field adjacent to the house and back on to the ridge. Trent rarely used that path, tending instead to just come down between the trees and over the low fence that delineated the farmyard. No police car stood in the lane and Trent wondered if there was anyone left at the house after all. Instead of crossing the stile, he opened the five-bar gate and walked into the yard.

The kitchen window had now been boarded over and crime scene tape fluttered pathetically on the fence, indicating the path the killer had taken that day.

'Oh, Ellen,' William breathed. 'Life is just not fair. Just not bloody fair.'

The door to the back porch was ajar. Never designed with security in mind but only as a means of keeping out the weather, William knew it just fastened with a roller catch. There was a bolt inside and hook and latch on the outside, purely to stop it blowing open in the bad weather. A strong wind could send it crashing wide and once, so Ellen had told him, had broken the hinges. Gingerly, William pulled it open now and peered inside. The inner door leading to the kitchen was closed but the bench seat and the collection of Wellingtons and outdoor shoes were still in their usual place. Late afternoon light streamed in through the little window and William recalled vividly just how it felt to sit on that rough bench, sun warming his back, Ellen calling to him from the kitchen that she'd just made cake, that she'd get the kettle on. Ellen used instant coffee too, William thought, but unlike Hilly's offering, it was served with a smile; served in friendship and that made all the difference. His gaze fell on what he realized had really brought him here. Ellen's old, laceless trainers were still tucked at the side of the bench, toes facing the wall so she could push her feet straight into them as she went out to attend to her chores. He bent down and picked them up, looked at the soles. Ridiculous to think the mud and muck from that night would still be there. Ellen would have scrubbed them, just like he intended to scrub his own shoes when he got back to the cottage.

But the more William looked, the more he realized that was wrong. The soles were a little muddy, true. Fragments of dried clay flaked from between the treads as he touched them, but the familiar staining on the old white leather, on the pink fabric, that was still the same. He would have bet his life on it. These shoes had been nowhere dirtier than the gravel yard and the surrounding verges or at most into the tiny scrap of a kitchen garden where Ellen grew her herbs and a bit of salad. Anything else she needed for the kitchen would have been collected from the market garden and if she'd gone to see to the chickens she would always have worn her Wellingtons. He glanced over at the boots standing side by side against the wall. A tiny smear of chicken shit and a wisp of straw adhered to the right one.

No, these trainers had been used for quick jobs in the yard only. Though, he supposed, Hilly could be correct. It hadn't rained for a while before Ellen's night time visit to their house and the cows were one field further over, so . . .

'I'm being an idiot,' William told himself. 'Looking for clues where there are none.' It was, he realized, because he felt so damned helpless. So utterly impotent. He wanted this to be solved and he wanted to be the one to solve it, however ridiculous that sounded.

'Can I help you, sir? You shouldn't be there, you know.' The young police officer seemed a little put out but also curious. 'It's Mr Trent, isn't it?'

'It is, yes. And I'm sorry. I just—'

The officer nodded. 'I'm sorry, sir, but you can't be here.'

'I didn't touch anything. Only the seat and the trainers.'

'It's all right, sir. Forensics have done here.'

Trent nodded. He thought about telling the officer about the trainers and then thought better of it. What could he say that would make any sense?

Trent left, aware that the officer watched until he was out of sight. No doubt he'd get another visit from one or other of the policeman he'd seen so far or maybe just the uniformed division if he proved unworthy of the detectives. He tried to turn his mind to other things on the walk home, to his research, to the book he had yet to finish, but Ellen's face seemed to be blocking his sight, Ellen's voice in his head preventing all other thought.

He had loved her, of course. William had acknowledged that long ago, even as he had accepted that Ellen would never see him as more than a dear friend. Perhaps he hadn't recognized until now, just how all consuming that love had been.

William Trent was tired when he reached his cottage. The walk had been a long one. He took off his walking boots, dropping them on the threshold and walked in his socks to the kitchen. The trainers would not be dismissed though and Trent knew he had to find something out before he could put it to rest.

He called directory enquiries and a few minutes later was on the phone to the farm next to what had been Ellen's.

'Mr Jenkins. It's William Trent, here. Yes, that's right. No the cows were fine, but that's what I want to ask you about. I know it may seem a strange question, but how long have you had them in that field? Two weeks. Right, and before that?'

Trent listened. 'So, just so I have this right. You moved them up from the field closer to the road. The field crossed by the other public footpath.' The path Ellen must have used if she'd come from her house across to the Richardses' place.

William replaced the phone on its cradle and stood for a moment, unmoving and deep in thought.

She could have cleaned her shoes. Of course she could, but the doubt, once sowed, would not go away. Something was wrong here. With the story the Richardses had told him or, possibly, though he found that harder to accept, with the story Ellen had told them.

TWENTY-THREE

C hris Shaw, Philip Soames' probation officer, was a harried-looking man. He summoned Mac into his office at precisely ten minutes to five and informed him that he really could only spare him until five precisely.

Mac got to the point. 'Any concerns about Soames?'

'None. He keeps to the rules, checks in with me according to our agreement and according to his employer is satisfactory.'

'Satisfactory?'

'Inspector, I'm happy with that. My expectations don't extend to anything spectacular.'

'Does he talk about his personal life?'

'No. He mentioned going to the pub with one of his work colleagues. That's all.'

'Is that unusual?'

'That he doesn't talk about his personal life or that he goes for a drink after work?'

Mac glared at him. 'He's never mentioned Ellen Tailor to you. She took out a court order against him.'

'Twelve years ago. I've been a little more concerned with his more recent career. And no, he didn't mention her.'

'Did he mention how he heard about the Marsden scheme?'

Chris Shaw paused and then nodded. 'I asked him, of course, when his case notes were transferred to this office. His first response was that a prison visitor had mentioned it to him. His second, later, response, was that the education officer had told a group of them about it. Either or both could be true. Neither could be. I didn't think it important at the time.'

'Strange coincidence, though, that Soames ends up down here, within spitting distance of someone he once persecuted.'

'Persecuted is an emotive word. As is stalking or harassing. Coincidences do happen, Inspector. Their relationship was a very long time ago. The trouble they experienced was, presumably, resolved. No one can guarantee that the past won't come back to bite them one day, wherever they move to or whatever life choices they make.'

'A woman is dead, Mr Shaw.'

'And I'm sorry for that. But if you had any evidence, even the hint of evidence that it was Philip Soames, then I'd already be passing his file over to his court-appointed solicitor, wouldn't I? So it seems to me, Inspector, that you are merely fishing. In a pond where there are no fish to catch.' He glanced at his watch. 'You have time for one more question, then I have to leave.'

Mac stood up and laid a business card on Shaw's desk. 'Call me if you think of anything,' he said. 'Soames may not have pulled the trigger, but he still turned up at the victim's home unannounced, he could still have—'

'Set up a hit?' Shaw laughed. 'Get real, Inspector. Where would a man like Soames find the money? Why would he bother? What was the woman to him now? It strikes me that Philip Soames has the sense to know that running as fast and as hard away from the woman that caused trouble in his past – and no, Inspector, I'm not blaming the victim, merely seeing it from Soames' perspective – would have been the sensible move. How do you know he visited her anyway?'

'He really doesn't talk to you, does he,' Mac said. 'I know,' he said, 'because Ellen Tailor called the police. Goodbye, Mr Shaw.'

Mac walked back down the busy shopping street to where he'd parked his car. He wasn't proud of such a cheap shot, but Shaw had irritated him and it had been a long and, he felt, unproductive day. One phone call between Shaw and Soames would destroy any impact Mac's words had had, but still, it felt like a small if petty victory in a day singularly without any real and solid ones.

His phone rang as he reached his car. It was Kendall.

'Go and meet Frank Baker at Daphne Tailor's place, will you. We had a call out to a domestic about half an hour ago. The address was on the open case list, so it flagged up. Uniform is there already and I asked Frank to take a look.'

'A domestic?'

'Yes. It seems Daphne and Diane went to the solicitors today to see what Ellen had put in her will. I don't think it was what Daphne expected.'

It took Mac about fifteen minutes in the evening traffic to make it to the house. He arrived to find two patrol cars parked outside and a young officer standing self-consciously beside one of them. Inside were the Tailor children, tearful and distressed.

From inside the house a woman could be heard shouting. She was calling someone a bitch and a tart and a treacherous little whore. Mac guessed this must be Daphne Tailor.

'What's going on?'

'Neighbours reckon she's been yelling like this for an hour or more before we got here. Sergeant Baker arrived about a half hour ago. He suggested we get the kids out of the way. She was chucking stuff about too.'

Mac nodded. 'And the aunt?'

'Still in there. Ask me, she's enjoying the show a bit too much.'

'And do we know what started it?'

'Apparently, the grandmother didn't get custody of the kids in their mum's will. That's what I can gather from all the shouting anyway.'

Mac nodded. He opened the front passenger door of the police car and sat inside, twisting round so he could talk to the children in the back seat. 'It's a daft question,' he said. 'But are you two all right?'

'Suppose,' Jeb shrugged.

'I want my mum,' Megan whispered. She'd obviously been crying and the tears began again now. Jeb, doing his best to be big brother, put his arm round her shoulders and hugged her but his gaze never left Mac's face.

'Do we have to stay here,' he whispered. 'Can't we just get in your car and go?'

Mac had the odd impression that he'd asked this question before. That it was a wish expressed often – and as often been denied. He remembered what Diane had told him, about the children asking her if they could just flit before their grandmother noticed and he also remembered her smile, her satisfaction when she had told him about her sister's will and the fact that she would be getting custody.

'You want me to try and get your aunt out here?' he asked.

Jeb thought about it and then shook his head. Megan's sobs grew louder and she buried her face in her brother's side.

'You need a break from both of them, is that it?'

Jeb nodded gratefully.

'OK, I'll see what I can do.'

Through the front room window, Mac could see Frank Baker and another officer trying to calm the scene. Diane stood beside the fireplace, leaning against the wall. Mac thought that the expression on her face looked oddly triumphal. He called Kendall.

'Can I borrow Yolanda and can we get a family liaison officer down here. No, the adults can take care of themselves. But the kids have had it up to . . . yes, I just want to get them out of the way for an hour while the so-called grown-ups get themselves calmed down. But I could do with an appropriate adult.'

Mac tucked the phone back in his pocket, smiling at the last comment Kendall had made. 'And you think that's Yolanda? You must be feeling desperate.' He turned to the officer. 'I've got a female officer coming down, then we'll take the kids off for a bit while tempers calm.'

'You can do that?' Jeb was leaning forward over the driver's seat, listening in to the conversation.

'Only for a little while, Jeb. Just until everyone is in a better mood.'

'Like that's going to happen now.'

'I'm going into the house for a few minutes,' Mac told the officer. 'Hold the fort; I don't think I'll be long.'

Mac took in the scene from within the room this time. Diane spotted him and her smile broadened. 'Inspector, come in, see the show.'

Daphne turned on her. 'Deceitful cow. Bastard fucking . . . I'll bloody kill you.'

She leapt at Diane, was intercepted by Frank Baker and wrestled back into a seat.

'Enough!' Mac took himself by surprise with the volume of his shout but silence fell as everyone turned to look at him.

'You pair are supposed to be the adults here. You are supposed to be looking out for those kids. I don't give a damn what your differences are or who did what to whom, but right now all the pair of you are doing is inflicting pain on a couple of kids that have already had enough of it, don't you think?'

Mac realized, belatedly that he was still shouting at the two women. That his anger and frustration had boiled over into a very unprofessional display. He tried and failed to feel bad about it, but continued a little more quietly. 'Now, you both sit down and calm down.'

He glimpsed Yolanda coming down the path and a moment later she was standing in the doorway. Mac nodded to her. 'Meantime, Yolanda and I are going to take Jeb and Megan out of the way while the two of you talk—'

'You can't do that—'

'You have no right—'

'I can. Or I can give social services a call and tell them the children are at risk.'

'I'll get my solicitor involved,' Diane told him.

'Be my guest,' Mac told her. 'From what I've heard, getting your solicitor involved hasn't exactly helped so far, has it. Frank will give me a ring when he considers the two of you are fit to have the children back. Meanwhile. Sit the fuck down and talk.'

He didn't wait to see the results of his pronouncement. Mac turned on his heel and left, Yolanda in tow.

'Wow,' she said as they reached the pavement. 'You will be in so much shit for this.' She was trying hard not to laugh. 'I can't believe you just did that.'

'Well, you'd better bring Kendall up to date,' Mac told her. 'I'll get the kids into my car. We can collect yours when we come back later . . . or something.'

What had he been thinking, Mac wondered as he walked Jeb and Megan to the car. This would be all round not just Kendall's HQ but all along the South Coast by morning. He glanced at his watch. Six o'clock and already getting dark. There would be rain soon, he thought. Yolanda hurried up behind them as Mac got the children into his car. 'Kendall wants to know where we're going,' she said.

Up until that moment Mac had given it very little thought. 'Rina's place,' he said. 'Kendall knows her.' He gave Yolanda the address and hoped Rina wouldn't mind four other guests for dinner.

'I just lost it, Rina,' Mac said quietly.

Bethany was teaching Jeb and Megan to play a card game he didn't recognize and Eliza was plying them with cake. They still looked tearful, but Megan, at least, seemed willing to be distracted. Jeb kept looking Mac's way as though for reassurance.

Yolanda had seated herself at the piano and was leafing through the sheet music.

'You were angry. We all get angry. Especially where the innocent are concerned.'

'Which is no excuse. Not really.'

'Do you play, dear?' Stephen Montmorency asked.

'I used to. Got my grade-eight piano, but I've not done in oh, five, six years.'

'And why ever not. Here, try this one.'

Rina smiled fondly. 'Well you came to the right place,' she said. 'I hope Frank is coping,' she added mischievously.

'Well, he's got back up if he needs it. He'll be fine.' Mac closed his eyes, relaxing for a moment and savouring the somewhat chaotic but loving atmosphere of Rina's eclectic household. To the sound of Yolanda playing the piano and, surprisingly, Stephen Montmorency softly singing.

Then his phone rang. It was Frank.

'Time to go home,' he told Jeb and Megan.

He took a moment to talk to Rina while the children collected their coats and put their shoes back on. He still had the diary and letters he had taken from William Trent in his pocket. It seemed like years ago and he had to remind himself that it had only been that morning.

'Rina, can you do something for me and make copies of these. Have a read and see what's in them.'

'Is it to do with . . .?'

'I don't know,' he admitted. 'But I'd be grateful if maybe you and Tim could take a look.'

'Of course we will. You take care how you drive back. You're still upset.'

Mac smiled at her and kissed her cheek and then he and Yolanda packed the children back into the car.

'Are they still shouting at one another?' Jeb asked.

'Frank . . . Sergeant Baker assures me they've calmed down. You have to go back sometime I'm afraid.'

Jeb nodded reluctantly.

Looking at the boy through the rear view mirror, Mac could see that he looked back, hungrily, at Peverill Lodge until they reached the end of the road, as though wishing himself back there.

TWENTY-FOUR

Yolanda had taken the children upstairs to watch television in Daphne's room. Mac had left them, perched nervously on the bed either side of Yolanda. She had an arm around each one, much to Mac's surprise. She was doing OK, he thought, for someone who didn't like kids or old ladies.

Diane, Daphne, Frank and the young officer he had seen posted outside were all gathered in the front living room and Frank was serving coffee. He should have called family liaison, Mac thought, and then decided that Frank was probably doing as good a job.

'Would you like to tell me what all that was about?'

'Are they all right?' Daphne asked.

'No,' Mac told her bluntly. 'Of course they're not. They've lost both parents. One of them they watched die from cancer, one they discovered with her face blown off on the kitchen floor.'

'Mac,' Frank reproved quietly.

Mac heard Diane gasp and saw Daphne blanch. He knew he was out of order but he wasn't sure he cared. 'You are now all they have left. Diane, you know how it feels to suddenly lose everything. Ellen made certain you were never alone, didn't she. Daphne, you know what it's like to lose a child, and, I suspect, to feel excluded and helpless when you thought that child should have needed you the most. The fact was, he needed his wife more. You didn't like that, did you?'

Daphne's stony face turned from him. 'How dare you,' she whispered. 'How fucking dare you.'

'That's enough, Daphne,' Frank soothed. He looked across at Mac reprovingly.

'And you,' Mac said, turning his attention to Diane. 'I don't doubt you want the best for your sister's children but have you actually given a moment's thought to what that might be?'

'They want to live with me,' Diane said hotly. 'Ellen wanted them to live with me.'

'According to her will, yes. But I don't imagine she ever thought the two of you would be so full of enmity it would cause this much pain to the people she wanted to protect.' He paused and looked at the two women. 'Or did she?' he asked. 'Did she know how much you hated one another?'

'We don't,' Daphne said hastily. 'And I had nothing but respect for—'

'Respect! Really?' Diane spat at Daphne. 'For the woman you accused of ruining your son's life? Turning against the family? If you could have found a way to blame her for the cancer, I'm bloody sure you would have done.'

'Enough!' It was Frank this time. 'Ladies, I thought we agreed to a truce, here. So settle down and drink your tea.'

'And while you're doing that,' Mac said, aware he was about to throw another match into the powder keg, 'Daphne, perhaps you'd like to tell me why you lied about Ray still being in New Zealand?'

Frank and Daphne both looked stunned. Diane opened her mouth as though to accuse him of betraying her.

'We checked with passport control at the border agency,' Mac said. 'He was in the country the day Ellen was shot, wasn't he?'

It was a bluff, of course. Mac had put in a request for a trace on Ray Tailor and phone calls had been made to New Zealand police, but he'd had no news yet. But from the look on Daphne's face, he knew he had hit the target.

'Ray didn't kill her,' Daphne said.

'We're going to want to speak to him, Daphne.'

Daphne Tailor placed her cup back on its saucer and set both carefully back down on the table. She looked Mac full in the face. 'I don't know where he is,' she said. 'And I wouldn't bloody tell you if I did.'

TWENTY-FIVE

Day five after the murder

Mac waited for Rina on the promenade the following morning and she brought the journals and letters to him. 'Tim and Joy copied them last night,' she said. 'They're going to take a look, later, and he'll have a chat to his Uncle Charles, see if he can make sense of the entries, but I don't see—'

'That it has anything to do with Ellen Tailor's death. No. I doubt it has at all. If I'd thought that I'd not have brought them to you. I've bent enough rules without all out breaking them.'

'Stephen and Matthew have taken a shine to Yolanda,' Rina said. 'Did you manage to get things settled for the children?'

'As settled as we could.' Mac sighed. 'I suppose it gets to me,' he said. 'Adults, theoretically at least, get the option to walk out of a situation. Kids don't even have that theoretical option, you know? And the truth is it's hard enough for an adult to break away from a bad situation, what chance do you have when you're that age?'

Rina gripped his arm gently. 'I know,' she said. 'You'd best get off to work, you know. I've seen Andy come to the door twice now to look for you. I think your friend Dave Kendall is there too. I caught a glimpse of him just now.'

Mac laughed. 'I'd best get an extra coffee then,' he said. 'See you later, Rina. Have a good day. At least one of us ought to.'

Kendall first took the proffered coffee and then Mac's seat behind the desk. Mac considered this the first stage of the coming reprimand.

'I suppose I should ask what the hell you thought you were doing,' Kendall said. 'You know she's filed a complaint?'

Mac nodded. 'I had Yolanda take her through the forms,' he said. 'I told her, if she wanted to complain, she should do it right.'

'What's with you, Mac?'

'Truthfully? I don't know. I just seem to have less and less patience with stupidity. With cruelty, maybe.'

'Then you're in the wrong job, Mac, and neither of us believe that. Look, I'm going to have to let this run its course. You might face a suspension, you know that?'

'It won't be the first. I'll get over it. The woman was and is being obstructive. I suppose that's not an issue though.'

'Of course it is. But that's a *separate* issue. Anyway, while you're still part of the team, you and Frank had better bring me up to speed.'

Frank Baker sank carefully into the third chair and Andy took up his usual position by the door, ready to return to the front desk should anyone urgently require help with a lost dog.

Mac took a swallow of his coffee and gestured to Frank to begin.

'Well,' Frank Baker said. 'It all began with the reading of the will, yesterday afternoon. Diane had been privy to the information, but to Daphne it was all a bit of a shock. It seems that Ellen left the guardianship of her kids to Diane. The farm and everything in it to the kids to be sold and split between them, should that be what they wanted. Diane was to be allowed a certain amount from the proceeds not exceeding ten per cent of the sale price, to help support the kids. Daphne not only was to get nothing from what had been family land, but was to be excluded from caring for the children. Ellen had said she could visit and be visited, but not be considered a full-time carer in any sense. And from the sound of things, she'd had the solicitor go over it with a fine-toothed comb to make sure the will couldn't be challenged.'

'I can see why the grandmother went ballistic,' Kendall said.

'Well, quite, especially as it seems the kids had already been asking their aunt if they could go and live with her. In the grandmother's hearing.'

'Did the children know about the will?'

'Apparently not, but it seems they couldn't hide the fact that they were pleased, which must have gone down like a lead brick.'

'So, what's wrong with the grandma?' Andy asked. 'Mine used to spoil me rotten as a kid. They used to try and outdo one another. Drove me mam mad.'

'Apparently she insulted Ellen on a regular basis and made it clear that she'd never approved of the marriage. She apparently told Jeb that now Ellen was gone they could get the farm back on track but, granted, that bit of information was filtered through Diane, the sister. So we have to take it with a large pinch.'

'So, the solicitor delivers the glad tidings, and—'

'And things kick off in his office. The kids are in the waiting room. The secretary goes in and asks if she should call the police. The solicitor tells them to take it somewhere else and throws them out. They all go back to Daphne's place and the argument continues, gets so loud the neighbours try to intervene. Daphne tells them where to go and they call us.'

'And has anyone checked in with them this morning?' Mac asked.

'I had Yolanda do a welfare check. It seems the injured parties are now not speaking to one another and Diane has been asked to leave. She says she's not going without the kids, so things are . . . uncomfortable but stable, I suppose you might say.'

'And Ray Tailor. What are we doing about him?' Mac asked.

Kendall produced his notebook. 'Returned to the country, alone, ten days ago. We've spoken to his wife. She says Daphne arranged the trip, but just for him. She bought the ticket. From what the wife said, the marriage hasn't survived the trip to New Zealand very well and she'll not be sorry if he doesn't come back. She gave us his mobile number, but it seems to have been disconnected. Probably switched off or the Sim changed, or it's easy enough to buy a pay-as-you-go phone.'

Mac nodded. 'I'm betting Daphne knows where he is.'

'Agreed, and we will apply pressure, bring her in for interview under caution. Ray Tailor is a legitimate suspect. But I think finding him will be something we have to do without his mother's help.'

Mac nodded. 'She insists he's innocent. We know they fought over the farm and that Ellen's husband cut Ray out of the will. We know that Ray is always short of cash and that he's careless with money. But does all that really add up to murder?'

'People have been killed for a lot less.'

'I know that, but the Tailor family don't seem to have even garnered a speeding ticket between them. It seems a leap.'

'Passions run high when there's an inheritance at stake,' Frank noted. 'It must have hurt like hell, seeing what you'd always believed was your birthright go to some outsider, just because she happened to have married your brother.'

Mac conceded the point. 'And Philip Soames?'

'His alibi for the day Ellen Tailor was shot seems watertight. He appears on the CCTV cameras at work at regular intervals. The video is all time-coded, saved on to a hard drive, the hard drive is locked in a computer, locked inside a purpose made box. So—'

'And the night Ellen was scared out of the house?'

'He seems to have been in the pub until nine, but no one can be totally sure what time he left. He's still in the frame for that.'

'Where were the kids that night?' Andy asked.

'At the grandmother's. Why?'

'So, the relationship was OK at that point?'

'Seems to have been,' Mac said. 'I spoke to William Trent about Ellen and Daphne's relationship and also Terry Bridger, the part-time farm hand, they both agree that the relationship had been stormy, but seemed to have settled down this past year.'

Andy nodded. 'Did they do it regularly? Stay over with Daphne Tailor for the weekend?'

'Apparently not. The Richardses told me this was the first time Ellen had been alone for the weekend since her husband died.'

'So—'

'So, yes. It is an interesting coincidence. Though, according to the Richardses the silent calls had been going on for a while. They were inclined to blame telemarketing companies, but—'

'So, we have two suspects and a broken family,' Mac said. 'Where from here?'

'Track down Ray Tailor, look deeper into Ellen Tailor's life before she came down here, check and recheck Soames' alibis. I've sent the copy of the card Soames claimed to have received from Ellen for analysis. We've got samples of her handwriting from the farm, so we'll see what that brings up. My guess is that Ellen knew nothing about that card.'

'If that's the case, then who sent it? Who was intent on bringing Philip Soames back into her life?' Mac wondered. 'I'd like another word with Diane Emmet.'

'No,' Kendall told him. 'The questions will be asked but not by you. Mac, you'll stay away from both Daphne Tailor and the sister for the time being. Is that clear?'

He could have argued, Mac thought. Strictly speaking, Kendall didn't outrank him, but he was lead officer on the case, so . . . Mac nodded. It really didn't feel worth the extra hassle. 'I promise to stay out of their way,' he said.

Aunt Diane and their nan seemed set on outdoing one another in the surveillance stakes and it was only when Jeb had set up the chess board in his room and invited Megan to play that they had finally been left alone.

Jeb was not, in fact, very good at chess and he didn't rate it much as a game either. Had his games console and all his games not still been back at the farmhouse he would have selected something noisy and violent and turned the volume up high. But, you had to work with what you had, didn't you.

Megan, on the other hand, was a member of the school chess club and was actually a pretty good player. Figuring out Jeb's strategy had also been easy and after a few interruptions from Diane and Daphne, Megan had got impatient and tearfully begged both women to go away.

'I want to practise,' she said. 'Dad taught me to play and I want to practise. It makes me feel like he's still here, you know?'

Jeb had looked on admiringly as Megan had summoned more tears and Daphne had found a few of her own before retreating downstairs.

Diane had shrugged and left them to it as well.

Strictly speaking it was true that their dad had taught both of them to play chess. Megan had only been about five at the time and Jeb could vividly recall the circumstances. A prolonged power cut in the middle of winter and parents at the end of their tether trying to keep the kids entertained. Their dad had known how the pieces moved and the basic rules, but that was about it. Megan, on the other hand . . . well, Jeb knew he could never beat her.

He got up from the board and crept over to the door. Opening it a crack he could hear Daphne downstairs. Diane was out in the garden and Jeb could see that she was weeding or something. Or maybe just pulling up Daphne's plants.

'Good idea,' Megan said. 'We'd better look like we're halfway through a game in case they come back.'

Jeb watched as she arranged the board, playing an imaginary game from both sides until she was satisfied. Neither Daphne nor Diane played, but Jeb agreed that they should be thorough.

'I heard them talking about an old boyfriend,' Jeb said. 'With that policewoman. She wanted to know something about a letter.'

Megan nodded. 'Nan was telling someone on the phone. She said Mum must have been seeing him behind Dad's back.'

'Dad's been dead nearly three years,' Jeb said. 'If she was seeing someone, he's not going to have much to say about it, is he.' He saw Megan's lip quiver and felt immediately bad about that.

'She liked Dan,' Megan said.

'Yeah, but he's married. I don't think Mum would do anything like that.'

'What, like Miss Greasely did?' Megan giggled briefly and Jeb smiled at her. Miss Greasely had been a teacher at their primary school and she'd caused a bit of a fuss when she'd run off with one of the fathers.

'Did Mum talk to you about her old boyfriends?' Megan asked. Jeb, being that bit older, did sometimes glean tit bits of information that Megan didn't.

Jeb frowned, thinking. 'No, she didn't talk much about anything before Dad. But there was that man who came over that night. When the police came as well.'

Megan nodded. She'd slept through it and Jeb had been sent back to bed, but there'd been a strange man sitting at the kitchen table and their mother had said it was an old friend. But she'd not told Jeb his name.

'Diane keeps saying Mum wasn't worried about anything,' Megan said. 'But she was, wasn't she?'

Jeb nodded. In the weeks before she died, their mother had been jumpy and anxious. Ignoring the phone and getting a new phone with a caller display box. And twice or three times she'd not been home when they got there. Jeb had let them in with the spare key and Ellen had arrived not long after saying that she'd got struck in traffic or there was an extra long queue at the bank. Little things had made her angry and that had been unusual. She'd just not been herself, but neither Jeb nor Megan – and they'd talked about it a lot – had been able to figure out what was wrong.

'Do you think they'll ever start talking to one another again?' Megan asked.

'Nan and Aunt Diane? I don't know. I don't really care to be honest. I thought I liked Auntie Diane but I'm not sure now.'

Megan looked stunned and then she looked sad. 'Well, we've got to live somewhere,' she said. 'I suppose Auntie Diane is better than Nan.'

Footsteps on the stairs drove them back to their game. The door opened and Daphne came in with pop and biscuits.

'How's the game?' she asked cheerfully.

'Check and mate,' Megan said.

TWENTY-SIX

Tim had run into William Trent a few times at *Iconograph*, but never really spoken to him. He knew that neither the designers nor the programmers really liked the man, but he hadn't been sure why. At lunch in the canteen he spotted Dennie Miles, someone Tim had worked quite closely with on the *Magician's Quest* series Tim had been involved with for the past eighteen months or so. Dennie was now doing some of the preliminary storyboards for the wartime project Trent was consulting on. He was exactly the person Tim had been hoping to see.

Dennie looked up as Tim plonked his tray down on the table. 'Timothy. How the devil are you?'

Tim grimaced. He hated his full name and Dennie knew that.
Dennie laughed. 'How's it going,' he said.

'Not so bad. You'll be getting my research notes in about a
week or so, you'll be able to tell *me* then.'

'Look forward to it. And how's the night job going?'

Tim smiled with a little more enthusiasm. He worked at
Iconograph anything between one and three days a week. Three
nights a week he worked at the Palisades Hotel, performing his
magic act. He was gaining a considerable reputation and was
gratified to know that hotel bookings were some twenty per cent
up on the nights he performed. The refurbished Art Deco theatre
and restaurant at the hotel was an additional draw and was open
to the public as well as hotel guests. Most nights sold out in
advance and Tim enjoyed his theatrical persona. 'It's all going
very well,' he said. 'We're doing the final prep for the Christmas
programme now. More research.' Tim laughed. If he was honest,
researching the history of stage magic was actually the best part
of his job. He had successfully revived several classic but not much
used illusions over the past couple of years.

'Anything we can use?' Dennie asked.

'I hope so. Yes. Dennie, I wanted to ask you something. You've
been working with William Trent, I think?'

Dennie rolled his eyes. 'Working with is stretching it a bit. I've
been listening while he lectures me, yes. Look, no offence to the
man, he's probably a fantastic historian or whatever, but he doesn't
have a clue as to what's useful in our field. We don't need someone
to create backstory; we've got writers already doing that. What
we need is the action stuff. Who did what and how and where.'

'I thought Lydia wanted him on board precisely for the back
stories,' Tim argued. 'All the bits of hidden history.'

'Sure, that was the original idea, but all the really unusual stuff
is practically unusable. At least in the timescale we've got.'

'Oh, why's that?'

Dennie stirred his tea. 'Look,' he said. 'I don't want to be
unfair to the man. He's filled in a whole load of background of
how people lived, the civil defence side of things, the restrictions
on movement and all that, but the bits he's really obsessed by
we wouldn't touch with a very, very long barge pole. He's got
a bee in his bonnet about there being a training school for SOE

somewhere hereabouts, so we looked deeper into that. You know, that's the sort of thing we had in mind. All the hidden stuff that no one knows about. Trouble is, some of it, we're still not supposed to know about.'

'Really?'

'Really. He reckons there was something as significant as the work they did over at Bletchley, but we don't know what, he can only guess and when we put in a freedom of information request we were told that the thirty-year rule didn't apply. I mean, why, for God's sake? They've even released all the cold war intel – well some of it anyway.'

Tim shrugged, his mind drifting towards the journal that Mac had brought to them and which he'd only had time to glance at yet. 'Did he say anything more?'

'No, he just got annoyed. Said there was more than one way to skin a cat or something and muttering about oral history. Thing is, he gets annoyed with me and my team. Like I can do anything about it. I just design the damned games. I don't run the government, do I?'

'Why use a freedom of information request?' Tim asked.

Dennie grinned. 'Because that way someone else has to do the leg work for you. They search the archives so you don't have to. Give him his dues, Trent was right about that part. Pity nothing came of it.'

Dennie tapped his watch and nodded at someone on the other side of the canteen. Glancing over his shoulder, Tim could see another member of Dennie's team waiting for him. 'Playtime's over,' Dennie said. 'Do you know this Trent, then?'

'Not really. He was a friend of that woman that was shot. Ellen Tailor.'

'Ah, so your Mrs Martin is investigating is she? I heard about it. Sounds terrible. Look, got to go.'

Tim nodded and glanced at his own watch. He too had another meeting. He drained the last of his tea and tucked the pack of biscuits he'd bought into his pocket for later.

The journal, Tim thought. Was that what had convinced William Trent that something mysterious, something secret, had been going on in wartime Frantham? It wouldn't be all that surprising, Tim thought. It was hard to go anywhere on the South Coast without falling over some symbol or memory or relic from the second war as his mother always called it. Coming from a military family, Tim's youth had been imbued with stories and family legends and his two uncles were still actively involved in the shadier aspects of that world. One had spent a lifetime in diplomatic protection and one was something vague and mysterious in military intelligence. Tim and his father were the only members of the extended family for whom the attraction of soldiering of one sort or another had passed them by. His father was an engineer and Tim . . . well Tim had only just found his direction.

TWENTY-SEVEN

'I told you, I didn't want to see you again.'

'Tough. Makes a change for you to be telling that to someone else, doesn't it? It's usually you being told to piss off.'

Philip Soames scowled at her. 'What the hell do you want anyway?'

'Well—' Diane settled into her chair and added sugar to her coffee – 'I just thought you'd want to finish what you started, so to speak. A job half done is only half a job. Did your mum never tell you that?'

'Piss off, Diane. This is your game. I never wanted any part of it.'

'You think anyone will believe that?' She leaned forward. 'Phil, my sister's dead. You are number one on the list of guilty parties. You surely don't want me to make life even harder for you than it already is.'

'Like you've already done.'

'Believe me, I've not even started.'

Philip Soames pushed his own cup aside and stood up. 'Piss off, Diane,' he told her again. 'You want something done, you do it yourself.'

She watched him leave, a frown creasing deeply between her brows. 'Damn.'

Diane sighed. Nothing was ever bloody simple. She glanced at her watch and knew she must think about getting back. Daphne would be taking advantage of Diane's absence to sow her poison.

She finished her coffee, glancing around the little cafe and feeling suddenly very obvious. The cafe was round the corner from the Marsden warehouse. It catered for the factory workers and the warehousemen and the bacon butty brigade and Diane was very obviously not one of the usual clientele. She'd been dressed for another visit to her solicitor and the impulse to drop in on Phil Soames in what was one of his usual haunts had just been overwhelming.

Now she began to wonder if it had been a major error of judgement.

Diane got up and left, aware that her departure had been watched by the woman behind the counter and the two men perched on high stools seated beside it.

'Think she's lost,' one of them joked.

'Think she rubbed Phil up the wrong way,' Jake said. His companion laughed. 'She can rub me any way she likes,' he said and earned himself a reprimand from the owner.

'Sorry, Mel. He's a dark horse, our Phil.'

Jake's companion nodded. He watched through the window as Diane walked back to the end of the street and disappeared round the corner. He wondered if his boss knew that Ellen Tailor's sister was coming round asking questions. Decided that maybe he should be the one to make certain that he did.

Megan was playing on the swing again and Jeb, in desultory mood, kicking a ball around the garden. They had discovered that their nan left them alone if they went into the garden and 'played'. If they hung round the house and tried to talk, she'd be there, listening in at their conversations or checking to make sure they were out of earshot when she made her phone calls. They had spent a lot of time outside these past few days and thankfully the weather had held for them.

Jeb was dreading the winter.

On his list of things to dread, though, he was dreading the funeral first. The body would be released ready for next Friday. He had heard Daphne tell someone that on the phone – he found it hard to think of her as nan these days; his mother's voice seemed to echo in his head whenever he tried to say the word. She hadn't told him that though. And he wasn't sure that Diane had heard the news either.

'I want to go back to school,' Megan said. 'I want to see my friends. I want—' She broke off and looked at her brother.

Jeb nodded. 'She's not going to let us, though. She doesn't want us out of the house and talking to other people, does she?'

Megan shook her head. 'I don't get why.'

Neither did Jeb, but he knew he was right. Daphne had watched them like a hawk. The only respite had been the afternoon that Diane had taken them out to the beach. The day she had met up with that policeman. They'd got home just ahead of Daphne and Jeb knew it was more by luck than organization on Diane's part. He knew how relieved his aunt had been though. The only other respite had been when the policeman had taken them away for a bit on the day of the Big Argument. That couple of hours at the old woman's house had been a major relief. Rina and everyone had been nice to them and not asked stupid questions.

Daphne had been furious about that and he had overheard her telling someone on the phone that she was making a complaint about the inspector. She had quizzed them frequently and at length about that couple of hours away. What did people ask them? What had they done? Who were these people they had been with? What had the policeman asked them?

She hadn't believed Jeb at all when he told her that he and Megan had learnt a card game with a weird name and eaten cake. Even when Megan, questioned separately, had given the same responses, Daphne had still yelled at them for lying to her.

Frankly, Jeb didn't get it. His grandmother had always had a bit of a temper and he knew she'd never liked their mum, but she'd never gone off on one like that. She'd never been this mad.

Turning with the ball, he caught a glimpse of Daphne in the upstairs window, looking down at them, a fierce expression on her face. She'd threatened not to let Diane in when she came back. Diane had then threatened her with the police or even that she'd call social services. Jeb felt like he and Megan were caught between two crazy women. Like they were a living rope in a tug of war. He didn't know what he could do about it.

Megan slipped from the swing and aimed a kick at the ball.

She missed, so Jeb nudged it back to her so she could try again. 'You think Auntie Diane will take us up to York?' she asked.

'Probably. She says it's up to us. That she'd move down here if we wanted, but I don't think she means it.'

'You want to stay here?'

Jeb shook his head. 'I don't know,' he said. What he wanted wasn't going to happen. What both of them wanted was never going to happen. They wanted their mum back. They wanted it to be all like it was before.

'You're sure it was her?' Dan asked.

'Certain. Ellen was with her sister when I ran into her one day in town. I came to pick you up – she was with you, and her sister was with her.'

Dan nodded. He remembered the occasion now. Diane looked a lot like her sister. Jake would remember meeting her all right. 'So what was she doing with Phil Soames?'

'I don't know. Couldn't very well go and listen in, could I, but he wasn't pleased that's for sure. He told her where to go and left and she didn't hang around afterwards.'

Dan nodded. 'Thanks, Jake. I'll have a word with him.'

Rina and Tim had been scanning through the documents Mac had left with them. '*I had a meeting today with Richard Freeman, head of the Home Guard Auxiliary Unit for this area. He seems like a sensible man and looking at his record is well equipped, mentally and experientially at least. I'm going to try and arrange a weekend up at Farnham for him and maybe a couple of his men. I'm trying my best to pull strings to get him the equipment he's requested but it's a slow process. I'm due for a visit to the Diamond Company next week and I've promised to put his case.*'

'I think I'm in need of an interpreter here,' Rina said.

'So did I, so I called Uncle Charlie. The Auxiliary Units were the home guard equivalent of commando groups, specializing in guerrilla warfare and trained to be the last line of defence in case of invasion.'

'Ah, I read something about that,' Rina said. 'And the Diamond Company.'

'Now that really is interesting,' Tim told her. 'At the start of the war part of the Secret Intelligence Service operated out of the eighth floor of Bush House in London. Cover for the operation were two shop fronts. One was—' he paused to consult his notes – 'Geoffrey Ruveen and Co and the other was Joel Brothers Diamond Company. I'm betting that's what this entry means.'

'No wonder William Trent was so interested. Did this come from the Tailor family, I wonder?'

'Well, that would be logical, I suppose,' Tim said. 'Ellen Tailor loaned them to William Trent.'

Rina nodded, but she was thinking about Vera Courtney. About the possessions missing from the storeroom at the airfield. Could Ellen have loaned Vera's family documents to William Trent? It was a consideration.

'Keep looking,' she told Tim. 'See what else you can find out, but it's no wonder William Trent was all excited by this journal, is it?'

TWENTY-EIGHT

It was two weeks since Ellen Tailor had been shot and her funeral took place at St Peter's Church where she had arranged the flowers.

The press were out in force, Mac noted, and for once Daphne and Diane presented a united front, shepherding the children between them and doing their best to keep them away from prying eyes and invasive lenses.

The children were dressed in black. Jeb looked mutinous. Megan had a bright red scarf wrapped tightly around her neck and Mac guessed this was her version of protest. From what he knew of Ellen, he didn't see her as being a woman who'd like to see her kids dressed in formal funeral clothes.

Still, what did he know?

Daphne looked suitably formal in a dark suit and Diane in a blue dress beneath a dark coat. Make-up couldn't hide the fact that she was tearful and had already been crying.

Funerals make everything real, Mac thought. His professional life had brought him to more than a few and he had seen the effect many times. Too many times.

'Any comment, Inspector?' A familiar voice at his elbow caused Mac to turn and smile. 'Thought you might be here. How's Simeon?'

'My brother is as fine as he ever is,' Andrew Barnes said. 'But he's no worse and for that I am grateful. It's a bad business, isn't it?'

Mac nodded. 'Who are you representing today?' he asked. Andrew wrote for a couple of small locals, but he was also a stringer for a few of the nationals these days which was a change due in no small part to his coverage of some of Mac's earlier investigations.

'Actually, though I will no doubt write about it, I'm here on my own account. I knew Ellen's husband really well so I thought I ought to come and pay my respects.'

'I see,' he said. 'What was he like?'

Andrew laughed softly. 'A genuinely nice man,' he said. 'Down to earth, kind, loved Ellen to bits and the kids too. Fell for her hard and never fell out of love. Same for her, I'd have said.'

'So you must know Daphne?'

'So I must know Daphne,' he agreed. 'She's an odd one, our Daphne. Can be the kindest woman you'd ever want to meet. Can also be the most bloody-minded and awkward and miserable sod you could run into. Trouble was, not even her kids knew which one they were going to get.'

'Must have been tough?'

The journalist nodded. 'She married another moody bugger. Jeb's father was as changeable as the proverbial. I wouldn't say he was an unkind man, just a bit of a loner. Preferred his cows to his kids, Jeb always used to say. He died when Jeb was just sixteen, you know.'

'I didn't, actually. That must have been tough, too.'

Mac saw Dan Marsden arrive with an older woman he assumed must be his mother. An older man got out of the car straight after. He walked with two sticks. 'You know Dan Marsden too?'

'Oh yes and Carrie and the rest of the Breed Estate lot. We're all of an age, went to the same schools, and Dan, of course, I interview on a regular basis about whatever scheme he's involved with.'

Something in his voice made Mac ask, 'Do you like him?'

'Dan? No not that much. He's . . . too glib, too consciously good if you know what I mean . . . or maybe I'm just an old cynic.'

Mac waited, sensing there was more.

'He's married now, of course, got a couple of kids, but he's always been a bit of a womanizer.'

'Is he still?'

'I really wouldn't know. I should be getting inside, seeing as how I'm a participant and not an observer today. Take care of yourself, Mac. My best to Miriam.'

Mac nodded, making a mental note that he should have a further conversation with Andrew Barnes – or maybe he should ask Rina to do so; she was much better at wheedling the gossip than Mac. Frank, across the road from him, was chatting to the press corps. Kendall's men mingled with the crowd. The flower-arranging committee arrived together. William Trent came alone. He spotted Mac and came over. 'Are you going inside? I feel a bit awkward.'

Mac was slightly surprised. He nodded. 'I may as well go in now,' he said. 'I'll be staying at the back, though.'

'Best place to be,' Trent agreed. 'I take it the family have arrived? I hoped to say hello to the children. Maybe as they leave.'

Mac remained close by the door as William was, reluctantly, directed to a seat. The little church was full and Mac supposed that those he didn't recognize must be local people who had known Ellen and the Tailor family. He found that he was looking for Philip Soames, however unlikely that might seem.

A young man slipped into the church just as the service was about to start and stood at the back close to Mac.

Mac recognized him from a photograph he had seen at the farm. As the first hymn began he sidled over.

'Ray Tailor, I presume?'

'And I believe you are Inspector MacGregor. Inspector, I'm not going anywhere. Can we just wait until after the service? Then I'll come along and you can ask me anything you like.'

Mac hesitated and then nodded. 'I take it your mother doesn't know you are here?'

Ray smiled wryly. 'I told her I was coming, but she didn't

believe me. And I'd sooner not get embroiled, if you know what I mean.'

Mac nodded again. The organ had begun to play and the congregation rose to sing the first hymn. He stood in silence beside Ellen's brother-in-law, watching the two women, so at odds with one another, either side of the two children. Jeb's shoulders were rigid, Megan leaned into her aunt and Diane's arm was wrapped tightly round her shoulders.

'Ellen was a lovely woman,' Ray said quietly. 'It should never have ended like this, no matter what our mum thought.'

Diane approached Frank Baker after the funeral. 'I though DI MacGregor was here.'

'He was; he's just had to go. Something came up. Will I do?'

Diane nodded. 'I just wanted to let him know that the kids and I are leaving tomorrow morning. Make sure he's got the address.' She handed him a slip of paper. 'I think he's already got all my contact details, but just in case.'

Frank thanked her. 'I imagine Mrs Tailor isn't best pleased about that?'

Diane shrugged. 'The kids and I spent the last few nights in a hotel,' she said. 'It seemed easiest. I agreed to ride in the same car with her today just for the look of things. I don't want to give the gossips more ammunition. Daphne can do enough of that, all on her own.'

'Does she still plan to challenge the will?'

'Oh, yes. Of course she does. My solicitor says there's nothing she can do and he's spoken to her solicitor who agrees and is trying to get her to see sense. But if she wants to waste her money, that's up to her. The only trouble is it ties everything up until it's all gone to court or whatever. It's going to make things harder for us all.'

'She'll probably back down. I figure she's just angry and hurt. Give her time.'

'Maybe. Frank, do you know when we'll be able to get into the house? I mean, not the kids, but all their stuff is there. Clothes and games and whatever. It would be really helpful if I could collect some of it? Or maybe arrange for someone else to.'

'I'll have a talk to the boss,' Frank promised. 'What would

probably be easiest is if I could get Yolanda to gather some bits together for you. You could give her a list?'

She smiled. 'Thanks,' she said. 'That would be a big help. It's sorting out all the little stuff that's so hard.'

Ray had been shown into an interview room and cautioned. Mac set the tape running, reporting his own presence and that of Kendall.

'Why did you come back to the UK, Mr Tailor?'

Ray sighed. He looked, Mac thought, a lot like the pictures he had seen of his older brother. The same dark hair and eyes and slightly square chin. Ray looked a little rounder; a tad softer, maybe, but the family resemblance was strong. Jeb junior had his father's eyes too, Mac recalled.

'Mr Tailor?'

'I came back because she summoned me,' he said at last. 'I told her, I didn't want anything to do with it, but she was throwing a hissy fit and in the end it seemed better for me to come back and settle things once and for all than to let it all build up again. I came back because I thought I owed Ellen and the kids and I know what my mother is like when she gets an idea in her head. But I told her. This would be the last time. I'd got a new life and I wasn't going to be at her beck and call after this. I'd had enough.'

'I understand she helped finance this new life,' Mac commented.

'She helped a bit. Chucked a grand into the pot. Ellen and Diane did a lot more. Ellen split some of the money from the land sale with me. I didn't deserve it, but she did and Diane managed to get a cheap deal on tickets and even fixed a place for us to stay while we got sorted out. She works for a travel firm. Some little family company, specializes in holidays for the "independent traveller".'

Mac could hear the inverted commas. He hadn't known that was what Diane did; he hadn't asked.

'So she used her contacts.'

Ray nodded.

'And are you and your wife settled there now? You'll be wanting to go back.'

'Go back, yes. But we'll be getting a divorce, I think. We thought, fresh start, new life . . . we might be all right. But all it showed was how far apart we'd drifted. Thank fuck we've no kids.

And we're not fighting over anything, just want to go our separate ways.'

'You say your mother "summoned" you.'

Ray laughed. He sounded uncomfortable. 'Sound like a right mummy's boy, don't I. Look, Daphne called. Again. She said Ellen was selling off stuff that was rightfully hers. Something she'd found at the farm. Daphne was in a right state, said Ellen had found some money or something and now Ellen was refusing to let her into the house and refusing to give her whatever it was she'd been selling or . . . I don't know, she wasn't making any sense.'

'So, on the strength of a garbled accusation, you came all the way back here?'

Ray shook his head. 'No, on the strength of a threat I thought she might actually carry out I came back. I owe Ellen. No, more than that. I loved Ellen. If Jeb hadn't got to her first, I might have—'

'Hence the cracks in your own marriage?'

'I should never have even got married. It wasn't fair, not to either of us. I thought I could make it work out. I was wrong.'

'Did Ellen know how you felt?' Mac asked.

Ray shook his head. 'I don't know. I never told her. But she might have.'

'And these threats your mother made.'

'Were just noise. She'd never have carried them through.'

'You were worried enough to come all the way from New Zealand. You must have thought she might.'

'She says a lot of stupid stuff.'

'Like what? Did she threaten to kill Ellen?'

'No, of course not. I mean, not that she ever meant. Daphne is volatile. She says stuff, flies off the handle.'

'But Ellen is dead.'

Ray closed his eyes and was silent for a few moments. Mac prompted him again.

'Mr Tailor. What did she threaten to do?'

'Oh, I don't know. She said she'd see to it that Ellen was ruined. That she'd accuse her of ill treating the kids. That she'd take her to court over . . . whatever it was Ellen had found and was now profiting from.'

'And did she say what that was?'

'She didn't make a lot of sense. One minute it was money and the next minute just something that belonged to my dad. Look, I've only seen her once since I got back. Twice if you count today. I stayed away, called her a few times, but I realized as soon as my plane touched down. Maybe sooner than that. The truth was I didn't want to be here and I didn't want to be sucked back in. I called Ellen a couple of times, told her to be careful. Ellen said I was welcome to visit, but I never went.'

'Was Ellen scared? Did your mother threaten to harm her?'

'Mum says things. Things she really doesn't mean.'

'Did she threaten Ellen?'

Ray shrugged. 'A couple of times, yeah. But she didn't kill her. She wouldn't really have done that.'

'But the threat was made?'

'Yes, I suppose the threat was made. She can be a dumb bitch at times, she really can.'

'And what did she want you to do?'

'Go to the farm, search the place, see what Ellen had found. Persuade her to hand it over, maybe. I don't know.'

'She must have had something specific for you to do, otherwise why want you here. You're telling me she didn't spell it out?'

Ray laid both hands flat upon the table and studied his fingers as though this might be an exam and the correct answers might be written there. 'She said she'd had the kids over to stay with her one night. Ellen had agreed because like she always said, her quarrels with Daphne were hers not theirs. She said they had to make up their own minds. Anyway, she got them settled and asleep and asked a neighbour to keep an eye and then she went over to the farm. Parked a little way off and went across country to get there. She said she wanted to frighten Ellen out of the house. I think she'd been ringing her and sending letters and generally winding her up for a couple of weeks before. This time she actually broke into the house. I told her, if Ellen had actually confronted her, she'd have been in real trouble.'

'But Ellen didn't. She ran. She was scared.'

Ray nodded. 'At first I think she was. Ellen told me about it a couple of days before she died. Like I said, we spoke on the phone a few times. That's when I really decided not to have anything more to do with whatever Mum wanted. She'd lost it as far as I was concerned. Lost it big time.'

'At first?'

'Yeah. You see Ellen saw the car, didn't she? She said she dragged on some clothes and got out of the house. Her first idea was to get to her car and drive to the village.'

'Her car?'

'Yeah. You see Ellen parked the car at the bottom end of the lane, in the field closest to the road. We all did. That lane is on a slope. Midwinter and it can ice up like . . . anything less than a four-by-four and you're skating. So we all just got in the habit. You park close to the main road and it saves a lot of trouble. Mum must have assumed she'd run straight across the fields. Not cut back to the lane. But Ellen didn't. She saw the car and knew who it was.'

'So, why didn't she call the police right then?' Kendall asked.

'Because you can't get a signal in the lane,' Mac said.

'Exactly. Ellen said she gave up on the idea of driving anywhere then. She wanted time to think. I don't think even Ellen had thought Daphne was that crazy. So she went by road to the Richardses' place.'

So, no mud on her shoes, Mac thought. 'Why didn't Ellen let the Richardses call the police?'

'I think because she didn't want to cause more conflict in the family. She maybe planned to confront Mum later, I don't know. I asked her but she said she just wanted time to think. I think she'd reached the stage where she didn't know what to do for the best. Then it was too late, wasn't it?'

'And it never occurred to you that you might tell us this before?'

'She's my mother. I tried to make her see sense, leave Ellen alone. Then Ellen was shot and I knew you'd have Daphne in the frame for it.'

'Actually,' Mac said. 'You were top of our list. Once we knew you were back in the country.'

Ray nodded, seeming to accept that. 'I suppose Mum told you?'

'No, it was Diane. Jeb overheard Daphne speaking to you on the phone and told his aunt. The children don't know what to think or who to trust, Ray.'

'I don't suppose they do. We've made a right hash of it all, haven't we?'

'Yes, I think you have. You seem very certain that your mother didn't shoot Ellen.'

Ray laughed. 'Daphne? With a shotgun? She couldn't hit a barn door.'

'I'm not sure she'd need much in the way of accuracy, not from such close range,' Mac said. 'It's hard to see how she, or anyone else, could have missed.'

Ray paled a little and leaned back from the table as though Mac had just threatened him with contagion. 'I can't believe she'd go that far. She doesn't have a shotgun anyway.'

'I'm not sure that would stop her,' Mac said. 'Your mother is a very determined woman and right now, Ray, I'm still inclined to put the two of you top of our list. I'll be bringing her in for questioning. See what she has to say about all this.'

'She didn't do it.'

'Then who did? You?'

'No! Of course not. I'd never hurt Ellen or the kids. Never. I—'

'Loved your sister-in-law. So you said. Did she reject you? Did you turn up out of the blue and—'

'No! Nothing like that. Look,' Ray took a deep breath and tried to keep his emotions under control. 'I came here today because I wanted to clear things up. I knew you'd want to talk to me so here I am. Now, if we're going to talk about this any more, I—'

'Want a solicitor present,' Kendall said flatly. 'For the record, Mr Tailor has just requested legal counsel. Interview terminated at three fifty-five.'

TWENTY-NINE

Daphne arrived 'under protest' as she put it. Actually, Mac would have described her as incandescent. He had arranged with Kendall that Ray would be moving from the first interview room into a second, at the same time that Daphne was brought through into the corridor. Ray stopped in his tracks, but his mother merely glanced at him and then looked away. Then she looked at Mac. I'm better than that, the look said. You can't force me to say anything I don't want to say.

Ray's solicitor had arrived – the ostensible reason for his move to a larger room – and Daphne's had been summoned. Whereas Ray had to wait for the duty solicitor to make his way, Daphne had demanded her own. He was, he said when called, already examining the matter of her daughter-in-law's will. He didn't, Mac thought, seem terribly keen on attending Daphne Tailor at the police station.

Daphne was shown into the room her son had just vacated and offered tea or coffee. She refused both and so they left her alone until her legal counsel decided to show up.

Mac had the odd feeling that Paul Montague, Daphne's solicitor, would not be hurrying. He felt tired and oddly dispirited and wondered if Kendall would want him to stay for the interview. He wanted to call Miriam, needing to hear her voice and know that she was all right when so much of his world was not. He was still scared, Mac realized; afraid of losing her. Afraid of the world impinging on their lives again. Afraid of the violence he knew was out there. He found his mind drifting to the journals and letters and mementoes Lydia had gathered for the exhibition. People living every day with the level of fear he recognized within himself. A more acute level in all probability. He could call Miriam any time he wanted to; hear her voice, know that most nights he would be going home to her, know that the likelihood of the violent world he had so nearly lost her to infiltrating again was actually very remote. The individuals who had written those letters, made those records, been in that time, there had been no possibility of escape and Mac could not help but marvel that it had not driven them all insane.

'Solicitor's arrived.' Kendall's voice broke into his reverie. 'You want to sit in? Or do the sensible thing and get off home.'

'You mind?'

'No, I'm planning on keeping it short and sweet. I want to establish if she's got an alibi and give the lady reason to believe we're watching her. From what you've all told me, she's going to take some wearing down. I've handed off the Ray Tailor interview to one of my people.'

'Any particular reason?'

'Keep him off balance, I hope. Mac, the fact that Ray Tailor came to you of his own free will probably means he's feeling comfortable about you. He sees you as a known quantity, not as a threat. No offence, but I think there's more to all this than he's telling us and I want to keep the bugger off balance.'

'You like them for the shooting?' Mac asked.

'I've not ruled them out. But I don't for one minute think either of them are going to give anything away. Not tonight. So, you may as well clear off home. We'll keep the pair of them here for a bit, then let them have some thinking time before we bring them in again. Attrition, not a frontal assault, I reckon.'

'Is that just false optimism talking?'

Kendall laughed. 'Maybe, who knows? Go home, Mac, you look all in.'

'I'm not arguing with you,' he said.

'Anyway, Daphne Tailor is still refusing to speak to you and she's got her solicitor all prepped to complain if she has to, so . . .'

It was Mac's turn to laugh at that. 'She really doesn't like me,' Mac said.

'No, she doesn't and, Mac, I'm not going to risk losing anything on a technicality.'

'You want me off the case?'

'No, I want you off Daphne Tailor's radar.'

THIRTY

Lydia was surprised to see Vera Courtney alone. She had grown so used to seeing the flower-arranging committee as a single body it was a slight shock to find that they existed separately. She was also surprised to find Vera waiting for her so early in the morning.

'Hello Vera, have you been waiting long? I didn't expect anyone yet.'

'I couldn't sleep,' Vera said. 'I went for a walk and then I thought I'd come straight here. I want to collect my things if that's all right?'

'Of course it is. Come on in.'

Lydia unlocked the double doors and led Vera through to her office. She dropped her coat on to her chair and retrieved the storeroom keys from her desk. 'Are you OK?' Lydia asked. 'If you don't mind me saying, you look a bit peaky.'

Vera smiled. 'I'm just tired, I think, that's all.'

Lydia looked concerned, but didn't press the point. 'Right, let's go and find your things, then.'

Fifteen minutes later, it was very clear that Vera's mementoes weren't there. Thinking they'd been misplaced, Lydia went through each box in turn and even searched her office desk but it was obvious that Vera's possessions had gone.

Lydia consulted her master list. 'Ellen put everything on here,' she said. 'And where everything was placed. In the second C box. They should be there. I don't understand it, Vera. I really don't. I'm so sorry. I'm sure—'

'It's all right,' Vera interrupted. 'It's not your fault.'

She turned to go.

'Vera?'

But Lydia was ignored. Vera headed for the double glass doors and then was gone, leaving Lydia distraught and embarrassed.

He must have taken them, Vera thought as she drove away. She was certain of it. He'd known what she'd had and he'd got into the storeroom and taken them away. Or maybe even taken them from Ellen. Thinking about it, Vera couldn't remember if she'd changed her mind about loaning her things before or after Ellen had brought everything to the airfield.

Ellen had asked her permission to read through the journal and Vera had been oddly pleased to say yes. It had felt good to share something so personal and precious with this young woman she loved so dearly.

Now she thought about it, she was even more certain that William Trent must have taken her things from Ellen at the farm. And then her Ellen had been killed and, of course, no one would have known about Vera's little bits and pieces. Well, she wasn't going to let him get away with it. He couldn't just think . . . he couldn't just do . . . Vera realized she could hardly see. Tears blinded her and she pulled over on to the verge to wipe her eyes and take back a vestige of control. Had Ellen known? The thought came unbidden and knocked her sideways.

No, Vera thought. There was no way Ellen would betray her like that. It was him, all him. William Trent.

Mac had planned to drive over and join Kendall's morning briefing but Dave Kendall phoned him first thing and saved him a drive.

'Daphne has no real alibi for the day of the shooting. She says she was at home. Ray Tailor thinks he was in Exeter, but has no corroboration. And you asked me to check out Dan Marsden. Carrie Butler says she thinks he left around two but she can't be sure. He's given us his CCTV recordings and he was definitely at the warehouse by four fifteen.'

'So, we're back where we started, aren't we. Philip Soames is a non-starter, we know nothing about the whereabouts of either Tailor and I'm not sure we needed to know anything about Dan Marsden anyway.'

'He seemed too keen to rule himself out. He's known to be a womanizer. He knew Ellen and admits to being attracted,' Mac argued. 'Which I know means absolutely nothing.'

'Nothing at all,' Kendall agreed. 'So, we wait, we keep pushing, we see what cracks.'

Vera hammered on William Trent's door but she knew he wasn't there. At first she had convinced herself that he was just ignoring her but she had circled the cottage, peering in through the windows and there was no sign of the man anywhere. She stood back and yelled up at the bedroom window.

'William Trent, you bastard. Come and face me. Come and admit what you've done.'

She shouted until her lungs burned and her head ached and her limbs felt drained. Vera who never swore, who never raised her voice.

But in the end, she had to admit defeat. What else could she do? He wasn't there and short of breaking into the cottage – a thought that appealed for long enough for her to look for a means of breaking the glass in the kitchen window – she had no means of getting inside.

Finally, she drove away, blinking back the tears and feeling the adrenalin draining away, leaving her exhausted and bereft.

*   *   *

Rina arrived at the airfield a few minutes after Vera left. She found Lydia in a very distressed state.

'Oh, my dear,' Rina said. 'Lydia, it's not your fault. I don't believe Vera's things ever made it to here. I think she left them with Ellen and Ellen . . . Ellen must have let William Trent take them. Did she say what she had lent to Ellen?'

'Oh, an old diary and some letters and . . . she said something about a tape recording. But she was really distraught by then, Rina, and wasn't making much sense. She kept saying that he must have stolen her things. Rina, I don't know what I should do.'

'Nothing,' Rina told her. 'Lydia, there is nothing you can do. And I think I may know where some of Vera's possessions are. The diary and the letters at least. I think Mac took them from William Trent the other day. I think we can get those back to her at least.'

'Oh, Rina, that would be wonderful. What about the tape?'

'I don't know anything about that,' she told Lydia. 'But I'll have another word with Mac when I see him next. It might have turned up. And it's not your fault, Lydia. It's really not.'

'But people trusted me with their things,' Lydia said. 'I feel so guilty, Rina.'

Gently, Rina hugged her friend. 'It will be all right,' she said. 'We can sort all of this out and make it right with Vera. I'm sure we can.'

Reluctantly, Lydia nodded. Rina hoped that she was right.

THIRTY-ONE

In the end it was Mac who ferried Jeb and Megan's belongings up to York. Diane's list had been given to Yolanda and she and Frank had gathered possessions together when they both went off duty the day after the funeral.

Mac, with new questions to put to Diane, loaded up his car and headed north the following day. It was a long drive and a late start meant he crawled through the city just as everyone else wanted to leave and got caught up in a one-way system he found baffling.

Driving with the city walls on his left, he looped around St John's College and then headed into a side street in what was obviously a student area. Diane's flat was in a more modern block of red brick, set slightly back from the line of terraced houses. He parked as close as he could and plucked the first of the boxes from the car.

Diane met him at the door, the children crowding in behind.

'Come in, come in. This is really good of you.' She took the box from him and handed it to Jeb. 'I'll come down and give you a hand.'

She propped the door open with a wedge and followed Mac back down the stairs. 'You said you'd got a few questions? Have you eaten? I can make you a sandwich or something.'

'I could do with a cup of tea,' Mac confessed. 'And, yes. I've talked to Ray. It's a conversation that's left me with a few loose ends I hope you can clear up. How are they settling?' he added.

'Well, all things considered. Megan's sleeping with me and Jeb is sleeping on the sofa bed. It's not ideal, but—'

'Is this where you lived with Ellen?'

'For my last year of uni, yes. She was working full time and I had a bar job, so we managed to rent this place. Been here ever since. It's going to seem strange moving out.'

Mac nodded and opened the car boot. It took them two trips to get everything upstairs. The children pounced, diving into boxes and bags.

'Yolanda sent sweets,' Mac said, 'and William Trent sent this for you.' He handed them a fat folder full of press clippings and maps and photocopies. 'William said he didn't know if you'd still want it,' Mac added as Megan looked suddenly bereft and Jeb handled the folder as though it might bite.

'Tell him thanks,' Jeb said finally. 'He was helping us with a school project. We'd all got to write something for the end of term performance thing. Uncle Bill said he'd find us sources no one else had got.'

'I bet he did.' Mac smiled. 'Your Uncle Bill is a very know-ledgeable man.'

Jeb was clearly confused about what to say. Gently, Diane took the folder from him and peeked inside. 'Looks great,' she said. 'Look, it's going to be a little while before we get a new school sorted out, maybe this could be something to do in the meantime. Something to really impress them with?'

Jeb nodded though Megan still looked a little doubtful.

'In the meantime, why don't you two go and sort through these boxes. Meg, if you need more hangers, you can take my jumpers out of the wardrobe and put them in . . . oh, I don't know. Stick them in one of the cupboards, OK?'

Relieved, Mac watched as the children turned back to their boxes and bags.

'Shall we leave them to it? 'Diane asked. 'I'll get you that cup of tea.'

'Do I know you?' Vera asked. Then her expression cleared. 'Oh, you're that friend of Lydia's, aren't you. Rina . . .'

Rina nodded. 'That's right, my dear,' she agreed. 'Rina Martin.' She held out her hand and Vera shook it, automatically. 'Can I come in? I think I have something of yours. A notebook and some letters?'

Vera's expression changed. A sudden hopeful, relieved look in her eyes touched Rina painfully. 'You have my things? Do you have the tape recording too?'

Rina shook her head. 'I'm sorry. That hasn't come my way. Can I come inside?'

'Oh, of course. I'm sorry. I'm just . . .'

She opened the door wider and allowed Rina to enter, then led her through to the small living room at the front of the bungalow.

'You have a really pretty garden,' Rina said.

'Thank you. It's a little sad this time of year. Won't you sit down? Can I get you some tea?' She was staring at Rina's bag, guessing her possessions must be inside the blue leather. Rina took a seat and withdrew the diary and the bundle of letters. She held them out to Vera who practically pounced on them and then held them close to her heart. Vera closed her eyes and Rina could see that she was close to tears.

'Thank you,' Vera said. 'Where were they? Did that man have them?'

Briefly, Rina thought about lying. About saying that they had been at the airfield and just been mislaid but Lydia had described the thoroughness with which she had searched every box and every possible hiding place. Instead, she went for a version of the truth. 'They were given to Inspector MacGregor,' she said. 'He brought them to us and Lydia realized they must be your missing documents.'

'But did he have them. William Trent?'

Rina hesitated but knew that Vera had already made up her mind. 'I believe he may have done,' she said. 'The main thing is, you now have everything back.'

'Not everything,' Vera said. 'No, not everything.' She walked over to an old bureau and opened a drawer, slipped her letters and her book inside and then turned to Rina. 'I'm grateful to you,' she said. 'And I'm sure you'll think me very rude, but would you mind terribly if . . . Would it be awful if . . .'

'You'd like me to leave,' Rina said gently and Vera nodded.

'I'm not offended,' Rina assured her. 'I can see that you're upset. I understand that you were close to Ellen Tailor. This must be a terrible strain.'

She busied herself with her bag and then stood up. Vera had turned away and Rina knew that she was crying. 'I can see myself out,' she said.

'Ellen told me that it was Vera who gave her the impetus, really,' Diane said. 'That it was Vera who gave her the confidence to make changes. At the farm. And that was what set everything in motion, I suppose.'

'In what way?' Mac asked.

'It was in the church. They were arranging the flowers one day and Ellen was talking about the exhibition, I think.'

Vera Courtney had discussed the exhibition with Ellen Tailor as they arranged flowers in St Peter's church.

'Part of me thinks it's a good idea and part of me thinks it's terrible,' she confessed, 'putting people's private letters and diaries on public display.'

Ellen paused, a puzzled expression on her face and a long-stemmed rose in her hand. 'It's all old news, Vera. So old the younger generation, like my two little monsters, know almost nothing about it. History matters. You have to make history real for it to matter to the ones who come along afterwards.'

Vera shook her head, watching critically as Ellen plunged the stem of the rose into the oasis. 'Your children are lovely,' she said. 'Certainly not little monsters. Not like some . . . anyway, I'm not against people learning about the history, it just goes against the grain do put, well, private stuff on display.'

Ellen viewed the flowers critically. 'That's not right, is it? Vera, how do you get yours so perfect every time?'

Vera laughed and eased the rose from the green foam, placed in back in just a slightly different position. 'Ellen when you've been doing church flowers for as long as I have, you'll be able to do it in your sleep. Place the others round that one and then infill with the gypsophila. Lovely little flower, that is. Hides a multitude of sins.'

She fussed with greenery for a moment longer and then asked. 'Is Daphne contributing anything?'

'I asked her. She said if there was anything left at the farm I could take that along. The kids want to get involved. I don't think Daphne's that interested, to be honest.'

'She can be a stubborn woman,' Vera said. 'But she was a stubborn child too. These traits get set early if you ask me.'

'I called her twice about it,' Ellen said. 'Does that look better?'

Vera nodded approval.

'I thought, you know, sorting through old stuff together, it might be something she could do with the kids. I know Jeb hated the fact that we didn't get along and when he was alive I think we both made the effort, but you know.'

'As I said. Stubborn. Ellen, you can only do so much.'

'She doesn't even come to the farm. And she doesn't want me in the house. If she wants to see the children I have to take them to her place and drop them off outside, or arrange a meeting somewhere. She barely speaks even when we're making arrangements.'

'You've done all you can, my dear.' Vera patted her hand.

'I've even left all her stuff out at the farm. She's got more shelf space in the living room than we have. I just don't feel right, putting it all away, you know?'

Vera laid down her secateurs and straightened her back. 'Ellen, my dear, I sometimes despair of you, I really do.'

She noted the younger woman's surprise – and a little hurt.

She softened her tone. 'Daphne will never approve of you. She wouldn't approve of anyone. Jeb knew that and you should accept it. Let her go her way and you and your children go yours. If you want my advice you'll hire a skip and have a sort out.'

Ellen laughed uneasily, 'Vera, I couldn't do that. It wouldn't be right.'

'Then box up what's hers and put it in the attic or in one of the outbuildings. Tell her she can come and get it if she wants, but your home should be yours. Not a place you feel you are still living under sufferance.'

'Even if that's true.'

'The only truth is, Ellen, that you and your children own that place now. Jeb left the place to you and to them, not to his mother. You both did your best by her and by that useless brother-in-law of yours. Now your only duty is to do the best by yourself and your children.'

She picked up her secateurs again and snipped the stem of a spray chrysanthemum. 'You listen to an old woman, Ellen. Get out from under her thumb. There've been enough members of the Tailor family put down by their womenfolk for you to be another one.'

Ellen had cast a curious look in her direction, but Vera had chosen not to elaborate. Instead, she had carried her arrangement to its place in the side chapel and announced that she was getting the kettle on.

'When Ellen got home that day,' Diane said. 'I happened to phone and she told me what Vera had said. I'd been saying the same thing for ever, but this time it seemed to have stuck. She said she was going to start with some of the cupboards in the spare room and what had been Daphne and her husband's room. Ellen had hardly gone in there. Just covered everything with dust sheets and let it be and I said it was just a waste. The only time she used the guest room was when I went to stay. I don't think Daphne's old room ever really got used for anything except storage and as a general dumping ground.'

'So,' Mac asked. 'Did she start to clear stuff out?'

Diane nodded. 'Ellen said she got a load of bags and started with the wardrobe. Daphne had left a couple of old coats there

and some shoes and other bits. I swear, when you went into that
room it was like she'd never really left. Like she wanted to keep
an outpost in someone else's house.'

'She never thought about it as someone else's house, though,
did she?'

Diane shook her head. 'It was still her farm. Even though she'd
only married into it. The Tailors had kept the place going for about
four generations but each new generation had sold off a bit more
and a bit more of the land. Ray had inherited from Daphne's father;
she told you that, didn't she?'

'Yes, and she said he'd run the place into the ground and then
sold up.'

Diane nodded. 'She was mad as hell. As far as Daphne is
concerned she'd lost her entire birthright and what she'd married
into to strangers. I mean, I could understand what she must have
felt. Ellen really felt for her, which is why she felt so bad about
everything, put up with so much from her, I suppose.'

'So, she started sorting through the cupboards.'

Diane nodded again. 'The first day it was just bits and pieces.
Clothes, ornaments, all her father-in-law's old clothes too. She put
them in bags and sent the lot to charity, I think.' Diane smiled. 'I
remember reminding her to check the pockets. She said she found
a twenty-pound note in a coat of Daphne's. I told her that was
Daphne's bad luck. She put it in the kids' account. Somehow, if
it went to the kids, then it was all OK.'

'And the deposits she made later. The bigger deposits?'

'It was about a couple of weeks after she'd started. There's like
a built-in cupboard in that room and it was full of junk. There was
an old vacuum cleaner in there, Christmas decorations, lord knows
what else. At the bottom was a whole stack of books. Old
encyclopedias that she thought the kids might like to look through.
So she took them out. When she had, she noticed that the floorboards were loose. Under the floorboard was a box and in the box,
wrapped up in a cloth, there were all the coins. All the time they'd
struggled and penny-pinched, especially when Jeb was so ill and
all the time—'

'All the time she'd had a fortune hiding in the wardrobe.'

'Yeah. All that time.'

'She told you about them?'

'Not at first. She said she felt so guilty. It was obvious Daphne
had no idea. She said she told Daphne that she'd found a few old
coins and let the kids have them, was that all right? Daphne was
sniffy, said her husband had collected a few when he was a child
and she didn't care one way or another. The kids must have told
her that Ellen was having a clear-out because she was furious
about it. Ellen told her she'd bagged everything up and put it in
the barn and Daphne was welcome to come and get it. She never
did and like I said, I think Ellen gave anything she could to charity.'

'And Daphne continued to see the children?'

Diane nodded. 'We'd had no family so Ellen didn't think she
could say no. She thought she ought to keep the peace for the
sake of the children. But we decided, after her husband was diag-
nosed, that there was no way Daphne was going to get them if
anything happened to Ellen. Not that we ever thought it would.
The will was just a precaution, you know?'

Mac nodded. 'And the reality is hard, isn't it?'

'It is. I'm not ready for kids. I'm about the most unprepared
person you can imagine, but I guess we'll make it through one
way or another. Not much choice, is there?'

'And the coins?'

'Ellen had done her homework. She figured she could sell the
sovereigns without too much trouble. At bullion prices, they made
a good amount and she spread herself around. A couple here, a
couple there, but it was a slow process. The more specialist stuff,
well that was more complicated. It meant finding dealers who'd
know what the coins were and give her a good price. I wanted her
to just get shot of the lot in one go. I knew she might not get quite
as much money that way, but it would still be a lot more than
either of us would ever see in our lifetime short of robbing a bank.
She was scared stiff of being found out but I was pretty sure that
Daphne would get wind of things sooner or later and I was right.'

'How?'

'Little Megan. She noticed that her mum was researching coins
and their values and looking at gold prices. Ellen wasn't very
savvy when it came to covering her tracks but both the kids are
really computer literate. Megan must have mentioned something,
and Daphne remembered what Ellen had said about finding a few
old coins and put two and two together. She was furious. Came

to the farm one day and demanded Ellen hand over what she'd found. Ellen said that anything in the farmhouse now belonged to the children. Daphne threatened police and lawyers and trouble. Ellen called me. Really worried. That was about a month before she died. Before she was killed.'

'So where does Philip Soames come into the picture?'

Diane sighed. She got up and filled the kettle, rinsed their mugs at the sink. 'Philip Soames,' she said. 'Right. That was one hell of a stupid idea, wasn't it?'

'What did you do, Diane? Was it you who sent him that card?'

She shook her head. 'No. I persuaded Ellen to do that. She really didn't want to but . . . Look, I hated the man. Still do. I saw what he tried to do to my sister and then . . . then I suppose I threw her back into his path again, didn't I?'

'How?'

'Because I'd been keeping tabs on him ever since he went to prison the first time. I was scared that he'd go looking for her.'

'All this time, you've kept track of him?'

'Yeah. You see, whatever you may think, Inspector, I actually loved my sister very much. I didn't want to see her hurt again. There was this young PC, not much older than us and well, we saw one another for a bit and we stayed friends and he helped me at first, then I hired a private detective when Soames came out of jail the first time. Then again when he came out this last time. In between, well you could say that the stalker got himself a stalker of his own.'

'That takes a certain single-mindedness.'

'Wasn't that hard. We'd got to know him because we had mutual acquaintances. They kept an eye open for me, told me what he was up to. He was in and out of jail like a bloody yo-yo anyway.'

'And when he came out this time?'

'Seemed like a lucky break when he got a job down south. So I made use of it.'

'And did you have anything to do with that?'

Diane frowned but did not reply directly. Instead she said, 'We needed someone to fence the coins for us. We needed to act fast, before Daphne could interfere. I was banking on the idea that Phil would listen to Ellen. She wanted no part of it, but I managed to persuade her, just to talk. What I didn't bank on was Soames telling us to fuck off.'

'I can see that would have been a shock. Did he say why?'

'Seems he really did want to go straight this time. He'd had enough. Marsden offered him a job, he'd got a place to stay and he'd come to view Ellen as trouble. Me, even more trouble.'

'But he went to see her.'

'Ellen said he just wanted to check things out. He'd convinced himself we were trying to set him up. That we'd found out where he was and were still out for revenge.' She laughed harshly. 'The stupid thing was, he was now as anxious about us as Ellen had been about him. Ellen said he begged her just to leave him alone and she told him she would. She called and told me, just after he'd left, that we'd carry on doing things her way, Daphne or no Daphne, but we'd just try and speed up the sales. I said to send some of the coins up to me and I'd see what I could do in York and Leeds. Manchester, maybe. More jewellers in a big city, easier to get lost in the noise and not be noticed.'

'And is that what you did?'

'That's what I'd started to do. I'd got two grand stashed away waiting to go into the account. Now it'll go towards getting somewhere big enough for the kids.'

'And you still have some of the coins. Diane, don't lie to me. I'm not interested in taking them away from you. Just in catching who killed your sister.'

She nodded. 'Everything in that house belonged to Ellen. Now it belongs to the children. I've got to have money to look after them until the sale of the farm goes through.'

'You are determined to sell then?'

Diane shook her head. 'Not up to me, is it? Look, I don't know what will happen yet, Daphne's determined to challenge everything and it could drag on forever. It's all such a bloody mess.'

'You managed to keep your job?'

'Yeah. I have a good boss. Actually, I hope he's a bit more than a boss, if you know what I mean.'

Mac smiled at her. 'And how does he feel about a ready-made family?'

'Oh, he's got to get used to the idea, I guess. I'm hoping he will, but frankly that's the least of my worries right now. You still have no idea, do you? Who killed Ellen?'

Mac shook his head. He watched as she suddenly remembered

she had promised more coffee and bustled with the kettle. 'It was one sugar, wasn't it?'

'Thank you, yes.' He took the mug from her. 'I think Philip Soames is probably out of the frame. What about the family? Daphne? Ray?'

Diane grimaced. 'Look, I can't stand Daphne. She's a spiteful cow, but to take a shotgun and walk up to the window and shoot someone. Actually look in their eye and shoot them and that's what the killer must have done with Ellen. No, I don't see Daphne doing that and certainly not Ray.'

'No? He must have been resentful?'

'Ray?' Diane laughed. 'No, I'm not sure he was. I think he was just relieved, you know. He took the money and ran – and I expect the money did too. He never could keep it for long, you know.'

'Strange that he came back when he did?'

'No, not really. Daphne sent the summons and he came running, I suppose.'

'And why did she want him to come back? Diane, the night Ellen ran to the Richardses' house, do you think she was genuinely frightened?'

'What sort of question is that?'

'One that has to be asked. If she'd pretended to be upset, to be persecuted, put the blame on Daphne, it would have made things look bad—'

'If it ever came to court. Hmm, I see what you mean. But no. She was scared that night and I do think Daphne was behind that. I've thought so from the start. Ellen was alone in the house, Daphne knew that. What better opportunity to get in herself and try to find the rest of the coins?'

'Are they still at the house?'

Diane gestured that she didn't know. 'Ellen didn't say they had gone. But she didn't tell me what she'd done with them either. I can't believe she'd have left them where Daphne could get at them, but she might not have had the chance to do anything else and obviously, I've had no chance to go back to the farm.'

Mac shook his head. 'There was nothing there. It would have been found.'

'That's what I thought. So Ellen must have moved the box. That would make sense. But where?'

Mac got up and took his coat from the back of the chair. 'I'll be off,' he said. 'If you think of anything else?'

'I have your card.'

'Just one small question,' Mac said as he was standing at the top of the stairs. 'Ellen had an old pair of trainers. No laces. I'm told she kept them in the porch and used them in the garden. Is it likely she'd have had them upstairs with her for any reason?'

Diane's look was quizzical. 'That's a strange sort of question?'

'I know. It's just a loose end. They nag.'

Diane frowned and thought about it. 'I know she'd been clearing out the attic space,' she said. 'She said there was no proper floor or anything. Jeb wanted very badly to go up there. Ellen wouldn't let him. She said it was all rough joists and big nails, so I imagine she'd have wanted something on her feet. I suppose the old trainers would have been an obvious choice.' She shrugged. 'Sorry, I really wouldn't know.'

Mac thanked her, and left.

Glancing back, he saw her waving from the kitchen window. Sitting in his car he called Miriam and told her not to wait up. He'd stop on the way and get something to eat, but expected to be late home.

Back in the flat, Diane watched as the car pulled away. She stood beside the window until she was certain he had gone and then turned back to face Jeb and Megan. Jeb stood in the doorway, a look of suppressed excitement on his face. He held his games console.

'You'll need a screwdriver,' Megan said solemnly as he set it down on the table.

'Second drawer along. There's a Pozidriv.'

Diane almost held her breath as she undid the screws and removed the case. A small, cloth bag had been secured to the inside of the case with strips of tape. It chinked gently as Diane pulled it free. She emptied the contents on to the table and felt the tears pricking at the corners of her eyes.

'Is it all right?' Jeb asked.

Diane nodded. 'Thank you Ellen,' she whispered softly. 'We're going to be OK, now,' she told Jeb and Megan. 'It's all going to be all right.'

THIRTY-TWO

943. Vera closed her eyes and imagined. She had read her father's journals enough times to understand what they said, so that she could place herself where he had stood and imagine what he had seen.

He stood on the ridge overlooking the farm. Smoke rose from the kitchen chimney and he could see the women moving about in the kitchen, drifting in and out of his field of view as they came to the sink or reached for plates from the rack. He could imagine the scene in the kitchen, table being set for the evening meal, the scent of food – rabbit stew, probably, if it was Nora's turn to cook, and she'd probably have managed to rustle up a few dumplings as well. Nora could make a feast out of nothing and that was a skill of even more value now than it had ever been.

He sat down with his back against the old beech tree whose branches hung low, almost brushing the ground. He'd climbed this tree as a child, hidden out beneath its branches when his mother was mad at him or when he just wanted to get away from everyone and read a book. His grandfather tolerated bookishness but his mother was all for practical skills. A favourite question was: 'And what good will that do you? How will that help you out in the world?'

He was starting to think it might be a better question than she knew.

He wondered if they had heard that he was back. He doubted it. Most of the time he was based not ten miles from the farm but moving in such different circles and so confined by duties and commitments that he rarely even glimpsed his old life.

He could have gone down now, though. Could have visited and sat down at the scrubbed table and eaten a great plateful of Nora's cooking and the thought was, briefly, an inviting one.

Fleeting.

He knew in his heart that he had moved so far beyond them, so far in some other direction that he no longer belonged, either

*at their table or in their hearts. Not even in Nora's. He thought
of his parents, settled still in the little house back down the track
from here. His grandfather was long gone and he was glad of
that. The old man would have understood and right now, Bob
could not bear to have anyone understand. That would mean that
someone else had faced the hell he was going through and he
found he could not bear the idea of that. Especially not of someone
he knew and loved.*

*Bad enough to be sharing his fate with strangers though he had
decided that he could not even countenance that any longer.*

Slowly, Robert got to his feet and started his slow walk back.

THIRTY-THREE

October

I t had been a gloriously sunny day. Rina had wandered happily
among the stalls in the large marquees and between the
thronging re-enactors, escorted by Tim, looking very dapper
in a pinstriped suit and Joy and Miriam, both sporting their hair
in extravagant victory rolls.

It was, she thought, excellent to see the old airfield brought
back to life again and the owners, Lydia and Edward de Freitas
had been very wise to stage the opening a couple of weeks before
Armistice Day. A full service and concert had been organized
for the weekend before November the eleventh. Frantham had,
for a full month now been the focus for plays and music and art
events, culminating in a weekend of activities at the refurbished
aerodrome, including a fly-past by local enthusiasts and a half-
dozen tanks, brought in on low-loaders and now excitedly used
as climbing frames by the local kids. There were many locals
among the crowd, but Rina was delighted to note the number of
tourists and outsiders who had been drawn to the weekend and
she'd had people knocking at her door, asking if she had any
vacancies, Peverill Lodge still being, ostensibly a guest house,
albeit with guests that had no desire to leave. It was a good sign;
the extra trade at what would have been the end of the tourist

season would be extremely welcome, Rina thought, after the past few recession-hit years. She could almost hear the community breathing a collective sigh of relief and any misgivings they may have had – incomers taking over the airfield and opening a computer games business, of all things! – had largely evaporated in the unexpected autumn sun which blessed the weekend. The de Freitases, it had been collectively decided, were doing all right. Not local yet of course, but they had made a promising start.

Rina basked in it all, enjoying the sunshine, the company and the music. She had even taught Joy and Tim to jive in readiness for the NAAFI dance scheduled for that night. Joy had taken to it immediately; Tim could now move without falling over his feet and she figured they would both have a good time anyway.

The only fly in the honey jar so far as Rina was concerned was the assumption by some of the local youth that she and the other older residents of Peverill House might actually be old enough to remember the war.

She hadn't even been born then, the world having to wait another five years for that significant event to take place.

Mid-afternoon, she ran into William Trent. He looked harried.

'I hear you're giving a speech,' she said.

'Not a speech, no. I'll be officially opening the exhibition later and Edward will be doing the announcement of the new computer games.' William shook his head. 'I'm not sure what I was thinking when I agreed to become involved. The idea of a game about war seems distasteful, somehow. I hope I've at least managed to inject a little history.'

'From what I've heard, you've injected a lot of history,' Rina said. 'And to be fair, there have been games of strategy for many thousands of years, I suppose you should just see this as the latest incarnation.'

William harrumphed and excused himself. Rina watched him go. He looked old, she thought. Greyer and not just his hair. Life was taking a toll on William Trent. She'd meant to ask him for news of the younger Tailors. Had Jeb and Megan settled with their aunt? Were relations between Diane and Daphne still as frosty? But she was almost glad she hadn't done so. He probably knew no more than she did; he certainly had more of an emotional

investment in a situation that was, to Rina just another example
of local tragedy. She didn't want to pick at what were obviously
still unhealed wounds.

Joy had been examining some vintage clothing and now returned
with her purchases. 'Tim's gone off to look at a tank,' she said.
'Edward has this idea about making one disappear and maybe
doing a Christmas show.'

'Won't that clash with the Palisades performances? It's also not
going to be long enough to set up the staging. We're almost in
November.'

'That's what Tim said, so Edward suggested getting the hotel
involved too. Anyway, let them argue it out. They'll have more
fun doing that than they will shopping with us. Miriam's just
nipped off to the loo; she'll meet us in the cafe. Don't know about
you but I'm starving.'

She slipped an arm though Rina's and they wandered back
towards the main building. The tower was now fully functional
again and the main concourse beautifully restored, Rina thought.
The de Freitases had thrown money at the project. What had been
offices had now been converted into tea rooms and Lydia's museum,
as she rather grandly called the two areas of display and the long
glassed area linking them. Miriam was waiting for them at the
entrance to the cafe.

'It's pretty packed. Joy, nab that table over in the corner, Rina
and I will order. Mac phoned, said he's on his way.' She smiled
and Rina found herself transferred from the attentions of one young
woman to another as Joy skipped off to capture the corner table.

She was very blessed, Rina thought. She had loving friends and
a good home and a sense of belonging. Precious things.

Glancing around the room she caught sight of familiar faces.
Celia Marsden sat with the flower-arranging committee.

'Ah, there's Mac,' Miriam said. 'Where did Tim get to? Should
we order for him?'

'No, don't bother. He's off with Edward discussing how to make
a tank disappear. I'm guessing that could take some time.'

Minutes later they were seated at the corner table distributing
tea and sandwiches. Rina leaned back in her chair and surveyed
the two young women and the man she had come to regard almost
as affectionately as she regarded Tim.

Life was very good, Rina thought. So why, looking over at the little group of women on the other side of the cafe, did she feel such a sense of something being very wrong?

THIRTY-FOUR

The official opening of the exhibition, press call and performance by local school children was scheduled for three p.m. and William Trent, in his role as historian, was due to make a speech.

Rina spotted Andrew Barnes amongst the press pack and exchanged a smile. The children's choir assembled in front of the platform and a small troupe of Irish dancers – also children – prepared for their performance on a specially constructed stage that would be ready for the musicians at the evening dance.

Edward took his place before the microphone stand and thanked everyone for being there. He looked happy, Rina thought, and genuinely excited by the official opening. He spoke a little about the history of the airfield and the role it had played in both world wars. He talked about the tin huts and that they had been a POW camp. He mentioned that several of the Italian prisoners had stayed on after the war and become part of the local community and that links had now been forged with Pisa and Rome because of that. He spoke of the future and the children who would be singing and dancing later and then he handed over to William Trent.

Rina's attention had drifted a little and she let her gaze travel around the crowd gathered in the auditorium. Faces she knew, people she had come to see as friends and neighbours. Tony from the cafe, with his wife and children. Andy Nevins and his mother.

The women from the flower arranging committee. Celia Marsden looking attentive. Martha and Julia whispering to one another.

Vera Courtney staring hard at William Trent, a look of pure hatred on her face.

Rina, her gaze fixed on Vera, tuned back in to what William was saying.

'This exhibition represents all of those forgotten voices. All those whose stories might otherwise have not been told. There are those I know who believe that the past is the past and that we should not disturb the dust of those who are so long gone. But I disagree. We must remember and acknowledge the past, we must listen to those voices and we must tell their stories to the world.'

Vera Courtney turned on her heel and left. Glancing sideways at William, Rina saw that he was looking in Vera's direction.

THIRTY-FIVE

Monday

'William Trent,' Kendall said. 'His wallet was still in his pocket and nothing seems to have been taken.'

Mac nodded. 'I've not seen him since the Ellen Tailor murder went cold. Though Andy told me he came into the police station last week, looking for an address or something?'

'Oh? Andy tell you who for?'

'He did, but it didn't mean anything to me at the time. He came into the police station wanting the address and Andy told him that we weren't in the business of giving out addresses. Trent got annoyed and left. I ran across him briefly in the cafe on the prom. He apologized, tried to explain why he was looking for the person in question, I told him I still couldn't help, he got annoyed again and then left.'

'And?'

Mac frowned. 'And a couple of things, I suppose. The woman he was looking for was someone called Wenda Carson.'

'Gwenda?'

'No, definitely Wenda. She was the daughter of the vicar here, apparently. The vicar was the son of the chaplain at the POW camp during World War Two.'

'Out where the tin huts are now?'

Mac nodded. The so called tin huts were now a collection of small businesses, some still housed in the old Nissen huts, now substantially refurbished and made more fit for purpose, that had formed part of the accommodation. It had always surprised Mac that the camp had been just on the outskirts of town. The fence must have run right along the main road in places. Rina Martin had told him, when he first came to Frantham, that it had housed mainly Italian prisoners and that many of them had worked out the war on local farms, returning to the camp at night. Some had stayed on after the war, including the grandfather of the owner of Mac's favourite little cafe on the promenade.

'It seems William Trent had got wind of the fact that Toni's grandfather had been a POW.'

'Toni? That's the guy who runs Tonino's?

'Yes, he'd been asking all sorts of questions, wouldn't leave when Toni asked him to and upset Toni's wife, Bee.'

'What sort of questions?'

'About the grandfather. Who he was, what he did here after the war. Why he stayed. Personal stuff.'

'Why *did* he stay?'

Mac laughed. 'He worked on one of the local farms. He met the daughter of the farmer and fell in love. Her dad thought he was a good worker and a good man, but couldn't possibly approve of a relationship with the enemy. The story is that on the evening of VE day, Tonino senior proposed to Martha and the father gave them his blessing. He wasn't the only one around here to stay on. Rina always reckoned that a lot of them were just farm boys and teenagers.'

'All the same under the skin,' Kendall said thoughtfully. 'But still, the father must have been open-minded.'

'The way Toni tells it, the farm would have gone under without the extra help. They'd got a couple of land girls, but the government demands on food production sound back breaking. I suppose when you've worked beside someone for three years or so, you get to know them and the barriers come down.'

'And this William Trent, he was making trouble?'

Mac shrugged. 'If you recall, he always had an acerbic manner,' he said.

He and Kendall looked down at Trent's body and considered thoughtfully. The knife stood out from the body, angled just slightly as though the assailant had struck upward. There were no other signs of violence and no signs of any struggle or defence.

'He turned away and was stabbed in the back,' Kendall said.

'So he didn't think he had any reason to be afraid. He knew his attacker.'

'That seems likely. Either knew them or felt he could safely ignore them. But what were they doing out here in the first place?'

Mac glanced around, getting his bearings. They were halfway up the bank that separated the airfield from the town and the beach. A footpath ran across the top of the bank at the point, popular with hikers and dog walkers and often thronged with tourists in the summer. Popular too with plane spotters lately.

But pitch dark at night. They were about three hundred yards, Mac estimated, from the control tower and ancillary buildings that had been the focus of the Saturday night dance. The de Freitases had managed to get an extension on the usual eleven p.m. shutdown and the dance had finished just before midnight. For the next half hour or so, Mac thought, the main external lights would have been on as people left either on foot or picked up their cars from the area close to the entrance that had been turned into a temporary parking spot. But the lights would not have illuminated the body. The best preliminary guess, judging by the state of rigor and also that there had been rain on the Sunday – the ground beneath the body being dry – was that he had been killed on the Saturday night.

The last time anyone recalled seeing William Trent had been at nine forty-five, when he'd been bought a drink by the host of the dance, Edward de Freitas. Mac gathered that everyone had been quite relieved when, just a little later, they assumed he had returned to his cottage. What was strange was that no one had found him on the Sunday when the airfield had again been thronging with re-enactors, stallholders and visitors. True, the body lay in long grass hidden by scrubby hawthorns and gorse and was somewhat away from the action, but Mac was a little surprised that no child had run up and down the steep bank and tripped over him, no couple looking for a bit of privacy had come through this way. It seemed likely that the dance had continued after he was dead, that the festivities had gone on all day Sunday and his body had gone unnoticed. The man had gone unmissed and unlooked for.

'From what I can gather, no one liked him very much,' Kendall said.

'He could be a bit sharp. I don't imagine he was an easy conversationalist or that he socialized at the dance. But still . . . sad, but from what I've been told I think everyone was just relieved he wasn't there.'

THIRTY-SIX

'He wasn't an easy man to get along with.' Lydia de Freitas sipped at her tea and considered what she had just said. 'I mean, I know you are not supposed to speak ill of the dead and I suppose especially of the murdered, but all the same, he wasn't a nice man.'

Rina nodded solemnly, agreeing with both sentiments. 'Tim said he was very knowledgeable,' she offered, feeling that maybe she should, for form's sake, soften the judgement.

'Oh, undoubtedly. And what he knew he *knew*, if you see what I mean. There could be no variation, no argument. What William Trent believed and thought was gospel and you couldn't get him to shift or modify one millimetre once he'd got his ideas fixed. I know Edward wished he'd never taken him on as a consultant.'

Rina nodded again. She knew from Tim that the rest of the team had felt the same way. He'd explained that. William Trent had been consulting on the follow up to a newly launched first-person RPG, based around some of the lesser known aspects of the World War Two conflict, many of which had begun very close to Frantham. The D-Day landings, for instance, which had been launched from along that same stretch of the south coast.

'From what Tim said, William Trent really knew his subject but he had no feel for fiction or for game play and what was required in a field that was, first and foremost concerned with entertainment.'

'He was a royal pain in the arse,' Lydia said bluntly. 'He upset the storyliners and the animators and the programmers by telling them that they were either missing the point or telling the story wrong. He had no patience with the idea of fusing real action with fiction. For him it was all or nothing; one or the other. At one point Edward had threatened to terminate their agreement and ban him from the site.'

'But he still let him make a speech at the opening,' Rina said.

'Yes, and look how that turned out. Edward thought he owed him that, though. He'd brought some good stories to the table, some really interesting material, it wasn't that, it was his attitude, I suppose. He was just an awkward sod. But it's a whole different level, isn't it, between disliking the man and wanting to stab him in the back.'

'I suppose it's a question of. degrees,' Rina said. 'I suppose anything can build incrementally to that level and if he annoyed Edward as much as he did, then I can imagine he must have done the same and more to other people.'

'True,' Lydia agreed. He husband was not a man easily driven to anger or even irritation, but William Trent had managed to do both.

'I understand he was divorced,' Rina said.

'Years ago apparently. They had a son, too, but I don't think there'd been any contact to speak of, not since the divorce. Edward made the mistake of asking about it once and was treated to an hour long tirade on the . . . I think it was the inability of women to commit to anything that wasn't a pair of shoes or a knitting pattern. Something along those lines, anyway.'

'That's sad though, isn't it?' Rina said. 'To have a child and then not have any contact. You'd miss so much.'

Lydia smiled a little sadly. Neither she nor Rina had been blessed with children and though Lydia had talked from time to time about adopting, Rina thought it unlikely she would ever carry the idea through. She was no stranger to violent death. Her brother-in-law had been killed violently the year before and her marriage to Edward rocked by those events. It would, Rina thought, take time and energy to restore their own equilibrium, never mind taking another person into their family.

'It happens a lot,' Lydia said. 'But in this case I find it hard to blame the mother. I just wonder what on earth made anyone marry him in the first place.'

'Maybe he was different then?'

'Maybe so. And you're right, of course, it is sad. Having contact with his son might have changed William's perspective. It might have mellowed him.'

'He seems to have liked Ellen Tailor's children,' Rina observed.

'Oh goodness. You know, you're right, I'd forgotten that,' Lydia confessed. 'He came over a few times with Ellen and sometimes with the children. They called him Uncle Bill and he was really gentle with them, you know?'

The two women looked speculatively at one another and then shook their heads. 'No,' Lydia said. 'I don't believe that. How could there be a connection between Ellen Tailor's death and William Trent's?'

'I don't know,' Rina admitted. 'But it is a terrible coincidence, isn't it? You have to wonder.'

Lydia set her cup back on the little table. 'Anyway, I'd best be going. Is it selfish to say I'm glad he didn't get himself killed before the weekend?' She smiled wryly. 'I know, terrible thing to say. And you, Rina, are the only person I'd ever say it to.'

'And your secret is safe,' Rina told her. 'And I do know what you mean.'

She stood too and made ready to see Lydia off.

'I don't suppose your pet policeman has any further clues?'

'Not that I know of,' Rina said. 'But I'll let you know if he lets anything slip.'

Rina's 'pet policeman' was at that moment standing in a chilly room, watching a post-mortem.

'So, how's Miriam?' Mason, the pathologist, glanced up from his work as his assistant prepared organs for weighing and measuring.

'She's well, thanks. Sends her regards and says we must get together for a meal or a barbecue or something. Apparently your chilli dip is legendary?'

Mason laughed. 'Miriam was always telling me it was a bio hazard . . . It would be good to get together over something other than a dead body, though.'

Mac wasn't sure a barbecue qualified if you wanted an absence of dead things, but he nodded. 'She's getting over it,' he said, knowing that was what Mason really wanted to ask. 'She still gets bad dreams and flashbacks, but going back to academia seems to have settled her down.'

Mason nodded. 'It'll take time. Thinking you are going to die focuses the mind somewhat abruptly.'

Mac looked expectantly at the man, wondering at the comment, but Mason did not elaborate.

'She's still serious about the doctorate?'

'Yes, absolutely. It's going to cost a bloody fortune, but I think she should do it. And there's a possibility of part funding she's looking into.'

'Well, if she needs any references, you know I'm available. So, back to our man here. Not a lot to tell you that you couldn't already figure out for yourself. He was healthy enough for a man of his age. A little overweight, but generally fit and he met his demise courtesy of a single stab wound.'

'Did the killer get lucky or did he know what he was doing?'

'He . . . or she . . . seems to have had a fair idea. Your man must have turned his back and the knife went in from between the last two ribs.' He broke off. 'Tom, help me lift him will you.'

The assistant came over to the bench and between them they lifted the body for Mac's perusal.

'Here, see? Then at an upward angle and into the heart. Your man would have been dead before he hit the floor. Efficient, eh?'

Mac nodded and Mason lowered the body back on to the table.

'Any great strength required?'

Mason considered. 'That depends. If the killer had hit the rib on the way in, then it would have taken some strength and presence of mind to shift the blade, or push through against the rib. If they'd got the position right from the outset, then no, just about anyone with enough resolve could have done it.'

'And the weapon left in the wound?'

'No reason to suppose that's not the murder weapon, no. Whoever killed your man, here had a certain . . . well I hesitate to say style, but their weapon of choice certainly does. And had it been me, I'd have not wanted to leave it behind.'

'It's a Fairbairn Sykes, isn't it?' Mac said.

'Oh, well give that man a biscuit. But what you probably didn't know is that it's a period piece, not a later reproduction or even a later authentic model. This is the real deal as they say. I'd have not wanted to cast that aside.'

'Any evidence they tried to remove it?'

'None that I can see. I'll be checking out the wound again, but

I'd have expected to see marks on the ribs or sawing at the edges of the wound and I've seen nothing of that so far.'

Mac nodded. 'What would a weapon like that be worth?'

'In monetary value? I don't know. You'd have to ask our friend the Internet. But as a sentimental piece, I'd say it would be priceless to someone.'

'It was developed for the first commando units wasn't it?' Mac asked.

'It certainly was. You know I don't like to speculate, but you do wonder if someone was somehow making a point, don't you?'

Mac smiled at him. 'I wouldn't like to speculate,' he said.

But given what the man was researching, Mac thought, you did have to wonder if the choice of weapon used to kill William Trent might have relevance to the murderer.

Miriam was home when Mac called her as he drove back towards the airfield. 'What time will you be home? I thought we might have a meal at the marina tonight.'

'Sounds like a plan,' Mac told her. 'I should be back for six. Mason sent his love and threatened you with chilli dip.'

She laughed. 'See you later, then. Take care.'

It was, Mac thought, good to hear her sounding so positive. He tried not to think back to events more than a year before when she had almost been taken from him.

He turned through the airfield gates, pausing to check in with the officer on guard and exchange a few words with the security guard the de Freitases had left in the booth by the gate. Then he drove his car across to where the body of William Trent had been found.

It wasn't the first time that an incident room had been set up on the airfield. The discovery of bones in the excavation for a new entrance gate had brought Mac and his colleagues to this place before. But that had been a sad little death for which the arrest of the killer had brought no one satisfaction. This was something different and, given the circumstances, seemed almost staged, almost overdramatized.

He found PC Andy Nevins in a tent itemizing the contents of evidence bags before stacking them into cardboard file boxes.

'That looks fun.' Mac smiled at the younger man.

'God, you wouldn't believe the amount of rubbish. I doubt any of it's relevant.' He indicated the stack of crisp packets and coke cans and unidentified wrappers he was working his way through. Mac glanced at his watch. He had a meeting with Edward de Freitas scheduled, but that wasn't for another hour.

'I'll give you a hand,' he said.

'Thanks. There's flasks of tea and coffee and sandwiches if you're hungry.'

'The airfield staff are looking after you then.'

Andy nodded. 'Apart from the fact they keep finding more rubbish for me to work through.'

Mac glanced over to where three desultory individuals paced along the bank at the perimeter of the airfield. Along the top of the bank ran a section of the coastal path and a half-dozen onlookers watched curiously. The body had been found by a member of the clean-up crew litter picking early on the Monday morning after the re-enactment weekend. The CSIs and police officers had collected everything close to the murder scene, and for half a day the place crawled with white-clad CSI and blue-clad officers practically falling over one another. Mac and his colleagues from Exeter had agreed that a wider sweep would be a good idea for the sake of thoroughness. Edward had volunteered some of his staff for the job, the steep bank beside which the body had been found making it logistically difficult, as they had discovered earlier, to organize a larger search team and Andy got stuck with the initial collation.

Thousands of people had attended the celebration weekend, Mac thought, and they all seemed to have dropped at least one piece of litter.

'So, how are you tackling this?' he said.

'Well, the random rubbish, crisp packets and the like, I'm consigning to a single box. If there's anything useful among that lot, well . . .'

Mac nodded.

'Chewing gum and cigarette butts are all in there.'

'Chewing gum?' Mac pulled a face.

'Oh, I have a glamorous life.'

'Anything that might be more interesting, tickets, scraps of paper with writing on . . . that's over there. The smallest stack.'

'Good,' Mac approved. 'I've got a meeting with Edward in an hour. I'd like you to come along to that and then we'll go and see what Kendall and his colleagues have turned up. Your local knowledge could prove really useful.'

Andy grinned. 'Thanks,' he said. 'I'm bored out of my skull here. How did the PM go?'

'Nothing we didn't know before. Single stab wound – and you were right about the knife. Have you followed up on local collectors?'

'Um, yes. Three that knew William Trent, all of whom were here at some point over the weekend. They've given names of other enthusiasts who might be able to tell us more. William Trent interviewed a whole load of people for his book and I've yet to meet one that actually liked the man. No one in the re-enactment community has reported a Fairbairn Sykes knife missing and Sergeant Baker and me, we double-checked with all the stallholders this weekend. None of them have reported anything like that stolen. There were a couple had thefts, and one of those was an SS dagger, apparently.'

'Which wasn't what killed William Trent. So as long as we don't end up with another body, we can safely hand that complaint off to uniform.'

He glanced once more at the three searchers. They had all settled down in the long grass, sharing a bottle of something Mac hoped was not alcoholic. Now the main body of searchers had gone it all looked terribly leisurely, considering they were involved in a murder enquiry. In truth, Mac's colleague, DI Kendall and his team were doing the heavy lifting on this one, carrying out the background checks and the interviews. Frantham's little outpost again found themselves peripheral to the main action.

'Has Rina been over?' Mac asked.

'Brought cake for elevenses.'

Mac shook his head indulgently. 'And a list of questions?'

'No, actually. Just cake. I thought she was supposed to be off filming that TV series of hers.'

'One series is finished, I believe. *Lydia Marchant Investigates* is scheduled for the spring season. Rina told me the pre-sell has been so good that a second is already commissioned. She's off again in March, I think.'

'Good for her. My mum and nan are really looking forward to it. They were fans the first time round. My nan just hopes they haven't spoiled it by going all fancy.'

Mac guessed those were Andy's nan's words and that Andy probably didn't know what she meant either.

THIRTY-SEVEN

When Mac and Andy joined Edward de Freitas in the airfield's newly restored control tower they found him poring over a selection of old maps and, Mac noticed, a number of tracings and overlays that looked more recent.

'William left these with one of the artists,' he said. 'I thought I'd better bring them across. I think you've got the bits and pieces he left in his locker and his desk?'

Mac nodded. 'There wasn't much. I'm off over to the cottage later. CSI finished up there about an hour ago.'

'CSI, at the cottage? Did something happen there?'

'No, just routine.' Mac told him. 'Trent's home and car and desk, they're all regarded as potential secondary scenes.'

Edward still looked puzzled. 'Oh,' he said. 'I see. Anything turn up in the search of the airfield?'

'A lot of rubbish,' Andy said with feeling. 'Nothing that looks useful, yet. What are these maps, then? That looks like the tin huts.'

Edward tapped one of the maps. 'It is,' he said. 'I'm not sure where William found these, but they seem to be plans of the POW camp from about 1942, about six months after it was set up. And this,' he produced one of the overlays, 'is what remains now. As you can see, many of the units still in use are there on the plan. A few have been rebuilt but the basic footprint is the same.'

'That's the car repair place,' Andy said. 'And the kitchen fitters and the MOT test centre.'

Mac nodded. 'And this?' He pointed to a group of buildings on the original plan, set just behind the twin lines of huts. 'Isn't that where your place is now?'

Edward nodded. 'Look, William did an overlay of that too from the plans our architect drew up. *Iconograph* made use of the original buildings so far as we could and we kept to the footprint of these original buildings, infilling the space between. When we first started to look into the project we were advised that it would simplify the planning application and the whole process if we were seen to be integrating what was already there. Expanding between the existing structures more than doubled our potential ground plan, but we kept within the original bounds. None of the outer walls extend beyond what was already present.'

'And that worked? With the application process, I mean?' Andy was curious.

'I think there were two modifications. It took, in all, just over a year to get the approval. Not bad compared to some of the projects I know of. It actually took longer to get approval for the work we wanted to do on the airfield. The tower has listed status and there were all sorts of hoops to jump through getting the restoration done. I'm sure there are some people who would rather a place fell apart than let the horrors of commercial enterprise get a look in. But anyway—'

Mac was leafing through the maps and noticed something about the buildings behind the POW camp. 'Trent lists this as an admin building for the camp and this as a guard house. What's this section here? It looks as though it goes down another level?'

'It actually went down two,' Edward told him. 'That's now our R&D department. It was, if you remember, my brother's side of the business.'

Mac nodded. Edward's brother had been involved in a lot of government work. *Iconograph*, the public face, had provided an ideal screen for other projects. Mac wondered if it still did but knew he wouldn't get a straight answer anyway.

'William was convinced there had been some kind of bunker down there. That it had been designed perhaps as some kind of monitoring post or something. To be honest, I'd stopped listening to him by them. I wish that wasn't true, but it is, so—' he gathered the maps and plans together and handed them over to Mac – 'no room in life for regrets is there? But that doesn't stop us having them.'

*   *   *

Thursday was a regular day for Rina to do a bit of extra shopping at the general store along the promenade. She wasn't much of a one for supermarkets and one of the reasons she had chosen Frantham as her home was the abundance of small shops and independent retailers. The Grant Emporium was the closest thing Frantham had to a mini supermarket and it did a good trade in the summer from the visitors and the rest of the year ticked over keeping the local community supplied with everything from woolly hats to loaves of bread and household candles.

Thursday afternoon, just before closing, was a regular date for Rina when she was at home. Her journalist friend Andrew Barnes and his brother came on their weekly shop and Rina made a point of trying to be there.

Simeon, Andrew's brother, didn't cope with crowds. A childhood accident had left him brain damaged and, in the eyes of most people, severely disabled. Andrew and his brother still lived in the old family home high up on the cliffs. Simeon loved to watch the sea and the ships and the night sky. He kept detailed records of everything he saw and once a week, when he came to Frantham with his brother, he showed them to Rina. While she had been away, Andrew had been responsible for posting these observations to her and Rina had made a point of posting her usual responses and comments back the following day, no matter how tired or busy she had been.

'Hello, Rina,' Grant, the shop owner greeted her with a smile. 'The boys are down that aisle over there.'

Rina thanked him. She collected a wire basket from beside the till and went off to find them. Simeon was holding two packets in his hands, trying to decide which he wanted. They contained gas lighters, Rina noted, the sort used to light a stove or a fire. One contained a red and black pair and the second black and blue. For Simeon, such a choice was a difficult one. Andrew waited patiently beside him and it was clear that they had been working on the conundrum for quite some time.

'Blue and red,' Simeon said as Rina appeared. 'I want the blue and red.'

'You don't like the black ones?'

'I like the blue and red, but they don't do the packets of blue and red.'

'We could buy both,' Andrew said gently. 'Then you could have both.'

Simeon shook his head urgently. 'No. Then there'd be two black ones that wouldn't get used. That would be wrong. It would be sad. Things have a purpose. If they don't get used it would be . . .'

Rina exchanged an anxious look with Andrew. Simeon could get terribly upset about what others saw as irrelevant things. For Simeon, there was little difference between hurting the feelings of a person and those of an inanimate object. For him, they all had the right to be cared for. When Simeon's anxiety levels rose, he had been known to lash out and it would not have been the first time that Andrew had to pay for damage done to Grant's store.

'Could I share them with you?' Rina asked.

'Share them?'

'I could have the black ones and then you could have the red and the blue. We use those lighters for our fire at home. That way, they'd all get to do what they were made for.'

Simeon's expression of anxiety faded and Rina saw Andrew's relief.

'Yes,' Simeon said. 'That would be a good plan. Now I need lunches.'

'Thank you,' Andrew breathed as Simeon, on familiar ground now, chose five cans of soup and two of spaghetti as he always did and two loaves of bread. One white and one wholemeal. Then his chocolate and his biscuits. 'Do you have enough coffee?' he asked his brother.

'I think I could do with some. And I'd like some of that tea you chose for me last time.'

Simeon nodded and added the tea and coffee to the basket. Rina, adding the few things she needed to her own basket, didn't attempt to speak to Andrew until they'd reached the checkout and Simeon had explained that he and Rina were sharing the packs of lighters. Simeon needed full concentration for the shopping, and conversation, even not directly with him, was just an upsetting distraction until after he had paid.

'We can go for coffee now,' he said and the smile lit his eyes. 'I have my writing to show you, Rina. I saw three new ships this week and five new birds on the bird table and the squirrels are back in the garden because the weather is getting colder.'

They sat beside the window in Tonino's and Andrew fetched the coffee while Simeon talked Rina through his discoveries. Simeon's handwriting was careful and neat and his observations precise. Andrew sipped his coffee as his brother and their friend talked their way through the extensive list and it was only when Simeon, satisfied and now tired by the talk, put his list away that Andrew made any comment. Simeon stared out of the window, watching the sea and Rina knew from experience that he was unlikely to want to speak again until they all said goodbye.

'I saw Mac the other week,' Andrew said.

'At the funeral? That was a sad business. I get the impression he's not making much progress.'

Andrew smiled at her. 'And?'

Rina laughed. 'And, he asked me to have a quiet word about your friend Dan Marsden next time I saw you.'

Andrew laughed softly. 'Dan turned up at the funeral, of course. I thought Mac seemed a bit too interested. Rina, what can I tell you? He and his family are well off, have a philanthropic bent and a hell of a lot of business acumen. They found a way of combining the two, I suppose.'

Rina nodded. 'I've already done some background research,' she said. 'But I think it's Dan that he's interested in.'

'Dan. Right. But what does he want to know? Dan's never got on the wrong side of the law as far as I know. He went off to university and then joined the family business. I think he studied business and law, but it might have been accountancy or something. I don't remember. He's married with two kids. I've met them a few times. Her name's Holly but can't say I know her.'

'He'd been engaged before,' Rina said.

Andrew thought for a moment. 'I'd forgotten about her. Not that I really knew her either. He was away at university, I think. So was I. Before that, when we were both at school, he'd dated a girl called Yvonne Castle. Lucky beggar.' Andrew laughed at the memory. 'Blonde hair, legs up to . . . well, you get the picture. I think they broke up just after he'd gone away, then something happened. Car crash, accident. I don't remember what.'

'And the first engagement?'

Andrew shrugged. 'Sorry, Rina. We weren't close friends at school, moved into very different circles. He was one of the popular kids. I sat in the corner and read books. My Saturday nights were spent watching videos or maybe meeting mates in the pub. I expect his were spent in nightclubs and posh hotels or whatever else young kids with money do, especially when mummy and daddy trot them out on every possible occasion and make sure they meet all the right people. I think he went out with Carrie Butler for a while.'

'Heiress to the Breed Estate?'

'Heiress is pushing it. Anyway, I suppose she's more like the owner now. I think she inherited more debt than cash, it's taken her the past five years and a lot of slimming down to get it back on track. She's a nice woman, is Carrie Butler.'

'And Dan Marsden is not a nice man?'

'I didn't say that, Rina.' He grinned at her. 'Look, like I said, Dan and I knew one another but we were never friends. I interview him on a regular basis, like I told Mac, and we run into one another at the same events. He's usually a guest and I'm usually one of the hacks filling space in the local rag.'

'But your impression is?'

'My impression is . . . what's Mac's interest anyway?'

'He knew Ellen Tailor, apparently. I think he's just spreading the net.'

'Rina?'

She raised her hands in mock surrender. 'I know nothing,' she protested. 'Really, Andrew, I think he's just at a loss and looking at everything.'

'I think it's one of the family,' Andrew said. 'Daphne isn't a nice woman.'

'But a murderer?'

Andrew shrugged. 'Anyone can kill, I suppose.'

Simeon turned his attention back to the table and drained his coffee, a sure sign that he was ready to head for home.

'Look, I'll put a pack together for you. Interviews I've done and that sort of thing. You might find something interesting, I suppose?'

Simeon stood up. 'Bye, Rina. Are we going now?'

'Bye, Simeon. I'll see you next week.'

Simeon smiled and again the blue grey eyes were full of life and Rina fancied she caught a glimpse of the young man he might have become if the accident hadn't taken that chance away.

THIRTY-EIGHT

The curtains at Stone End cottage were closed. CSI had finished with the place, he had been told, and they had left the cottage as they had found it; as William Trent had left it, prepared for his return late, after the dance at the airfield.

This time, Mac had brought Andy with him.

No one had been left on duty but the front and back doors had been sealed with blue and white tape. Officially, this was only a secondary crime scene. No one had died here – at least not recently and violently. He'd been told that Carrie Butler had promised to keep an eye on the place, but he guessed that would just mean a quick check maybe once a day.

Mac unlocked the door and then broke the tape. He reached in and switched on the hall light before entering.

'Let's get the curtains open,' he said. 'Then we'll start upstairs. CSI have taken the computer but everything else is in place.'

'Right,' Andy said. 'Are we expecting any help or is it just us?'

Mac laughed. 'Actually, I told Kendall we could manage. I want to get a feel for the man. I can't do that with too many bodies around.'

'Right.' Andy sounded dubious.

'Frank says you've got a good eye for detail,' Mac said. 'So let's put it to the test, shall we?'

Upstairs was a single bedroom, a tiny boxroom used for storage and a neat bathroom with a very small corner bath.

'They probably split the second bedroom in half,' Andy commented. 'I can see why the estate sold this one off instead of making it into a holiday let. It's way off the road, going to be impossible to get to in winter and you could only really let to couples. Or maybe a couple with a baby. And there's no central heating.'

Mac nodded. It was chilly upstairs and he guessed it would soon be damp if the cottage was left unoccupied for long. An electric heater combined with a light kept the bathroom warm and another electric heater had been plugged into a wall socket in the bedroom. There had once been a fireplace. The surround and hearth remained but the grate had been blocked off.

'Start over there,' Mac said, pointing to the chest of drawers. 'I'll take the wardrobe and the bedside table.'

For a while, they worked in silence. Andy examining the socks and underwear and shirts. Beneath the newspaper liners and beneath the drawers themselves. Nothing concealed under the mattress. Trousers and jackets and a long winter coat in the wardrobe. Shoes and boots. Nothing inside. Andy helped Mac to ease it from the wall but apart from a coat hanger and a pile of fluff there was nothing to see.

No dressing table. The room was too small for that and William's hair brush and clothes brush were set on the chest of drawers alongside two candle sticks and a pack of household candles and a box of matches. He'd lived there long enough to be prepared for power cuts, Mac thought.

He checked the bedside drawers. Found a hip flask, half full of brandy, more candles and a little candle stand. A paperback book on the Spanish Civil War, an illustration of Guernica on the cover. Mac frowned; he'd thought that picture was done to commemorate something in World War Two but acknowledged he may well have been wrong. He flicked through the pages and checked the flysheet but there was no inscription.

A quick look beneath the bedside rug and a check of the floorboards and that was the bedroom done.

'You look at the bathroom and then join me in the boxroom,' Mac told Andy. 'Then we'll move downstairs.'

The boxroom had been given over purely to storage. There was not even a curtain at the window. Three – empty – suitcases had been stacked against the wall and most of the remaining space had been filled by boxes of books and, from the look of the dust, none of them had been looked at in a while.

Andy joined him with nothing to report from the bathroom and together they brushed off the dust and flicked through the books. Apart from the odd bookmark or the occasional sliver of paper serving the same purpose, there was nothing. Mac paused to look at the pages that had been marked, but could see nothing that identified the pages as important to anyone other that William Trent.

'Downstairs?'

Andy nodded. 'Cup of coffee? I've got a flask and Mum did me a pack up for us to share.'

'I always did like your mum.'

Andy went back to the car to collect refreshments and Mac went through to the kitchen. The units were old and basic but everything was very clean and very neat. A single mug had been washed and then inverted on the draining board.

Mac started on his perusal of the cupboards but found nothing out of place. He was checking behind the fridge when Andy returned.

'Thought you'd got lost.'

'Just talking to a farmer called Jenkins. He saw the curtains open and came to see who was here. Apparently he saw Trent regularly on the path to the Tailor farm and they talked sometimes.'

'And did they talk about anything relevant?'

'Probably not. Jenkins has a bit of a bee in his bonnet about this place, though. Says it's always been unlucky.'

'Oh?'

'Apparently someone was murdered here. A couple. With a shotgun. But don't get excited, it was years ago, during the Second World War.'

'Right. And did this Jenkins enjoy watching your reaction when he told you that?'

'I think you could say that. Find anything yet?'

'Not so far, but I'm not even sure what we're looking for.'

Andy poured coffee and handed a mug to Mac. 'There's sandwiches and cake and a couple of packs of crisps,' he said. 'What do you want me to start with?'

'Pick a corner. Lots of books to look through. Manuscripts too, from the look of things. I'll take the desk; you start in the book room.'

They took a break to eat and then fell quiet again as Andy started on the books and Mac skimmed through papers in the desk. One drawer contained bills and receipts. Another, a folder labelled tax which seemed to be a collection of expenses and bank statements. Mac examined the statements and set them aside for further perusal. Letters and contracts from his publisher, printouts of emails, also dealing with business or expenses. Stacks of research notes filled another drawer. Mac flicked through the pages but there seemed nothing untoward. He wondered if he'd even recognize something wrong if he saw it.

In the final drawer he found something a little different. In plastic wallets, were letters, ration books, notebooks, much like those he had seen in the boxes at the airfield.

Mac took everything out of the drawer and spread it out on the desk. So, it seemed that Trent had borrowed more than those artefacts from Ellen. In one of the packs was a reel of tape. Most of the wallets were labelled, in Ellen's neat script, the owner and contents described. But the tape had no such marker, no clue to the owner or what might be on the reel.

'You see anything that looks like a reel to reel tape player round here?'

'What, you mean like one of those old tape recorder things?'

'I think that's what I said.'

'No. Nothing like that.' Andy came over to the desk and looked at the folders Mac had laid there. 'It's like the stuff from the airfield,' he said. 'Look, all labelled up the same way.'

Mac nodded. 'I suppose they were for his research, but I wonder if the families knew about it or if he just helped himself. Lydia would probably not have noticed. I wonder if Ellen did.'

'I'll get a box from the car,' Andy said.

Mac stood up and stretched. Not much more to look through, he thought, apart from the rest of the books in the little side room. Though it looked as though Andy had made a good start. He checked up on the coal scuttle and the wood box, but they contained only what their names suggested and for good measure, he took a poker and rattled it up the chimney, gaining only a fall of soot for his trouble.

Andy returned with a box and they packed the folders inside, together with the bank statements and letters and a cheque book that had been filed alongside the tax folder.

'Books?' Andy said. 'I could do with a hand. I got to the middle shelf.'

Between them the last job was completed quickly. 'Who the hell would want to kill a historian, anyway?' Andy said. 'You think it could be linked to Ellen Tailor?'

Mac shook his head. 'I don't see how, but you never know, do you? Two deaths in the same vicinity.'

'Trent wasn't killed here.'

'No, but the same circle of people. What are the odds? But . . .' Mac shrugged. 'I think we're done here,' he said. 'Now we just need to find a way of playing that tape and try to figure out why Trent was so interested in it.'

THIRTY-NINE

Rina found an envelope on her mat when she came down in the morning. It was from Andrew Barnes and filled with copies of clippings about Dan Marsden. Happily, Rina dropped the envelope on her office desk in her little front sitting room – a private space; strictly invitation only – and then went through to the kitchen for her early cup of tea. She took her tablet computer with her and scrolled through a search while sipping her first cup of tea. The tablet had been a present to herself bought in celebration of the new series and she'd become very attached to it.

The Marsden family were easy to find, and Rina spent a half-hour bringing herself up to date on the family and their charity work. Three generations of Marsdens had, as their website put it, tried to 'give something back to their community'. Rina found herself agreeing with most of their assertions. That prison without the hope of rehabilitation was meaningless. That releasing people back into a community that didn't welcome them and with no skills to offer or to sell was just an invitation for them to reoffend.

That society should be judged on how it protected the weak and vulnerable and that often included ex-offenders or those that circumstance made likely to offend.

She read about the youth programme Ellen had volunteered for and about the work placement schemes the Marsdens supported. There were pictures of fund-raising events and charity balls. Smiling faces, well-dressed men and women, grateful recipients of cheques and donations of equipment. Success stories from those they had employed and got back into work.

On the face of it, impressive, Rina thought. She enlarged an image of Dan Marsden and his family, taken at a seaside event that summer. Dan Marsden smiled at the camera. The wife, holding one child in her arms and another by the hand, smiled at them. Rina studied the young man's face and thought about what Andrew had told her; what he had said.

Surface charm, she thought. But what about what was going on beneath?

On another page there were pictures of the youth project that Ellen had worked on and a tribute to 'Ellen Tailor, sadly missed' and Ellen's dates. She had been thirty-three years old, Rina noted. Ellen looked happy, surrounded by kids and teens who were obviously having fun. In a couple of the pictures Dan also featured. In one, he was looking at Ellen. Rina enlarged the image and studied both of them closely. Ellen, absorbed in painting with some of the younger children, seemed utterly unaware of Dan. Dan Marsden, on the other had, was gazing intently at her. Hungrily, Rina thought, and still she wondered what was going on behind his eyes.

'Do you know the Marsden family?' Rina asked Lydia de Freitas.

'Oh, socially, yes. Not well though. Edward made a donation to one of their projects last year. Why?'

'Oh, just curious. The name was mentioned.'

Lydia looked at her and raised an eyebrow. 'Rina Martin, don't you lie to me. You never *just* get curious.'

Rina laughed. 'All right,' she agreed, 'so it's more than just idle curiosity but, Lydia, I don't want to—'

'Give anything away. All right. So what can I tell you?'

'Anything you know. I understand he was engaged once before.'

'Sorry, wouldn't know. I've met his wife. She seems nice but like I say, we meet them socially. We're not friends.'

'Is there any reason for that? Or just circumstances,' Rina asked.

Lydia laughed. 'Oh, Rina, honestly. Look, Edward and I have

never chosen our friends on the basis of, well, anything but the fact that we like them, really. We meet a lot of people at fund-raisers and business events and corporate bashes but very few of those people make it on to our invited to the house list. And the Marsdens, well—'

'You don't like them?'

'No, it isn't that. I like Celia Marsden a lot. She's funny and clever and very caring, and her husband from what I've seen is equally pleasant to be around. But the conversations we've had have always just been about whatever we happen to have got together for. I might like them if I met them elsewhere but . . . I really don't know.'

'And Dan Marsden?'

Lydia grimaced. 'Not my cup of tea,' she said shortly. 'One of those people – and I include a fair few women in this number – that can't keep their hands to themselves.'

Rina was thoughtful for a moment. 'I've been thinking about Vera Courtney,' she said. 'How much she disliked William Trent. How resentful she was.'

Lydia's mouth fell open and then she laughed. 'Rina, for heaven's sake. You can't think?'

'I'm not thinking anything,' Rina said.

'Oh, really? Well, so far as I'm aware they hardly know one another. But, of course, they had Ellen in common, I suppose.'

Rina nodded. Of course they had, she thought. Of course they had.

FORTY

Rina used her main computer this time. Everyone was home and so it was easier to hide away in her office with the door closed and no one to ask questions. Her search was more random this time and guided by the press clippings Andrew had posted through her door. There had been a brief report of the car crash that had killed his girlfriend from his school days. She had been driving alone in bad weather and lost control on a bend.

On the face of it, a tragic accident and an inexperienced driver who had not long passed her test. Dan Marsden had made a statement for the report. He said that Yvonne Castle had been a lovely girl, but that they had decided it was better to go their separate ways when he went off to university.

She delved further, more pictures of fund-raisers and events. The odd feature in the society pages. She found his first engagement to a young woman called Elizabeth Rowley. Then the record of his marriage to Holly Whitely five years ago.

So what happened to Elizabeth Rowley, Rina wondered. A half-hour of further searching turned up nothing and Rina decided to call it a day.

What was she doing, anyway, Rina wondered. She was looking for something suspicious on the strength of two people she respected – Lydia and Andrew – not particularly liking a man who happened to also have known a murdered woman. Even for Rina, that was stretching things on the suspicion front.

She shut her computer down and went in search of tea and cake and company, wondering if Mac was getting any further along.

FORTY-ONE

Mac and Andy, with a little help from Frank, had been examining the letters and other ephemera that he had found in William Trent's desk. The documents came from four families.

The Courtney file contained copies of the journal and the letters that Mac had taken back from William Trent. The Marsden folder – Marsdens, again, Mac thought – contained a selection of letters and what looked like a recipe book. He put it aside to take a proper look. The third family were the Verneys and Mac knew nothing about them. Photographs of young men in uniform and some others of what looked like a wartime Frantham had seemingly attracted William Trent's attention to this file. Then there was the packet that had the reel of tape inside.

So what had led William Trent to pick these out from the pack?

What intrigued him about this information? And had he taken everything these families contributed to the exhibition or just selected elements? Thinking about it, Mac figured that it must just be extracts. Lydia had said there was far too much material to put into one exhibition and that she was hoping to be able to make regular changes, but he'd have made a bet that all the families who had contributed would expect at least something to be in the first exhibition and that William would have been selective in his borrowings. He'd have to have a chat with Lydia. See what else had come from these individuals and see if any light could be shed on why William had made his selection.

'Call it a day?' Frank asked. 'It's after six.'

Mac nodded. 'I'm going to get this lot copied,' he said, 'and see if Kendall's come up with a tape deck in the morning. See you then.'

Dinner over, Rina went back to her computer. The problem, she thought, was knowing how to search. She'd focused on Dan Marsden at first and found his first fiancée. Then the trail had petered out. But then, Rina thought, maybe the young woman hadn't done anything newsworthy after she'd broken up with Dan.

What other direction could she take, Rina wondered. She remembered something in the clippings Andrew had given to her about Dan and Elizabeth Rowley meeting at university. Sheffield, if she remembered right.

Rina tried another tack, inputting Elizabeth Rowley and Sheffield University. She found a couple of hits, little mentions in the university magazine. She climbed, apparently and ran. Rina glanced at the time and decided she would give herself another half an hour. She was getting bored now and also starting to wonder if there was any purpose to this. Then a few minutes later she found what she had been looking for but never expected to find. An obituary for Elizabeth Rowley.

Rina read on, eagerly. Elizabeth Rowley had died, aged twenty-one, in a fall. A climbing accident.

'Our thoughts and sympathies go to her family and her fiancé, Dan Marsden.'

'Three deaths,' Rina whispered. 'Surely, by any reckoning, that goes a bit beyond chance.'

FORTY-TWO

Reluctantly, Ray had agreed to see Daphne again but he found her in no better mood. He despised her, Ray realized with a bit of a shock. He really did.

'Mum, I don't think we should be doing this. It isn't fair.'

'What's being fair got to do with it? This is about justice. About restoring the natural order of things. Just grow a pair, boy!'

Ray sighed and leaned back in his seat. He glanced anxiously around the crowded cafe his mother had chosen for their meeting. 'Mum, the kids—'

'Should be with family.'

'Diane is family. It's what their mother wanted.'

'We get the kids we get our land back. What belongs to us, Ray.'

'What *did* belong to us, Mum. Look, Ellen and Jeb did their best by the both of us. They fixed you up with a nice house when they were barely making ends meet themselves. They helped me settle in New Zealand, they—'

'Which you bloody hate. For that matter, I hate that bloody house too.'

'Not their fault it didn't work out for me. Carol loves it there. And I like it too, come to that. She's got a good job and friends and it's no one's fault that—'

'Then let her rot there. You're back now and that's all that matters.'

'I'm back for a visit. That's all.'

'You can't go back. I bought you a one-way ticket.'

'Which Carol helped me upgrade to a return. I'm doing the right thing for once, Mum. I'm going back. We're going to arrange a divorce and then I'll make up my mind. I've been offered a decent job. I went for the interview just before I came back and I accepted. It starts next month and—'

'But this is your home. The farm—'

'Is no longer ours. Ellen did a good job with what she had left.

What happens now has to be in the hands of her kids and her sister. Not us. Our time has gone, Mum.'

'You don't mean that. You can't. She'll persuade the kids to sell up. She'll take them away.'

'Best thing for them if you ask me. I hope one day they might visit me. I hope we can heal the rift. I liked Ellen, liked her a lot. No, I have to say it, Mum, I loved Ellen. That was one of the problems between me and Carol. I married her because I couldn't have Ellen and I hoped getting together with a nice girl like Carol would make it all right.'

'You can't be serious.'

'Oh, but I am. Carol and me, we had a proper talk before I came back. Said things we should both have said a long time ago. She deserves better than me and I deserve to be able to make a fresh start, so it's all decided.'

Ray Tailor got up, scraping back his chair. Daphne was stunned, for the moment, but he knew that wouldn't last for long.

'They suspect you of shooting her,' she spat at him.

'Maybe they do. I'll have to sort that out, won't I? Mum, you told me to grow a pair and in that, you're right. I aim to. Everything else, well, you got it wrong.'

FORTY-THREE

Mac listened to Rina's description of her research and agreed it was a strange series of events.

'There are a lot of missing women in this business,' he said. 'William Trent lost a fiancée in a carjacking. Dan Marsden lost a girlfriend in a car accident and fiancée in a climbing accident – and Rina, that's unlucky, but it happens. We can't get carried away here.'

'But it's worth following up?'

'I'll talk to Kendall.' He sighed. 'Rina there's nothing I'd like more than a break in this case, but losing a girlfriend and fiancée to what were probably . . . almost certainly accidents, is not remotely related to taking a gun and shooting someone.'

'Oh, I know that, Mac. I just thought—'

'And I'm grateful. And now we have another death.'

'Ellen's friend, William Trent.'

'Which does not mean the two things are related. Though I agree, it's uncomfortably coincidental.'

'And any leads?'

'Rina stop fishing.'

'I'm not fishing, I'm asking a direct question. I'm not subtle, you know that.'

'No, no leads,' he admitted.

'Mac, this might sound like a long shot, but you should try talking to a woman called Vera Courtney.'

'Courtney . . . one of the flower ladies? I think uniform spoke to her. Why should I speak to her about Trent?'

Rina took a deep breath. 'Right, this is what I've put together. Might be adding two and two and making five, but . . . Vera Courtney said she'd lend some books and papers to the exhibition. Then she changed her mind. Trent was very keen to get his hands on what she'd brought along to the airfield. The journal and letters you brought to me to look at were Vera's. She was seriously upset about him having them. She went to the airfield to try and get everything back and it wasn't there. Ellen hadn't taken it over there. Which probably means that William Trent had persuaded her to let him . . . well, let's be generous and say *borrow* those things.'

'Others too,' Mac observed. 'We found some other items when we searched the cottage. Rina, you don't happen to have a reel to reel tape recorder, do you?'

She laughed. 'No, even we're not as old-fashioned as all that. Why?'

'There was a tape in amongst the stuff we found at Trent's cottage. I've nothing to play it on. I'm hoping Kendall will be able to help.'

'Who does it belong to? Vera mentioned a missing tape.'

'Did she, now. Well, there was no label on the packet so I don't know. Did Vera say what was on it?'

'No, but she was very upset about it. Actually, she was incandescent, if I'm honest. Actually she was extremely upset by the whole thing.'

Mac nodded. 'Do you know why?'

'I know that the journal and letters were very personal. I read them and frankly, I think I'd have wanted them kept private too. And then there's the secrets the writer hinted at. Tim and I did some digging and a lot of it seems to refer to an SOE operation based here. It's still sensitive stuff.'

'I've not had time to read everything,' Mac admitted. 'It is all ancient history though, isn't it?'

'Not to everyone, it's not. I think that Trent persuaded Ellen to lend the journal to him. But she didn't tell Vera, for obvious reasons. I think Vera guessed that Trent had her documents.'

'But, Rina, if you're right, all he did was borrow a few research sources. Someone stabbed him to death, that's—'

'I know, but the link is there, isn't it? Vera and Ellen and Trent. Look, I saw the way Vera looked at him when he made that speech. She was furious. It was almost as though he was speaking directly to her. Secrets should be exposed. That's what he was saying. Forgotten voices should be heard. I saw her face, Mac, she was dreadfully upset. She looked as though she really hated the man.'

FORTY-FOUR

'*You think you can scare me? You're even more pathetic than I thought.'*

He turned his back on me then and that's when I did it. I don't think I went out with the intention of killing him, but then, you never know what you're really capable of until it's done. But I just wanted some acknowledgement. Some consideration. Some sense that the bloody man actually understood what he was going to do to people if he carried on. To good people, honourable people. Not like him. He was not a man who even understood the concept of honourable.

So I killed him.

And I'm not sorry.

And I'm not going to give myself up.

I bent down and used my sleeve to wipe the shaft of the knife and then I walked away. Just like that. I was amazed, if I'm honest, at just how good it felt to know that he was no longer in the world. Could no longer torment and persecute and malign. If I'm honest I was almost proud of myself – though I didn't expect that feeling to last long. I'm a realist after all and I know that euphoria is the least real, least permanent of all emotions.

But, boy, did it feel good at the time.

What did I do then? Oh, I came back to the dance and bought a round of drinks. My own private little celebration. And then I danced what was left of the night away.

I wondered if that was what psychopaths felt like all of the time. That feeling of power, of lack of control and yet being in control all at the same time. If it is, then I can understand it totally, why they do what they do and yes, I do know how that sounds.

And how do I feel now?

Well, of course the emotion has cooled a little and I'm terribly conscious that there may be consequences, but I can't bring myself to worry about that at the moment, I have to behave normally, keep my life as it was before I did this momentous thing.

But I will confess to one, small thing. Each night since, each night before I go to sleep, I do raise a glass to myself and to those he sent to die. Boy, but he was an arrogant sod. His way or no way, that was always his trouble.

A pause, only breathing and the sound of birds recording on to the tape.

So, I'll leave this as a record for those who need to know and I'll make whatever peace I have to make when the time comes.

Another pause and this time there is no doubt that the speaker is crying, softly and with great restraint, but also unmistakable pain.

I miss you so much, my lovely. And one day I will see you again. That's the one thing that makes it all bearable. That's all that makes it bearable.

'Who is this?' Mac asked.

Kendall shook his head. 'I have no idea. Perhaps Vera Courtney will be able to tell us. I'm not surprised she wanted this kept out of the way, but I'm not sure I understand why she kept it.'

'The similarities, though,' Mac said. 'The dance, the knife . . .'

'Mac, that's a stretch isn't it?'

'Maybe.' He told Kendall what Rina had theorized and also what she had found out about Dan Marsden.

'It's all hearsay, Mac. And much as I respect Mrs Martin—'

'I know. But we can at least put the questions, can't we?'

Kendall nodded. 'I'll . . . request that Dan comes in and we should see what Vera Courtney has to say.'

Mac took Yolanda and drove out to Vera Courtney's home, a bungalow on a good patch of land about two miles from Ellen Tailor's farm. He had the tape recording with him.

She seemed unsurprised when she opened the door and he explained who he was. She had eyes only for the plastic folder, containing the reel of tape that he held in his hands.

'You found it then. He did have it, didn't he? I knew he had.'

'The tape was in William Trent's drawer. We didn't know it belonged to you. Not at first. Rina Martin said you'd mentioned a missing tape. You can confirm that this is yours?'

She nodded. 'You'd better come in. Rina returned the journal and letters to me. She was very kind.'

Once inside, Vera stood uncertainly in the hall, looking at the tape. 'Have you heard it?'

'Yes, but we don't know what it means.'

They followed her as she walked unsteadily into the living room and sat down beside the window. 'The diary belonged to my father,' she said. 'He should never have kept it. The tape recording was made by the man who killed him. It was made many years later and sent to my mother, along with the knife that he used. I think Teddy was looking for absolution. I think he was dead before the recording arrived. My mother never said.'

'Who was Teddy?'

'One of those my father sent away, sent on missions. Sent to die, probably. Teddy went three times. My father went on four missions, behind enemy lines. Yugoslavia, Mitilini and twice in Crete. He was with SOE.'

'Special Operations Executive,' Mac said.

'Yes. He was fortunate to survive. After the fourth operation he was grounded, he trained the next cohort. Among them was Teddy. Teddy was broken by it all and my father knew it. He pulled him out, retired him. So many died, Inspector. Very few returned. My father found it hard to live with himself after a while. He sent others where he had been and knew that the odds of them living through the experience were minimal. He died a little inside with every death and so did Teddy, only Teddy blamed my father. One night, I suspect after a little too much drink, he confronted my father, Bobby Courtney, and he killed him. He was never caught, but at the end of his life he confessed.'

'And all of this interested William Trent.'

'Of course it did. At first, I thought perhaps I could live with that. I could tell my secrets and have the world know that Bobby Courtney was a hero. But then I remembered that he had seen himself as something very different from that. We'd not spoken of it in our family. We'd not acknowledged it. My mother had hidden . . . had suffered, had kept silent. What could I do?'

'Did you kill William Trent, Miss Courtney?'

She blinked. 'Do you know who killed Ellen Tailor?' she asked.

'Not yet, no.'

She nodded. 'Ellen was seeing Dan Marsden, you know. She thought she'd hidden it from me, but she hadn't. I told her he was not a good man, not really. I never forgot how unhappy he made that pretty girlfriend of his.'

'Girlfriend?'

'Yvonne. Such a pretty girl.'

'She was killed in a car crash.'

'She thought she was pregnant and she'd told Dan. He was furious and they argued. She drove off in the rain and must have taken that bend too fast. He said some dreadful things, Inspector. He drove her to her death, in a way.'

'And how do you know all this, Miss Courtney?'

'I know because Celia told me. She heard the argument and demanded to know what was going on. Celia and I are old friends. Sometimes the only people you can tell these things to are those you knew when you were all equally young and silly. Poor little Yvonne.'

'Did you kill William Trent, Vera?' Mac asked again.

Vera sighed. 'I need to get someone to feed Charlie,' she said. 'Charlie is my cat. Can you arrange that? I need to get my coat. It's in the hall.'

Mac followed her from the room and waited until she'd taken her coat from the hall cupboard.

'Did she do it,' Yolanda whispered.

Vera turned with a puzzled look on her face. 'Of course I did, my dear,' she said. 'I followed him out and talked to him, tried to get him to understand but he just laughed. What else could I do?'

FORTY-FIVE

D
an Marsden was playing with his little girls in the garden when Kendall and Mac arrived. Holly Marsden showed them through and asked if they'd like anything to drink. Kendall declined for both of them and went to talk to Dan in the garden while Mac remained with Holly.

'It's nice to see some sun,' he said.

'Yes. Is something wrong? Why do you want to talk to Dan?'

'How did the two of you meet?'

'Why? I mean . . . I was doing youth work. We met up at a conference.'

'You knew he'd been engaged before?'

'Of course. What's all this about?'

'Did you know Ellen Tailor?'

'Of course. She was a lovely woman. Helped out at the youth group the Marsdens run.'

The Marsdens, Mac thought. As though she was somehow separate from the rest of the family. 'Did you know that she and Dan were seeing one another? Outside of work, I mean.'

Holly looked incredulous. 'That's a stupid accusation,' she said coldly. 'You can't come into my home and make accusations like that about my husband.'

'Do you know a lady called Vera Courtney?' Mac asked, changing tack.

'Slightly, she's a friend of Celia's but—'

'We've just arrested her for the murder of William Trent,' Mac said. 'Mrs Marsden, on the day Ellen Tailor was killed, did your husband seem upset in any way?'

'What? Ellen, Vera, I don't understand. Dan heard about Ellen and was very upset. We all were. But what—'

Kendall came back into the kitchen accompanied by Dan Marsden. 'I've got to go out for a while,' he said. 'I won't be long.'

'Won't be long? Dan, what is going on here?'

'We'd just like your husband to answer a few questions,' Kendall said. 'After you, Mr Marsden.'

FORTY-SIX

Lydia de Freitas was on Rina's doorstep early before the rest of the household had got up.

'Have you heard? They've arrested Dan Marsden,' she said dropping the morning paper on Rina's kitchen table.

'I think he's just at what they used to call the helping with enquiries stage,' Rina argued.

'Well . . . One thing leads to another, doesn't it? And Vera. Surely you've heard about Vera Courtney. I mean, Rina. She killed him. She killed Trent.'

'I know,' Rina said sadly. 'I suspected she might have done.'

'And you set Mac on her? Oh, Rina. Is that what you were so upset about yesterday afternoon?'

'Lydia, I still don't feel good about it.'

'Rina, if she did it and you knew, what else could you do?'

What indeed. 'It was the missing documents,' Rina said. 'That's what upset Vera enough to kill him, I think and I believe maybe Ellen facilitated that. Though I'm sure she meant no harm.'

'Does Vera know Ellen did that? What a mess.'

Both women fell silent, troubled by it all.

'I'd better start getting breakfast,' Rina said. 'They'll be waking up.'

'I'll make us some tea,' Lydia said. 'Do you think Dan Marsden did it?'

'I don't know, Lydia, I really don't.' She picked up the paper Lydia had brought in and skimmed the article. Yesterday afternoon, she was told, Daniel Marsden, son of prominent businessman and philanthropist Christopher Marsden, voluntarily appeared at Exeter police headquarters in connection with the enquiry into the murder of Ellen Tailor. There followed a resume of the case and of Dan Marsden's charity work and the fact that Ellen had been a volunteer at one of Dan Marsden's projects.

There was nothing about Vera or William Trent Rina noticed, flicking through the paper, but the byline was an interesting one. The article had been written by Rina's friend Andrew Barnes.

FORTY-SEVEN

In his dream he stood on the ridge looking down at Ellen's cottage.

He could see directly into the farmhouse from his vantage point. Not deeply, but a bit of the kitchen through the big window, a little of the range and the corner of the table. She had stood at the sink for a while now, her gaze mostly down and he guessed she was washing pots or perhaps peeling vegetables. Her blonde hair was tied back. He was too far away to see the grey strands that he knew were annoying her so much. She kept threatening to dye it and he had always told her that he liked it. And asking why she thought it mattered.

'Oh, there's a *man* speaking,' she would say, as she shook her head fondly.

From time to time she glanced up from her task, looking out of the window at the sunlight and flowers in the yard. She'd have the radio on; she usually did when working in the kitchen, especially when the house was empty. She liked the sense of being in company and she loved her music.

Occasionally when she glanced up he got the feeling that she was staring straight out at him, but he knew that she wasn't. Not really. That she was unlikely to have seen him. The grass was long and the leaves of the beech tree against which he sat swept down, obscuring him from view.

He loved this spot. He loved the woman he watched now.

But that was hardly the point, was it. That was not important now.

As the afternoon crept on he knew that she'd be finished her tasks soon, would move away from the window, would get ready for the children coming home from school. He wondered if he should meet them off the bus, so that they didn't go up to the house alone.

Perhaps he would.

But he could delay things no longer. He left the ridge and followed the winding rabbit path down, climbed the low fence that separated the yard from the field and crossed towards the house.

Looking up, she saw him then. She smiled, her eyes lighting with genuine pleasure and welcome, filling him with so much happiness that he could hardly bear it.

Then, slowly, reluctantly, he raised the shotgun. He could see her clearly, even glimpse the strands of grey in her soft blonde hair.

He forced himself into wakefulness, struggling away from the dream, from the memory, from the shock of what he had done. Light streamed in through the window and in the distance he could hear the seabirds calling.

Dan lay in his bed looking up at the ceiling and listening to the sounds of Holly and the children drifting up the stairs. It had been the early hours of the morning when he'd returned home, anxious that there might be reporters in his street and not wanting to face his wife.

'Where were you when. At this time, at that. What time did you leave the Breed Estate. That would give you plenty of time to—'

Dan sat up and then got out of bed and walked to the window. His house was set well back from the road and he lifted the edge of the net curtain and peered down into the street. It had been empty the night before, but now a small gathering of men and women huddled together against the early morning chill.

Holly had called his mother as soon as the police had left and she had come storming to the rescue – as she always did. Solicitor in tow, she had arrived at the police station only half an hour after Dan and she had not been amused.

It had still been stressful, though, Dan thought. The repeated questions, the small variations, the demands that he should recall detail after detail and not just about Ellen but delving deep into his past. It had exhausted him.

Dan listened to the voices of his children and the laughter of his wife as she replied to them. He was glad the girls were not yet old enough to go to school; there would be no need to run the journalistic gamut or to explain that today was an extra holiday and they would not be going in. He wondered what this would do to his relationship with Holly. She'd said so little to him when he'd got home – but then, his mother had accompanied him and Celia had done most of the talking.

Dan recognized that he had cared a great deal for Ellen. Had enjoyed her company, had toyed with the idea of further involvement but not taken what would usually have been such an opportunity. Ellen had seen to that. She had been tempted, he knew, but she had drawn the line and not crossed it and Dan found he was unexpectedly grateful for that.

'You love your wife,' she had told him. 'You love your children and I love mine. I won't be the possible cause of a broken marriage and I certainly won't hand Daphne or your mother ammunition. Daphne thinks she has enough of that already.'

And she was right, Dan thought. He did love Holly and he did love his children. It had been a shock to realize the truth of that and a relief to discover that he was, in fact, capable of it. Dan would be the first to admit that most of his previous relationships had been shallow, surface. Engaged in because it was expected of him. This time, though, he had to make amends for something he really hadn't done.

Dan had once kissed Ellen Tailor. But there had been no second kiss.

And the thing was, the absolutely most important thing was. Dan had not killed Ellen.

FORTY-EIGHT

'So, what now,' Mac asked.

'Now, we wait.'

Mac nodded. 'Come and sit down.' Kendall had come to the boathouse that morning. The little outpost that was Frantham police station had been besieged by journalists looking for an angle and they didn't mind which narrative that angle related to. Vera Courtney was now as much of a story as the questioning of Dan Marsden. Andy and Frank were doing their best to run the front desk as normal while a couple of Kendall's uniforms kept the press in line . . . or the approximation of one. Mac had phoned a couple of times expecting to be told that they were having a quiet morning other than having journalists door-stepping them but to his surprise Andy told him there had been a constant stream of visitors.

'Everyone and their dog wants to have a nose and ask daft questions,' Andy told him. 'I must have said, "I can't possibly comment on an active case" about a hundred times.'

'You think Dan Marsden will sue?' Mac asked. It had been Celia's last threat before she'd driven her son home.

'I think the Marsdens will expect us to find a way to spin the story,' Kendall said. 'Explain to the press that Mr Marsden was helping us to flush out the real killer.'

Mac laughed. 'Police and local philanthropist in sting operation,' he said.

'I imagine they'll express it with a little more grace, but yes. So, now we wait. I've got a watch on the airports and ferries, just in case he decides to leave from Europe. Eurostar too and on Daphne's house. Either of them go anywhere and we'll know. In the meantime, I'm sure you've got TOIL time due. Break the pattern and take it.'

Mac smiled. It was a joke amongst police officers that there was only so much paid overtime to go around. Unpaid overtime was supposed to be accounted for by Time Off In Lieu but the joke was that no one ever got the opportunity to take all of it. He nodded. 'I might just do that,' he said. 'But I want to know if he turns up.'

Kendall nodded. 'Nice view from here,' he commented as he sipped his coffee.

Late in the afternoon, Mac took the risk of walking into Frantham and visiting Rina. Miriam promised to meet him there and they planned a leisurely walk back around the headland.

A few hardy souls still hung around outside the police station, but the doors had closed for the day and with no one but themselves to talk to, Mac figured they too would soon depart.

Tim opened the door at Peverill Lodge and Joy shouted her hellos from the kitchen. 'Matthew is teaching me to make goulash,' she told him. 'You'll get the chance to pass judgement later.'

Rina was in her little office working on some accounts. She put them aside when Mac came in. 'Glad to see you,' she said. 'Now tell me what on earth is going on.'

'You only want me for the gossip.'

'Of course. What other reason would there be? You look tired, Mac.'

'Long night,' he said.

'And is Dan Marsden guilty?'

'Rina, he can't tell you that,' Tim scolded.

'No, but he can give me a hint.'

Mac leaned back in the fireside chair with the wooden arms – one of a pair that sat in Rina's little room – and watched them both, relishing the smiles and the warmth. He wanted to sleep.

'And what about poor Vera,' Rina said, turning back to him. 'That's a sad business, Mac.'

'You were right,' he told her. 'Trent had her documents and was planning on using them in his book. I don't doubt he would have anonymized the account, but Vera had kept her father's life and death secret for so long it must have felt like a cruel betrayal. She won't countenance the idea that Ellen had anything to do with his having the journal and letters, but I'm sure she knows the truth of that really. I'm sure Ellen had the best of intentions . . . but.'

'She was grieving,' Rina said. 'Ellen meant a great deal to her.'

'She keeps referring to Ellen as a daughter. She feels she's lost a child. We've applied for psychiatric assessments. I think she was already in a more fragile state than anyone realized and William Trent just pushed her over the edge. She says he laughed at her, but, Rina, she was already carrying the knife. She was already prepared.'

'The knife was hers?' Tim was surprised.

'It was the weapon used to kill her father,' Mac said. He explained about the tape recording, about the confession that had been sent to Nora, Vera's mother, together with the weapon used to commit the murder.

'What a bizarre thing to do,' Rina said. 'What a cruel thing to do. But she never reported it?'

'Vera told us that by the time the package arrived the killer was dead. What would have been gained? Only pain for his family and a lot of questions no one wanted to answer.'

They absorbed that in melancholy silence, then Rina asked, 'So what now?'

'Now, we wait.'

'For what?'

'For the killer to think he's safe and come out of hiding,' Mac said. 'For him to want to leave the country and go home.'

'You think Ray did it,' Rina stated flatly.

'With a little encouragement from Daphne, yes. Ray dropped off our radar five days ago and his mother has been making a number of bank transfers to a new account.'

'So bringing in Dan Marsden?'

'A feint,' Mac said. 'Though the Marsdens don't know that yet. There's going to be hell to pay when they do.'

FORTY-NINE

Ray Tailor held his nerve for three days during which time Dan Marsden was questioned twice.

On the second day, Mac got a call from Diane Emmet in York. Daphne had been making threatening phone calls, she said. The kids were scared. She wanted money, she wanted custody.

'I've called the local police and they're supposed to be contacting DI Kendall. Mac, I'm taking the kids away for a few days. I've got friends in Scotland and they're up for a visit, so—'

'Sounds wise,' Mac said. 'Diane, I can promise you this will soon be over.'

'I hope so. You have a pen? I'll give you the address and phone number.'

Mac jotted it down. 'Diane, have you heard about William Trent. I don't know if—'

'Yeah, Yolanda called and told us. She told us an old woman who knew Mum had killed him. Vera something. I remember Ellen talking about her sometimes.'

Talking about her sometimes, Mac thought. It seemed scant description for a woman who had loved Ellen so much. 'Are the children upset?'

'It's just one more thing,' Diane said. 'But I think we'll take William's folder with us and I'll get them to do some work on it. And after Christmas, they'll be back in school, hopefully making friends and with a bit of luck able to start their lives again.'

Hopefully, Mac thought as he hung up. He called Dave Kendall straight after and asked about Daphne and if the local police had contacted him about Diane.

'She had the presence of mind to record the calls, after the first couple,' Kendall said. 'She's got an answer phone with a recording facility. She told Daphne what she was going to do, but I don't think Daphne cared. We'll be bringing her in later this morning.'

'Nothing on Ray yet?'

'No, but we'll be sure to release a statement about Daphne,' he said.

The next day brought news of Ray. Trying to get on to a flight for home.

EPILOGUE

'So, he confessed then?'

'Eventually. He blames his mother and she blames him, but thankfully he admits to pulling the trigger so we have an answer to who actually killed Ellen even if Daphne is culpable.'

'But to kill your daughter-in-law, just because . . . Mac it seems . . .'

'Daphne felt she'd lost everything. Her sons, her land, even her grandchildren. They made it plain they didn't like her very much, no matter how she tried to coerce them. And the final straw was when she realized Ellen had found something of value that Daphne believed should have been hers.'

'The coins. Have the rest of them turned up, by the way?'

Mac shook his head. 'The house will be searched again, but chances are when Ellen realized what lengths Daphne would go to Ellen hid them somewhere.'

Rina nodded. 'What a mess,' she said. 'Families can be the greatest blessing, but when it goes wrong—'

'Quite.'

'What I don't understand is what evidence you had against Ray. What made you think—'

Mac shrugged. 'In part because there were no other suspects to speak of. The more we looked, the smaller the pool became. It had to be someone that Ellen would if not expect to see at least not panic when she did. Someone that belonged. She knew Ray was back in the country because he admitted to having called her. So there'd have been no surprise, no fear, even when she saw him with the gun. Ray regularly used to come over and shoot rabbits for her before he left. Ellen wasn't a good shot and she didn't own a gun. And there were rabbits in the freezer with a date on them – after Ray came back.'

'Sounds tenuous.'

'Oh, it was but we took a chance, told him Ellen had labelled them as being shot by Ray. Told him that was proof that he'd both visited the farm and had access to a gun.' Mac shrugged. 'If he'd thought about it or allowed his solicitor to think about it, he'd have realized it was a whole load of nothing but I think he was ready to confess and that just gave him the final nudge.'

'I'm glad,' Rina said. 'At least the family now know. I suppose that's a good thing.'

'He says he loved her. He says his mother was going all out to ruin her life and take the children away. Daphne had written a letter to social services accusing Ellen of abusing the children. She'd already made a series of anonymous phone calls to that effect. He says he was saving Ellen from a slow destruction.'

'He says—'

'I say he was so used to being bullied by his mother that he couldn't refuse her in the end. I doubt she ever laid a finger on him, but she destroyed him all the same and in coming back he put himself back under her control. He pulled the trigger and killed the woman he loved.'

Mac took a walk to William Trent's cottage. It looked lonely and forlorn at the end of the track. The local farmers had promised to keep an eye on it but it might be a long time before anyone cleared it out or moved in. Trent had a son, but no one knew where he was and then there'd be probate. Mac wondered if he could arrange to have Trent's books and papers put in storage somewhere before the damp got to them.

His phone rang as he walked back to his car. It was Miriam. 'Thought we might go for a walk and then dinner at the Marina,' she said.

'It'll be dark by the time I get home.'

'We've got torches. Or maybe we could just stay in. You could bring a takeaway and then we could have a . . . quiet evening?'

Mac smiled. 'Sounds perfect,' he said.